Almost at once Rance arrived.

Sylvia met him with quick color in her cheeks that rivaled the depths of the talisman roses, and they had one moment of meeting that made them both very happy. Rance looked down at her as though she were something utterly new and wonderful in this world of human beings. As if she were a thousand times more lovely than he had thought her.

STRANGER WITHIN THE GATES

LIVING BOOKS®
Tyndale House Publishers, Inc.
Wheaton, Illinois

This Tyndale House book
by Grace Livingston Hill
contains the complete text
of the original hardcover edition.
NOT ONE WORD
HAS BEEN OMITTED.

Printing History
Grosset and Dunlap edition published 1954
Tyndale House edition/1990

Living Books is a registered trademark of Tyndale
House Publishers, Inc.

Library of Congress Catalog Card Number 89-50878
ISBN 0-8423-6441-2
Copyright © 1939 by Grace Livingston Hill
Copyright renewed 1967 by Ruth H. Munce
Cover artwork copyright © 1989 by Lorraine Bush
All rights reserved
Printed in the United States of America

95 94 93 92 91 90
8 7 6 5 4 3 2 1

THEY were sitting at the breakfast table when the mail was brought in, Mary Garland and her children.

It was three years since Paul Garland had died, and his children had begun to feel it was an event of the dim past. For things went on in much the same gentle pleasant way that they had when he was alive. But they still missed his gay smile, his keen eyes upon them, his eager interest in all that they did. He was still a part of themselves, and when any important event occurred they still in their thoughts turned their eyes to his to get his calm sane reaction.

Young Paul had been in college a year when his father died so suddenly. And the fortune made out of inherited capital had been sufficient to keep things going just as the father had planned for his young family. Not that they ever thought of themselves as wealthy, just comfortably off. They still lived in the old house their father had inherited from his father. It wasn't the last word in architecture, but it was substantial and handsome, and large enough for them all. They loved it.

Young Paul would graduate in the spring. Rex, the second son, two years later. Both boys were attending their father's college, a hundred miles away from home. Sylvia, the oldest daughter, was attending the university in the nearby city, and Fae and Stan were still in high school.

It was Fae who sprang to take the bundle of mail from the housemaid who brought it in.

"Oh, shoot!" she said, twisting her pretty young face into a grimace. "I thought my picture puzzle would come this morning. I sent for it a week ago."

"You did not!" said Stan gravely. "I carried your letter to the post box and it was only last Saturday morning you sent for it."

"Oh, well, that's plenty of time for it to have got here by now," said the positive young sister. "Mother, here's a letter from Rex. He must be sick or something. His letters are scarce as hen's teeth."

She plumped it down beside her mother's plate, and went on around distributing the mail.

Sylvia sat with a book propped open beside her plate. She was reading up for an examination. She cast the letter her sister laid beside her plate but a casual glance. Her brother gave her a mocking look. "Remove the debris Fae," he said, "it must be from the wrong fella. Look at Syl's face."

"It's only the notice of a class meeting," said Sylvia, looking up from her book with a withering glance.

Then there was an exclamation from their mother who had opened her son's letter and was reading it. They all looked up and saw that her face was white and drawn. Suddenly she bowed her head over the letter and sat there with her shoulders quivering.

Sylvia sprang to her feet and went over by her mother, her searching eyes spying the letter.

"What's the matter, mother? Is Rex sick?"

One week before Christmas! Was something like that coming to them to spoil Christmas?

Her eyes searched Fae's face.

Was that letter from Rex, Fae?" she asked under her breath.

Though the question had not been asked of Mary Garland it was her anguished voice that gasped out "Yes." Then as Sylvia stooped and gathered her mother's head into her arms and lifted her face from the table, Mary Garland fumbled at the letter and motioned Sylvia to read it.

The letter was brief and to the point:

> Dear Mom:
> This is just a short note to tell you I was married last week and I would like to bring my wife home for Christmas! She is a nice girl and I know you will love her. She hasn't any home, and I'm sure she'll enjoy our Christmas.
>
> > Your loving son,
> > Rex
>
> P.S. I haven't told Paul yet, he is so busy getting ready to graduate in the spring. You can do as you like about telling him.

Stan and Fae had come quickly around the table and were reading over their sister's shoulder to see what had upset mother. Mother simply never cried, not since father died. And mother was crying! Still, slow tears. And something like a suppressed groan whispered from her pale lips.

"Gosh! Can you tie that!" said Stan in a grown-up tone, still staring at the letter. "I thought he had some sense!"

"Oh, I *hate* him!" uttered Fae between her teeth. "He — he — he's *wicked!* Doing that to mother!" and Fae broke into violent sobs and went to the dining room couch burying her face in the cushions.

"Be still, can't you, children!" said Sylvia, gathering her mother closer in her arms, and looking at her brother and sister with angry stricken eyes. "Get up, Fae, and let mother lie down!" Her strong young arms drew her mother to the couch.

It was only a moment that Mary Garland succumbed to

her grief, as the three children sat silently, angrily dismayed, trying to wink the tears back and find some solution for this awful problem suddenly thrust upon them to solve. They were not used to solving problems. Their mother had usually done that for them. And now she quickly roused to her responsibility and sat up in spite of Sylvia's strong detaining hand.

"No, dear! I'm all right," she said in that hurt kind voice that was so familiar to their ears. "It—just—got—me—for a minute! But—to think it should have been *Rex!* Rex who isn't at all grown up yet. Oh, I thought the fact that Paul was there would have restrained him from doing anything—foolish!"

"But he said Paul didn't know it! Maybe it's all right, only he just hasn't got around to telling Paul yet," eagerly suggested fourteen-year-old Fae.

"It couldn't be all right, not at his age!" said Stan in a superior tone. "He's nothing but a kid! He's only three years older than I am. Getting married! Gee! Why even *I* would have had better sense than that, no matter how nice the girl was! And she couldn't be nice, not a girl that would marry a fella who wasn't half way through college yet, could she? No nice girl would do that. Not when she knew his folks didn't know her yet. Not when she must have known they wouldn't like it! Gee! Our Rex!"

"Hush!" said Sylvia sternly. "Can't you see you're making it terribly hard for mother?"

"Well, but Syl," urged Fae earnestly, "Haven't we got to help mother decide what to do? Haven't we got to do something about it right away?" Just as if the whole responsibility rested on herself.

"Hush!" said Sylvia. "That's for mother to decide. You wait till you're asked."

"You dears!" said the mother tenderly, and gave them a loving anguished look.

"Well, there's just one thing, mother," said Fae. "The rest

of us aren't married, and I think this'll be a good lesson for us. I don't think we'll any of us do a fool thing like this. I for one shall *never* marry!" And Fae suddenly beat a hasty retreat into the wide hall and cringed down on the old-fashioned haircloth ancestral sofa, hard and uncompromising, pouring her tears down its shiny old covering, weeping her young heart out over the catastrophe that had without warning come upon the house of Garland.

"Aw, heck!" said Stan. Diving his hands deep down into his pockets, he strode over to the window, blinking and gazing out with unseeing eyes.

Suddenly the dining room clock chimed out the hour. One! Two! Three! Four! Five! Six! Seven! Eight! Sharply, like an old familiar voice calling them to order. They all looked up and gave attention. Even Fae slid back to the dining room door and looked at the clock in startled meekness, as if it were something that had a right to reprimand them.

For the clock had been almost the last thing that the head of the house of Garland had bought and brought home before he lay down in his final illness and went away from them altogether. And in a way it had come to symbolize to them all the voice of authority, the voice of their dead father yet speaking.

When he had started that clock and they all stood about listening to its solemn ticking, its mellow chiming, Paul Garland had given them a bright little talk about it that they would always remember.

"When you hear that chime you must always give attention! Always about face and look up at the first stroke, and ask yourself what duty it is calling to remind you of. It is like a big musical conscience to remind you of work, or to tell you it is a time you may rest or relax, or go to your night's sleep. When it strikes eight on week days it will be reminding you that it is time you started to school—"

His words came back to them all now, and suddenly their several schools took form before their eyes. Their long habit of hurrying away to be on time asserted itself.

They gave each other startled looks, and then their glances melted into consternation as the new catastrophe thrust its memory in ahead of precedent.

"Oh!" quivered Fae, "we don't havta go ta school today, do we, muvver?"

"Heck! No!" said Stan whirling about and facing his mother almost defiantly. "Not me! To heck with the school! We got other business to attend to. Good night, moms, what we gonta do?"

Mary Garland lifted startled eyes, eyes that came back suddenly from gazing into the open door to despair, and went swiftly to the clock. For the clock had come to be a monitor to her also, a kind of religious obligation, representing her husband's loving authority.

Slowly, as her eyes took in the hour, and her ears recalled its chiming from the faraway seconds since it had struck, that wild desperate look faded from her eyes, and sane common sense took its place. Then her voice quavered forth, growing clearer and more firm with each breath.

"Why, yes, you're going to school! Certainly!" she said decidedly. "What possible good could you do staying at home from school? This is something that has *happened!* There is nothing you can do to prevent it. It's just a fact that we have to face, and you can't make it any easier to face by sitting around here at home and glooming over it. Especially when you would be leaving duties undone. You know what your father would say. And this is an important day. Every one of you have tests or examinations to be passed, and you must get such good control over your nerves that you will pass them all better than you ever passed a test before. That will help to keep your minds off of the happening that troubles you."

"*Happening?*" echoed Sylvia in an appalled voice. "I should call it a tragedy!"

"Yes," said the mother, wincing but nevertheless taking a deep breath and going on, "it does look like a tragedy at first sight. There's no point in leaving necessary things undone to make more trouble for ourselves afterwards. You know what it will mean to all of you if you don't pass your examinations."

"Afterwards!" said Sylvia dejectedly. "It doesn't seem as if there *could* be any afterwards."

"Oh yes," said Mary Garland with a sad look passing over her face, "there is *always* an afterwards! Now, finish your breakfast all of you, and then get away to school!"

"I don't want any breakfast!" said Sylvia, "and I'm not going to school. I couldn't think of leaving you alone with this thing to face!"

"Nonsense!" said her mother sharply. "I'll be quite all right! At least drink a glass of milk. I can't let you go without eating something. It's a cold morning!"

"But mother, you almost fainted away just now. I'd be seeing you that way all the morning," pleaded Sylvia.

"No, you wouldn't. You'd have your mind too full with your examination. And besides, I've done my fainting, whatever I'm going to do of it, at the first shock. Come, quickly. I want to get a chance to sit down and think this over."

"But moms, what are we going to say to people?" asked Stan with a troubled look.

"Say?" said the mother sharply. "Why should you say anything? Just keep your mouths shut about home affairs. There isn't anything to say."

"But suppose someone should ask us?"

"Why would anyone ask you?"

Stan stood preplexed.

"Well, they might ask when the boys were coming home, or if they were coming home," he explained lamely.

"No one would likely do that, but if they did you easily say they hadn't written what train. Now *go!* I don't want to talk any more about it. And don't put on such a hang-dog look. You don't want people to ask you what's the matter, do you? For pity's sake can't you have a little fortitude? Put on a smile and go bravely off."

"Aw gee, moms, but it's our *Rex!*"

"Haven't you any *sense* at all?" said the older sister with an angry glance, and then looking down at the stricken eyes of her mother she said:

"Now, mother dear, you are going up to lie down and rest. Come. I'm taking you, and putting you to bed. That's the only consideration under which I would think of going to my class."

Mary Garland arose and faced her fiery young daughter.

"Sylvia, that'll be quite enough! I'm not yet in my dotage! Drink that glass of milk, and then put on your coat and hat and go!"

She finished by giving the table bell a sharp tap which brought the maid at once. "Hettie, bring the toast and eggs. The children ought to hurry. Now, Fae, go put on your galoshes, and then come back and eat something."

Hettie brought the eggs, and they were soon all back at the table, well shod for the snowy streets. And though they protested they could not eat, their healthy appetites soon asserted themselves and they ate at least a sketchy breakfast before they left, their minds now turned toward the duties next in hand. For the time being they were diverted from the catastrophe that had come upon them.

Mary Garland watched them off from her window, her face as bright as she could force it to be until they were out of sight. Then she turned with swift steps and went up to her room with her letters in her hand, and locking her door sat down to read Rex's missive again. This time the tears fell thick and fast upon the page, as she tried to think how her loving Rex could ever have been willing to do this to her, and to the rest of the children. *Rex!*

Had she spoiled him? Of course he was extraordinarily handsome and they all adored him. Gay bright Rex! Always full of fun! But generous and loving. Still, he did like to have his own way.

And he had so longed to go to college, when she had wanted him to wait a year. He was so young, a year younger than Paul had been when he went. Even Paul had been dubious about it. He had felt that Rex should stay at home with her another year. But Rex had been so eager to go. The thought of those days wrung her heart. If she only had him back, just an eager boy of seventeen. He could just as well have waited another year at least, and entered college at eighteen. If she only had kept him back maybe this wouldn't have happened!

Rex had always been of a more social nature than Paul. Paul was graver, more serious, more intent on having a career and getting ready for it.

But she must not waste time in vain regrets. There in her lap was the letter, staring at her with bald startling facts. Rex was married! Married at eighteen. Poor foolish Rex! She had not thought he could be so weak as to do a thing like that!

She could almost see his handsome eyes looking at her from the hastily scrawled page, the appeal in his eyes, as if he were pleading with her to forgive, to excuse somehow this perfectly inexcusable thing that he had done. That appeal, that memory of the boy's eyes in times past when he had done wrong and had come to her for forgiveness made it impossible for her to harden her heart now. She had never turned away from appeal in the eyes of any of her children. Sometimes she had had to deny them of course, but always they knew that back of that denial there was her warmest sympathy in their desire, even if she felt it was wrong or unwise. There was still a sympathy with the childish desire.

Oh, had it been that quality in herself that had helped to spoil Rex, given him confidence that he could get away with anything if he looked at her with that warmth of appeal? Was she to blame for this? Probably, though she hadn't suspected it till now.

But now what was she to do?

There had never been anything like this before. Always heretofore the troubles had been things that could in some way be paid for by money, or an apology, or by some small self-denial required of him, and the would-be crisis averted.

But here was something that could not be paid for by money. She couldn't by paying even a large sum undo this thing, and wipe out the memory of it from his life. Not even his most humble self-abnegation could put him where he had been before this happened, with the future still unchanged before him. Of course the world today might think of divorce in such a situation, but not their family. Not quiet, respectable, Christian people like themselves. Not that they had ever made a great point of their Christianity, but they had been fairly regular in church attendance, and such a thing as divorce was scarcely considered decent in their family traditions. With a weight like iron upon her heart she flung the thought aside, and stared at the hopelessness of the situation. Of course, even if the girl were fairly nice, she would feel the same about it. And a girl who would marry a boy not yet out of his teens, not through with his college course, what could she be? No nice girl would do a thing like that. Or would she? Nowadays? Young people did such very different things now, from what they used to do when she was young. But she hadn't yet reached the point of considering the girl, whether or not she was a right girl for Rex. It seemed to be equally terrible for her son, whatever the girl was. Rex! Married at eighteen!

But what was the use of such thoughts! This thing was *done.* She had to face the fact!

Or was it?

Was it conceivable that Rex would write her a letter like

that just for a joke? He couldn't be so outrageous, could he? Though Rex was always full of fun, always planning some wild kind of performance to make them all laugh. But he couldn't be so cruel as to do such a thing as this. She thought she had brought her children up to feel that marriage was a sacred thing!

She groaned and dropped her face in her hands, her heart contracting with the utter futility of all she had tried to do, in the face of this sudden catastrophe.

Selma the cook knocked at the door.

"The butcher's down at the door. He says do you want to pay for the order today or let it go till tomorrow?"

"Let it go, Selma," said Mary Garland. "I'm—very busy just now."

She had sprung up and stood facing the closed door, trying to speak in a matter-of-fact voice, a business-like tone. Selma had seemed to take it that way. There was no question in her voice as she said:

"Yes, ma'am."

Mary Garland listened as Selma walked down the stairs, and drew a breath of relief. If only she might be able to keep things this way, with their quiet accustomed tread, as if there were nothing ahead to frighten her. But she couldn't. She had to do something. Perhaps after all it would be best to call up Rex on the telephone. Treat it as a joke for which she felt she must reprove him.

No, if it should be true that might antagonize him. After all he was her son. She must walk carefully. Oh, if she just had his father to advise her. If she had someone!

But she mustn't call in strangers until she knew the worst, and had control of herself. Paul would be the one, since his father was not here. Paul was reasonable, and sane, and had good judgment. His father had always said Paul had splendid judgment for a boy. Yes, Paul would be the one. But she could not call up Paul today. This was his important day, his mid-year examination. Or was it his thesis? But anyway she knew she must not disturb him now. Not till his important classes were over.

And even if she did succeed in getting him, would that be wise? He would be very angry with his brother for having brought such trouble upon them all, especially her. Even if it turned out to be a joke Paul would be unmercifully sharp and stern. He would precipitate a quarrel, perhaps, that might keep Rex from coming home at all for Christmas. Oh, there were so many sides to this question!

And even yet Mary Garland had not considered the girl in the question except in the most casual way. Just the fact of marriage in connection with her eighteen-year-old son was all she seemed to be able to think of yet.

But she must do something right away.

She looked around the room frantically and met the clear calm gaze of her husband's eyes, from his picture on the wall, and somehow that glance seemed to steady her. If he were only here! Then Mary Garland dropped upon her knees beside her bed and buried her face in her pillow. Up from her heart there arose a great cry of need. It was not in words, it was just her desperate acknowledgement that she was helpless to face this terrible thing that had come upon her.

If Rex Garland could have seen his little pitiful mother as she knelt there bowing in her desperation, he might have understood what a terrible thing he had done to her. His little sweet mother whom he adored.

Mary Garland knelt there for several minutes, just bowing before her humiliation and defeat, and then at last she arose, her face almost calm with a kind of deadly quiet upon it. She walked over to her telephone, dropping down upon the little desk chair beside the telephone table. Her hands were trembling, and her lips were trembling too, when she called long distance and then the number of Rex's college and waited, but there was about her a look of decision that her children knew well.

Oh, she didn't know just yet what she was going to say to Rex, but she knew she was going to say it, whatever it was that came to be said, and she knew she must speak to Rex himself right away.

It seemed interminable, that waiting, till she heard the operator at the college, and then her voice grew strong for her task; she was able to keep her tone quite steady as she spoke.

"Will you please let me speak with Rex Garland? This is his mother."

There was an instant's hesitation at the other end of the wire.

"I'm sorry, Mrs. Garland, but everybody's in class just now. We are not supposed to interrupt classes for anything except a matter of life or death."

"Yes?" said Mary Garland firmly. "Well this is a matter of life and death. I must speak with my son at once."

She could hear a whispered consultation, a little flurry of excitement, and then the young operator was back again.

"It's out of the ordinary ruling, Mrs. Garland, but if it's quite important—"

"It is," said Mary Garland steadily.

"Very well. I'll see what I can do for you. You'll have to wait till I can send to his class."

"I'll wait," said the mother firmly.

It seemed forever that she sat there with the telephone in her hand. She could hear occasional talking, some student coming in to ask about a letter. A professor to leave a message, the Dean to ask a question. She could visualize it all, for she had been in that office and knew pretty well what went on. She drew a brief quivering breath. She thought to herself that it was like the time she waited at the hospital when Stanley had his tonsil operation and wasn't coming out of it as well as they had expected. She had waited what seemed like eons for word to come from the operating room. Life was full of such breath-taking experiences. There was the time when Paul had been hurt in the gymnasium on the high bar and the doctor was going over him carefully. It seemed forever while she waited. And there was the time Fae ran a needle into her foot and the doctor had to cut her foot to get it out. And then there was the time — and just then the operator's clear-cut voice broke in upon her thoughts.

"I'm sorry, Mrs. Garland, but we can't seem to locate Rex Garland anywhere. He told his roommate he was going down to class, but he isn't there. Do you want me to give him a message if he should return? Or will you call again?"

"I would like you to find my son, wherever he is, and have him call me on the telephone as soon as possible. It is most important."

"Very well, Mrs. Garland. I'll do my best. If I hear anything before noon, I'll give you a ring, shall I?"

"Please," she said, and then hung up. Dropping her face down upon her hands she wept hopelessly.

"This is ridiculous!" said Mary Garland's cool calm self that had for so many years carried on through storm and calm alike. "It isn't like you to *cry* about a thing! Get up and wash your face and be ready for the next thing. Likely Rex will call in a few minutes. Get control of yourself!"

It was early yet. Perhaps Rex had gone down to the village to post a letter or buy some fruit or candy. Probably he had been late to breakfast and had gone down to the place they called the "pie-shop" to get something to eat before he went to classes. Well, when he came back they would tell him. He would at least find the message at the desk when he came to the dining hall at noon. But, oh, must she wait so long?

She glanced at the clock. Only ten o'clock. There were innumerable things she ought to do, but could she tear herself away from the telephone long enough to do any of them? The ordering must be done for the day.

She gave a glance at her mirror. Her face was desolate and there were signs of tears around her eyes. Selma was sharp, she mustn't be given a chance to watch her.

She went to the head of the back stairs and called down.

"Selma, I'm waiting for an important telephone call. You had better give the order to the grocer right away or things will be late coming up. Get fish for dinner tonight, fillet of sole, the kind the children like, you know. Have chopped creamed potatoes, stewed tomatoes and an apple and nut salad. Lemon pie for desert. And for lunch, isn't there enough cold roast beef to go with waffles or flannel cakes? You know what to get, Selma, call up right away before my call comes in. And don't forget to order that mince meat, three jars. Hurry, please, Selma. I want the children to have their lunch as soon as they get home."

She went back to her room, and stood listening a moment at her door till she heard Selma's steady voice giving the orders. There, she had hung up! Now, Rex might call at any minute and she must make up her mind just what to say to him.

But time went on and the telephone did not ring.

There were many things that demanded her attention. Christmas matters that she must finish, things that had seemed most important only last night. But now she couldn't keep her mind on them. She went over her list, but somehow they all seemed impossible to her just now. If Rex was married, and Christmas was going to be complicated, what did it matter whether the rosettes for Fae's party dress were finished or not? Of course Fae didn't know she was going to have a new party dress for Christmas. She wouldn't know it was to have had rosettes even if they didn't get finished.

And there was another thing. That party she had planned during the Christmas holidays. They had already invited some of the guests!

But one couldn't have a party when a thing like this was happening! Why, it wouldn't be possible! Oh, if it were only two years later, and Rex through college it wouldn't be so bad!

Then suddenly she dropped beside her bed and began to weep bitterly again! It seemed as if her very soul was torn and tortured. She tried to pray, because she told herself that this would be a time for prayer, but her soul was in a perfect frenzy of grief, and for a few minutes it seemed as if the fountains of the great deep in her soul were broken up. Why, she hadn't wept like this even when her beloved husband had been taken from her! Though it had been sudden and sharp, she had felt as if God were behind that and she must trust and be strong. But this—why this was *outrageous!* It was something that a laughing merry boy had done, carelessly, not thinking what disastrous results there would be, and she felt as if she could not stand it! She simply *could not* stand it!

Then suddenly there came the thought of the other children. They would be coming home to lunch in a little while, and they would see she had been crying. Selma would see, the waitress would see. There were footsteps coming up the stairs now! Selma or Hettie coming to ask some question. Oh, there was no time in privacy to weep. One mustn't weep! Not a mother! No matter what happened!

She got up hurriedly and dashed into the bathroom, turning on the cold water and plunging her face into it.

Yes, that was Hettie knocking.

"All right, Hettie!" she called. "I'll be there in a minute."

"It's only a special delivery letter, M's Garland," called the maid. "I'll put it under the door!"

And then she could hear Hettie's solid steps retreating down the stairs.

A letter! A special delivery letter!

Her heart leaped up with quick anticipation. Ah! This would be from Rex, explaining that it was a joke!

It was curious how her mind could fool itself in that one instant, and hope for the best!

She grasped a towel and dabbed at her face, and then went hurriedly for the letter.

There it lay half under the door, face up!

But the letter was not from Rex. It bore Paul's writing. Hurried writing. Had Paul found out?

And then as she stooped to pick up the letter, her hands trembling so that they would scarcely hold it, the telephone rang, and she tottered over to it and sank down in her chair, one hand reaching for the receiver, her lips trembling so that she felt she would never be able to speak coherently.

2

SYLVIA, hurrying out into the winter sunshine that morning, had a sharp passing wonder that sun could be so bright when terrible things were happening. Just as if God didn't care what His creatures had to bear. Probably He felt just as mother had, that things had to go on, no matter what some of His children had done to spoil everything. How brave mother had been, thinking those lessons of theirs had to be finished creditably though heaven and earth should fall! Poor mother! But she had looked just stricken herself! How could Rex have done such a thing!

And then she caught sight of her bus rounding the corner a block beyond the big stone gateway, and she clutched her pile of books a little closer and started to run. She must not miss that bus. Not this morning.

She caught the bus and swung into her seat breathless. Somehow nothing seemed worth-while any more. She ought to open her book and make certain of those two pages she was weak on. There would be sure to be a question on those.

She opened her book, but her eyes were dull, and communicated no information to her. Some sound out in the street attracted her attention, a school child trying to catch the bus, running across in the very teeth of an oncoming car. She caught her breath at the narrow escape, and her heart was going wildly. Rex had done that once when he had gone to school with her, and how dad had scolded him afterwards! She had felt it was her duty to tell dad afterwards, because Rex had almost been killed. He had fallen down in the road and only the skill of the driver swerving to the left had saved his life. But Rex had lived and now he had done this to mother! Quick tears sprang near to the surface and she had to turn her head toward the window lest someone would see her cry. Oh this was terrible! Why had she come to school today? A university student weeping on her way to class!

Then as she stared out of the window she saw Rance Nelius standing by the curb waiting for the bus to stop, and he caught her glance and smiled lifting his hand.

If it had been yesterday her heart would have quickened with pleasure. She liked Rance Nelius. He was one of the brightest men in the university, and good-looking too, in a fine strong way, with the kind of good looks she liked to see in a man.

But now her heart took a plunge downward, for this sudden sight of him came right into the face of her own quiet resolve that men and girls were fools to get married, look what a lot of trouble it made for everybody! Oh, she didn't want to talk to Rance now, her heart was too heavy about Rex. And what were a few smiles and silly words anyway? Why should a girl lose her head because an upper classman had lingered beside her, several times, with a pleasant greeting? Oh, yes, she had questioned in her heart whether she wouldn't ask her mother to invite Rance to the Christmas party, though of course he lived in another part of the city and they didn't know him very well. But he had seemed so worth-while and sensible, and there was such a light in his eyes when he talked. He could even discuss a prosy class and make it sound interesting.

But now of course that was all off, and it would be better not to have to talk to him at all. She would be sure to show her sadness.

She gave a quick glance down the aisle, and was almost glad when she saw a crowd of people pushing in and filling all the available seats and then crowding down the aisle. He wouldn't be able to get anywhere near her, and that was just as well. With this dark shadow over her life it was better not to have anything to do with anybody. Anyway not till all this trouble had been explained, or arranged or something, and maybe forgotten. Would they ever be able to forget it? Yet she couldn't keep her eyes down on her book much as she tried, and twice when she looked up she found Rance Nelius watching her, and giving her a special quiet smile as if they were very good friends indeed and understood each other. As if just a smile meant a good deal, and spoke a special language all their own.

She caught her breath at the thought. She couldn't remember that she had ever felt quite that way with any other young man. True, she hadn't thought much about such things before. She had been very busy studying, and had taken everybody for granted, and smiled on all alike. But now there was something warming and pleasant in Rance's smile, as if he saw that something troubled her and he was giving her heartenment by his glance.

Well, there! That was likely the way Rex felt about whoever he had married. That was probably why he married her. People ought not to allow themselves to think about love and things like that when they were young and studying, and had families who expected things of them.

Someone stepped past Rance and intercepted their glances, and Sylvia dropped her eyes to her book, and studied hard, though she wasn't just sure that she was remembering what she read. Somehow there seemed to be something back in her mind like a shutter, resolutely fastened against taking in knowledge that morning. She pressed her lips together and fastened her gaze on the words again. She must get that special wording in her mind or she would fail utterly in the coming test which meant so much to her standing. Back went her mind to its duty, and by the time that the bus had lurched to a stop at the corner where she got off, she felt sure of the difficult paragraph. Now, if she could escape walking with anybody down the one block she had to go to the building where she must enter, she could glance over the next paragraph, and then she would feel reasonably sure of everything important.

She got out slowly, lingering to be the last, but when she stood by the curb and looked around she couldn't see Rance Nelius anywhere, and she felt a sudden blank. Had she then been cheating herself, pretending that she didn't want to walk with him? For now when she saw he wasn't here she was actually disappointed that he hadn't waited. Well, it seemed that she was silly too, just like Rex. That showed that every young person ought to be careful and watch their steps. Love and foolishness must be waiting around every corner to catch the unwary, and she for one didn't intend to get caught. Didn't intend to bring any more of that kind of sorrow into her mother's life. With that she set her lips firmly and stepped up on the curb. Then suddenly there he was beside her!

"Well, you did decide to get out after all!" he said smiling down at her from his pleasant height. "I made a dash across the street to the post box and mailed a letter while I was waiting for you." He had the friendliness in his voice of a very old acquaintance, as if he had the right to expect to walk with her. And it really hadn't been so long that she had known him. Their first meeting had been quite casual. It was one day in the library, when they were reading at the same table, and one of the professors had stopped beside them to tell them of a change of date for a special lecture that was open to all classes. He had quite casually taken it for granted that they knew one another. He had discussed the morning chapel address with them. From that day they had always smiled and spoken as they passed. Occasionally Nelius had walked along with her as they went from one class room to another, and she had come to think of him shyly as a friend. But now he swung into step beside her with the atmosphere of having a definite purpose in mind.

"What," said he, "are you going to do Saturday evening? Are you free? Because I was wondering how you would like to hear The Messiah with me. I have a couple of tickets, and nobody to go with me. You see, I'm sort of a stranger around here, and haven't had much time to get acquainted during the term time. I've been carrying a pretty heavy schedule. I thought you looked like the kind of girl who like music so I decided to take the chance. Are you free?"

Sylvia caught her breath! The Messiah!

"Oh, I'd *love* it!" she said, and a soft flush stole up into her cheeks. "But—" and a cloud drifted over the brightness of her face as she remembered what had happened in their household.

"Oh, is there a 'but'?" he asked disappointedly. "I was afraid there might be, this time of year and all, and everybody has their own holiday affairs, of course."

"Well," said Sylvia looking up wistfully, "there isn't exactly a but. And it might not turn out to be anything after all. It was just that I wasn't quite sure but that I would have to be at home that night—Saturday night you said? I would love to go. I've never happened to hear The Messiah. But I couldn't be sure till I see—" her voice trailed off unhappily. "But that wouldn't be fair to you. You can get plenty of people who would just jump at the chance to go with you, I'm sure, and I might not be sure whether I could go till the last minute."

"That's all right by me," he said amusedly. "I'd rather take the chance with you than not. There's nobody I know that I want to take but you, so if it happens at the last minute that you can't go, I'll just give the ticket to the most wistful old musician at the door, standing in line."

Sylvia's laugh rippled out briefly.

"That's a nice thought," she said, "but maybe I'll get worried about the old musician by the door, and think I ought to stay home anyway."

He grinned.

"Now, just for that, I'll give him a ticket anyway, so you can't have him for an excuse."

"Oh, but I don't need an excuse. I would love to go if things at home are—so I won't be needed."

He studied her another instant, and then smiled.

"Thank you," he said. "I just wanted to be sure you would really enjoy going. Because since you've developed that unprecedented interest and charitable spirit toward the unknown elderly musician, I wouldn't want to be uncertain that you were classing me with him. You wouldn't go to a concert during holidays just to befriend a lonely student, would you?"

"Oh, I might," said Sylvia nonchalantly, twinkling her eyes toward him, and then growing serious suddenly.

"I really would love to go," she said gravely, "and I feel honored that you have asked me. You see, I heard Doc Wharton say the other day that you were the most brilliant man he had in his classes this year, and you were going to make your mark in the world some day, so I shall be terribly disappointed if I can't go."

"Bologny!" said the young man suddenly, "Doc Wharton is full of soft soap. You don't mean he said that to you?"

"No, but I sat just behind him at a table in the library, and he was talking to one of the English professors. He was talking in a low tone as if it were confidential. I shouldn't have been listening of course, that is, I didn't know I was listening until I heard your name, and naturally my attention was drawn. So, you see I feel very much flattered that you have asked me—"

"Say," he interrupted, "if you're going to get that way—"

Sylvia suddenly laughed.

"No, I'll not pain you with further praise," she said, "but seriously I just wanted you to realize that if I don't go it's not because I don't want to. I certainly do. I'm just afraid of how things are going to turn out. However, I'll do my best."

She gave him a bright smile as they parted and went to their different classes, and the morning was less gloomy because of their brief talk. How grand it would be if she could only go to that concert with Rance Nelius! But of course she couldn't. Even if mother didn't let Rex bring his wife home there would likely be a great gloom over the house, and it wouldn't be very kind or considerate for her to run away, supposedly to have a good time. Well, at least it didn't have to be decided at once. The time was three days off. Maybe Rex and—well—Rex, wouldn't have come home yet. She would talk it over with mother and see what she thought about it.

She settled to her studying, but all the morning whenever the thought of what Rex had done hit her consciousness with a sudden dull thud, there was also a luminousness in her thoughts that put a light of golden hope into things, as she remembered Rance and his invitation.

But oh, if things were only normal. If Rex hadn't written mother right out of the blue that way that he was married! How *could* Rex have done a thing like that? Rex, who loved mother so much! Oh, maybe it wasn't so. Maybe he just wrote that for a joke! Could he be so cruel?

And then it was all to do over again, her reasoning.

The high school was full of the atmosphere of Christmas. Holiday gaiety pervaded the atmosphere. It met Stan and Fae as they mounted the steps and went down the hall to their respective rooms. Spicy odor of spruce trees, festive garlands of laurel ropes and holly wreaths, mysterious packages carried furtively and hidden in desks.

"Stan, Miss Marian wants you to go up to the assembly room and help decorate the big tree on the platform," an excited brown-eyed maiden accosted Stan as he reached the door of his classroom. "She says it's necessary to have some-one at the head of it that has some sense and a little bit of artistic ability. I'm glad she picked you instead of that Rue Pettigrew. He takes so many airs on himself, and thinks he can lord it over everybody."

Ordinarily Stan was quite willing to perform such offices for Miss Marian who was a favorite teacher. And it would usually have been twice welcome to get such a message from the lips of Mary Elizabeth Remley who had sweet brown eyes and didn't seem to know it herself; in fact he had just now been thinking of letting her wear his class pin.

But the cloud of the family catastrophe had been resting heavily upon him on the way to school, and he drew a frown.

"Heck!" he said annoyedly. "I don't see how I'm going to do that. I haven't quite finished copying my essay, and it has to be handed in today." He put on an old worried look and met her eyes, the brown eyes with a sudden disappointed look in them.

"Oh!" she said. She had thought he would be pleased. "Well, I'll go and tell her. Perhaps she'll ask Hanford Edsell instead. He never gets to do anything."

But Stan shook his head.

"Naw! Don't say anything to her. She's got enough wor-ries of her own. I'll manage it somehow. But heck, can you beat it? These extras are always coming in just when you least expect them?"

"Couldn't I copy your essay, Stan? You're typing it, aren't you? I can do it without any mistakes." The brown eyes met his wistfully, and Stan's face cleared into sudden sunshine.

"Thanks, awfully, Mary Lizbeth, that's pretty swell of you to offer, but I've got to make a few changes in the last part. I guess I'd better do it myself. But don't you worry, I'll make out. Are you coming along up to the assembly room, or have you got something else to do? If you haven't you might hand me up things to put on the tree. You've got pretty good taste yourself!"

Mary Elizabeth's eyes blazed into pleasure.

"Sure I'll come. Miss Marian thought there'd be some place where I could help," and she swung into step with him as they climbed the stairs to the assembly room where the great tree was already in place in the middle of the platform.

"Oh, hang!" said Stan to himself in the midst of his answering smile to the brown-eyed girl. "There I go! Makin' up to Lizbeth! And I just got done vowing I'd never look at a girl as long as I live, after what my fool brother has done, spoiling Christmas and everything for us all, getting married before he gets educated!"

Thus he adjured himself as he climbed the ladder. And then Mary Elizabeth brought him a lovely silver star to hang on the very top of the tree, and he stooped over and looked into her sweet brown eyes that were so unaware of their own loveliness, and forgot all about his resolves, working happily away, the cloud all gone from his brow.

There were so many girls and fellows there, all working so eagerly, hanging laurel and holly and wreaths, and they were all so gay and full of laughter and jokes, how could one remember right steadily amidst all that about the sorrow that had come at home? He was here now, in school, and must go through with it. Mother had said that. This was what he must do now, and do it well. So he gave himself to the tree, and took each emblem or ball or crystal angel or thread of silver from the eager young hand of the brown-eyed girl and hung it in place, as though it were a sacred trust. So it was not till the tree was finished, every light in place, every thread of tinsel hanging straight like an icicle, and he came down from the ladder and went to his desk to try to work over that last page of his essay, that the horror of home came back to his young heart and gripped it with a more mature pain than any he had yet experienced in his young life.

Down on the floor below Fae had been surrounded by her special friends, all clamoring at once to tell her the latest developments concerning the Christmas play in which she had a part.

"You know Betty Lou is *mad,* Fae, and says she won't be in the play at all because Miss Jenkins won't let her wear pajamas instead of a nightgown when she comes out to hang up her stocking. She says everybody will laugh at her, that nobody wears nightgowns now, and anyhow she's got some lovely new silk pajamas and she wants to wear them. But Miss Jenkins says it's an old time play and pajamas wouldn't be in character, and if Betty Lou says any more about it we can't have the play. But I told her you knew the part and could take her place."

"Say, Fae," burst in another girl, "whyn't you go an' talk to Betty Lou? She likes you. Maybe you can make her see some sense."

"Say, Fae! What do you think!" cried another friend. "Helen Doremus says we're too old to be in a play that has dolls in it. Isn't she silly? The dolls aren't going to be in *all* the stockings, only the little ones. And anyhow I told her it was too late for her to begin to find fault. But she says she's not coming to the play unless they leave the dolls out of all the stockings. Someone might misunderstand."

"Yes, but you haven't heard the worst one yet, Fae," called her special friend, Ruby Holbrook. "Mae Phantom wants to be a fairy with a sparkling wand and silver slippers, and she's made up some poetry to recite while she goes around looking at the stockings before we wake up. Isn't that the limit? If Miss Jenkins stands for that I'm going to quit. I won't have her messing in our play. She hasn't been in our school long enough to go bossing things like that."

"Say, Fae," said the youngest girl of all, "Millie Burton and Howard Jenks have the measles, and I was over there playing games with them night before last. Wouldn't that be *awful* if I should come down with them before the play, when I have such a long part to recite!"

"It's lucky most of the rest of us have had the measles," said another girl coldly.

And amidst it all Fae forgot the sorrow she had left behind at home, and let the Christmas gaiety and excitement surge happily over her.

"Say, did you bring your money for the teacher's present? Well you better get it in pretty quick, or they'll not be able to pay for it, and I think it ought to be wrapped and ready, or there'll be some hitch."

"Say, who's going to present the gift to the teacher, now that Howard Jenks has the measles? I think Fae Garland ought to. She learns things quicker than anybody, and she's the best reciter. Besides she never makes mistakes!"

All these things warmed Fae's young heart, so that it was only now and then that a memory would come and hit her in the region of her stomach with an awful sickening thud, and make her dizzy and sick. Then some new excitement would banish it for awhile.

Back at home Mary Garland sat at the telephone and heard the bland masculine tones of the village butcher, instead of her son's voice:

"Mrs. Garland, I have some very nice fresh-killed capons this morning. I was wondering how you would like me to to sent up a couple?"

"No! No capons, thank you! No, not today!" Mary Garland's voice rose crisp and businesslike out of the depths of despair, with a touch of almost exasperation at the poor butcher who was doing his best to make a sale.

Then she hung up, and dropped her hand in her lap, coming into sharp contact with the letter addressed in Paul's handwriting. With a start she hastened to open it. Here, *here* would be the explanation at last! The consolation, perhaps! Her trembling fingers removed the letter, a hasty scrawl, and her anxious eyes read:

Dear Mater:

I'm sending home two suits that I shall need in the holidays. Please send for Harris to have them cleaned and be sure to get then back *by Saturday. Stress* that! No time to write more. Exams going well. Terribly busy! Take care of yourself.

> Hastily,
> Paul

The mother dropped back limply into her chair and tried to stop the whirling in her heart and head. Tried to think what she should do. Paul's letter hadn't told her a thing. What ought she to do? She *must* do something. Not Paul! She must not disturb Paul until his afternoon class was over. Painfully, carefully she turned the matter over, and at last decided to send a telegram to Rex. It might be that Rex would hesitate to talk to her on the telephone lest their conversation should be overheard. Very well, she would telegraph to him, and make him realize what he had done to them all. She would make it brisk and to the point. A message that he could not misunderstand. One that would at least bring him to the telephone at once.

She did not hesitate long for words, and she sent it forth, brief and clear-cut and unmistakable. It read:

> Come home immediately.
> Mother

After it was sent beyond recall she sat down again and stared at the wall, trying to figure out what Rex's reaction would be to it, and not till then did it occur to her that he might think she meant he was to bring his wife along, and that was the last thing she wanted just now. What she wanted was Rex by himself, Rex, her boy, that she might gently question him and find out by watching his clear eyes just what it all meant. That would be the key to what she ought to do.

Yet if it was really so, and Rex was married, there was nothing to do but make the best of it. Or was that right? It sounded heathenish.

With a deep pitiful sigh she dropped upon her knees.

"Oh, God," she prayed, quietly into her pillow, "have I done wrong? Have I somehow failed in bringing up my boy? I must have or he would not have done a thing like this. Even if the girl is all right, it can't be the best thing that he should be married so young, before he is ready to go out into the world and fend for himself. Even though there is money to start him, his father would never feel I should turn it over to him at this age. Oh, God, if I've wandered away from the right path, if I've failed miserably won't You set me right? Won't You show me what to do? Won't You take care of this for me? Because I cannot see the matter for myself."

The telephone began to ring, and Mary Garland arose and went to answer it, but somehow she felt as if the great weight of the burden had been rolled from her heart. She had done the only thing there was to do, she had put the matter in God's hands. It was too great for her to handle, and He was the only One who could possibly take care of it.

It was Stanley on the telephone.

"Say mother, Mr. Hanley wants me to help him a little while at noon. Do you mind if I get a bite here at the lunch counter and don't come home? There's still a lot to do about the decorations, and he doesn't like to let all the kids in on it. D'ya mind?"

"No, that's all right, Stanley."

"Say, mother, anything else happened yet?"

"No, dear. Not yet." Mary Garland's voice choked unsteadily.

"Don't ya need me, mother? If ya do I'll tell 'em I can't stay taday."

"No, dear, it's all right! Don't worry. There's nothing you could do now even if you were here."

She was trembling all over when she hung up. Now why should she get all wrought up like that? Hadn't she any self-control? Just because she had thought that might be Rex, and she wasn't sure what she ought to say to him! She must get hold of herself and not go all to pieces this way. She must be self-controlled by the time the children came home. Fae would be coming soon now.

It was Sylvia who called next.

"Mother, are you all right?"

"Why of course, child. Why shouldn't I be all right?"

"Well, of course," said Sylvia cheerfully, "you would be all right if the heavens fell," and she laughed a little catchy sorrowful laugh. "Well, mother, if you don't mind I'll get a glass of milk and not come home till two o'clock. There's a little studying I'd like to do before the examination tomorrow and if I do it here I won't have to lug so many books home."

"That's all right, Sylvia dear."

Mary Garland was getting control of her voice, and making it sound quite cheerful.

"Mother, did you do anything about it yet?"

"Don't let's discuss it over the telephone, dear," said her mother gently. "Don't worry. Everything will come right in due time."

"Oh, do you think so, mother?"

"Why, certainly," said Mary Garland trying to speak briskly. "Hasn't God always taken care of us?"

"Oh!" said Sylvia, startled that matters had reached the crisis of depending on God to straighten them out. "Mother, are you *sure* you don't need me?"

"Why, of course," said Mary Garland. "Now cheer up and get your studying out of the way while you have the time."

Fae was the last one to call.

"Muvver, they've got some awful nice smelling macaroni and cheese at the lunch counter, and some little raisin pies. Would you mind if I stayed for lunch? Stan isn't coming home, he says, and I just hate that long walk all alone. May Beverly is going to stay today. Most of the girls are staying. We have a rehearsal of the play after lunch, besides, so maybe I'll be late coming home."

"All right, dear!" said Mary Garland almost cheerfully. Now she wouldn't have to answer any more questions for a couple of hours, and maybe by that time Rex would have called, and she would know what to do.

Oh, but would she know any better after Rex called?

She hung up with a sigh of relief, like one who had a brief reprieve. How she dreaded to meet her children's dear clear eyes, demanding the dreaded truth! How she feared to see rebuke in them for their brother!

She walked to the head of the stairs and called down to Selma.

"Selma, the children are all staying at school for lunch. Suppose you just bring me up a cup of tea and a bite. Not much. I'm not very hungry."

Selma was silent for a full minute. She always liked to get up nice surprises for the children for lunch, and was mortally disappointed when they did not come home.

"Yes ma'am," she said reluctantly. "Telephoning at this last minute, after I've got my lunch all ready to put on the table."

"Well, it's too bad," said Mary Garland. "Never mind, Selma, I guess they couldn't help it this time. But—I'm coming down. I shall enjoy the lunch anyway. I guess I can eat something." She tried to make her voice sound natural. Selma must not suspect that anything was the matter yet. If Rex— well, when it had to be told she must tell it most carefully. There had never been anything in their family life to conceal. Whatever came must be adjusted. If it was to be a trial then it must be admitted as such, with their faces all set to take their hard things courageously, no hiding behind subterfuges. But no servant should suspect that aught was the matter until they understood just what it was to be.

So she dashed cold water in her face and tried to hum a

little tune. It is true the tune got tangled with a few tears, but she steadied her lips and went down to the dining room, spoke cheerfully to Selma, sat down before the nice lunch and talked to Selma about the Christmas dinner that was to be next week. She managed thus to eat a very respectable lunch, forgetting for a few brief moments the anxiety that had fairly consumed her all the morning.

When she had finished her lunch she went upstairs, and patiently, persistently finished doing up the rest of her presents, trying her best to keep her mind on what she was doing, and away from the fearful possibilities that were in the future for them all.

And still so far she hadn't thought about the girl. Just because she had a strong feeling that no right-minded girl would marry a boy while he was in college and his people knew nothing about it. Not a boy as young as that, anyway.

So the girl was kept persistently out of all calculations. Until Rex should account for himself and tell his story, the girl had no part in this matter. Not even if she had been very much to blame, she had no part as yet.

At last all the presents were tied and labeled and put away. Rex's present too, because it had been long ago bought and planned for, and she could not think whether Rex's marriage was going to make a difference in what she was giving him or not. She must go on and get these things off her mind, and somehow wait without agitation until she heard from Rex.

And then, just as the children were arriving up the street and walking into the drive, the telephone rang, sharply, excitedly, almost as if it were angry that it had been forced to have so great a part in this affair, and Mary Garland, taking a long deep breath, and crying out in her heart, "O God! Help!" arose and went to the telephone.

3

THERE was a long delay before the connection was established, and the three children had entered the house and were tiptoeing up the stairs when the telephone gave its final twinkle, and Mary Garland's breathless voice answered. It seemed as if she could not summon the breath to speak.

"Is that Mrs. Garland? Mrs. Garland, your son Rex has been located and advised that you wished to speak to him but he was on his way to catch the train for our basketball game tonight in Buffalo, and couldn't stop to go to the telephone. He asked me to let you know that he is playing on the team tonight, and it was important that he be there. They will not be back until very late tonight, but he will call you in the morning."

Mary Garland hung up the telephone with a dazed look on her face, and turned toward the door where stood her three troubled children waiting. Could it be possible that Rex, after having sent her such a letter, would let a mere basketball game stop him from answering his mother's call? Surely Rex knew what consternation he had brought to her. Surely he would not so far forget his love for her, and all their years of close confidence, as to send her a message like that, and then pay so little attention to her call. The telegram had probably not reached him yet.

"He's playing basketball tonight!" She spoke the words as if they were a lesson she had been memorizing, and looked at Sylvia as if she expected an explanation.

"Yes," said Sylvia, "he wrote, you know, that he was on the team, but I shouldn't think he would let that stop him talking to you for just a minute." There was indignation in Sylvia's tones.

"I gathered that he only got my message as he was leaving the building, running for the train," said the mother slowly. "He will telephone in the morning."

"Bologny!" said Stan indignantly. "He knew what he'd done to us all, didn't he? He's not *dumb*. He knew how you'd feel. Where's he been all day that he just got your message? Hiding? If it was an all-right marriage and he isn't ashamed of it, why does he hafta *hide?* I think there's something phony about all this. Mother, I think you better let me run over to college and find out about it."

Then Mary Garland pulled her mantle of courage about her again and summoned a wan smile.

"That's dear of you, Stan, to want to protect me, but you know we've got to be patient and not judge Rex too harshly until we find out all about it. This is a serious matter, and we mustn't risk making some terrible mistake that may make us infinite trouble the rest of our lives. Besides, Stan dear, if anybody had to run over to college and find out about things I would certainly have to be the one to go. But I have thought it over carefully, and decided for the present that is not the thing to do."

"Well, I should think *not!*" said Stan indignantly. "One of your children should go of course, and it ought to be a boy. Personally I think Paul should have done something about this before you ever heard of it. I'll be glad to run over there this afternoon and put it all before Paul, and I'll wager that before night Paul will get it all fixed up somehow."

"Mother!" spoke up Sylvia quickly. "Isn't there such a thing as getting an unwise marriage annulled, especially when the parties are so very young?"

"I suppose there is," said Mary Garland slowly, sadly, as if she had already considered that.

"Well, then, why can't you call up your lawyer and fix it that way, right now before Rex gets any idea of it and runs away to prevent it?"

"Oh, my *dear!*" said Mary Garland. "Rex is very young to be married, of course, but Rex is not a baby. He is old enough to have fully understood what he was doing. It isn't as if it were something somebody had put over on him. It may have been unwise; of course it was. But it is done, and I'm not sure I would have the right to do a thing like that. I'm not sure it would be a *Christian* thing to do. I would have to know all the circumstances before I could even consider such a move. If they are really married, have been married for sometime, 'what God hath joined together let no man put asunder,' you know. It is a serious matter. I wouldn't dare make a single move in the matter until I know all about it. I'm not sure that I would even then."

"Oh, *mother!*" wailed Sylvia, her bright hope dashed, the quick tears coming into her eyes. "Has our Rex got to go under this terrible mistake all the rest of his life?"

"That is the way life is, Sylvia. We have to bear the consequences of our sins and our mistakes through the days down here. But you know it may turn out that there is really a bright side to it. The girl may be fine and sweet."

"She couldn't be!" said Fae determinedly, tossing her arrogant young head fiercely. "A girl like that would never encourage our Rex to marry her when his people didn't know anything about her. Marry when he wasn't through school! When his mother didn't know it."

"Now, listen, Fae," said Mary Garland, "we don't know this girl, and whatever comes in the future we have no right to jump to conclusions. Even though she has done a terrible thing like this she may have only been silly. Remember that Rex said she had no home, no people, he said she was all alone in the world. She may have had no teaching, and does not realize what an unwise and silly thing she has done."

"A pretty kind of a wife she'll make for Rex then," said Sylvia with snapping eyes.

"There, Sylvia, it won't do any good to say a lot of things like that that will probably have to be lived down and wiped out in the future. It would be better if you were all to go up to your rooms and kneel down and ask God to help you to look at this thing as He wants you to do, and then put it out of your minds until we know definitely if there is anything to do but wait and bear patiently whatever is to come out of this for us."

Stan gave her a startled look, dropped his serious gaze to the floor, and said huskily, "Okay, mother!" and walked gravely up the stairs. When he had reached the top and turned down the hall to his room Fae made a dash for the stairs and followed him, and then Sylvia turned to her mother.

"All right, mother, I'll try," she said, but there was deep trouble in her eyes as she slowly went up the stairs.

After they were all in their rooms again Mary Garland went upstairs to the telephone extension in her own room and called up the college, asking for Paul. By this time his examinations for the day would be over, and she would not be disturbing him.

But there was another long delay again, and finally the college operator spoke:

"Mrs. Garland, Paul has gone to the basketball game too. Almost all the older boys have gone. It is a very important game. I can find out from the Dean if there is any place in Buffalo where you could reach him. Would you like me to try?"

"No," said Mary Garland, with almost relief in her voice. She had been fearful ever since she had put in the call for Paul that maybe she shouldn't have done it. Paul was so hot-headed, so apt to be bitter with Rex, so ready to defend his mother and blame his brother. She hadn't wanted to tell Paul until she had talked with Rex. And now she was shut up to waiting, shut up to trusting the whole matter in the hands of the Lord!

There came a tap at her door, and Sylvia entered with a subdued face.

"Well, I've prayed, mother," she said quietly, "but it's going to be frightfully hard to keep from blaming that girl, and I'm sure I never shall like her, even if she turns out to be bearable. It's so awful, mother, for her to have made us all this trouble, and right at Christmas time. Spoiling our Christmas! The nicest time of all the year!"

"Well, dear, we mustn't think of that. Besides, perhaps it won't spoil Christmas. Christmas is a thing you can't spoil by worldly things. It has a real lasting meaning, of which the presents and the trees and the stars and the wreaths and carols are only symbols."

"Oh, I know," sighed the girl. "But—we were going to have *such* a nice time! Our Christmas party, and being together for our presents like it used to be when we were little kids! And we wanted to have our old friends around us, and maybe some new ones, and now we won't want anybody around here to see our shame and disgrace, and we won't feel like having any fun or going to things."

"I don't believe it is going to be as bad as that," said the mother, looking at her sweet sad daughter with troubled eyes. "Surely this happening isn't going to hurt the presents we have bought, nor to hinder you from going places and having good times. If this is something we are going to have to bear and get used to and try to like, why then we might as well get used to it now as any time, and carry bright faces. Have a good time in spite of it!"

"But mother, do you think it seems quite right to go

around looking happy when we are very sorrowful? People will think we don't care for Rex."

"Oh, no," said Mary Garland. "That is a foolish idea. We are not going to help Rex any by going around as if we were at a funeral. There will be enough of that without trying."

"But how can we help it, mother? We all love Rex a lot and to have this — this — kind of a girl come into our nice times and absorb him is going to be perfectly terrible. I don't feel as if I could hold my head up, and I know you feel just that way too, mother."

"Yes! Those are our natural feelings, dear. But God is stronger than such feelings. He is able to lift us up beyond those things. He is able to give us strength to be brave for each other, and find and plan nice ways to help us all to trust instead of worry."

Sylvia was still a long time, standing at the window looking out, and then she said with a deep sigh:

"But we'd have to stay at home all the time and try to act polite to that new sister, wouldn't we?"

"Not necessarily. Not all the time. You could have your engagements as usual. You can't put everything aside, even if they should be here. What were you thinking of, dear? Was there something special?"

"Well, I had thought about going to a concert, but it isn't necessary of course. When do you think they will likely come? Would they be here before Saturday night?"

"Oh, I don't know," said the mother, with a sound almost like a suppressed moan in her voice. "I haven't thought that far yet. But I don't see why their coming — *if* they come — should affect a concert. What concert is it? Something at the university?"

"Oh, no, it's The Messiah, given by the orchestra and the choral society. You know I've never heard it, and I had an invitation to go this morning, but I didn't dare accept it." She ended with a prolonged sigh.

"Oh, my dear!" mourned her mother. "There's no reason why you shouldn't go, of course. Who asked you? Someone I know?"

She looked at her oldest girl keenly, realizing that there were possibilities and dangers ahead of all her young brood, and she must be prepared to expect them. She awaited Sylvia's answer anxiously.

"No, I don't believe you do," she answered. "I showed you his picture in a college group the other day, but I don't suppose you noticed it. He's a swell fellow. His name is Rance Nelius. I thought perhaps I'd like to invite him here some night during Christmas week, or to dinner some time, while they are all home, but now of course I can't."

"I don't see why!" encouraged her mother thoughtfully. "Of course, we'll wait a little to see how things turn out, but I certainly don't want any of you to have your Christmas time spoiled in such ways. I would like very much to meet him, and we'll try to plan it so that it will be pleasant all around. But certainly go to your concert Saturday night. Just plan for it as a matter of course."

"But it doesn't seem right to desert the rest of the family at a time like this."

"No, dear. I'll be glad to have you having a nice time and getting your thoughts away from disappointments. Just who is this young man, dear? Is he in your classes?"

"Only in one. He's a senior. He's awfully bright, and I heard Doctor Wharton tell another teacher that he was the most brilliant man he had ever had, and he was sure he was going to amount to something great. Besides that he's awfully nice and full of fun, and not a bit stuck on himself. I'm sure you'd like him. But I told him I wasn't sure but things at home would be so I couldn't be away that night, and he said it was all right. I might call him up at the last minute if I found I could go. He's very—sort of—understanding, you know. Nothing silly about him."

"Where does he live?"

"I don't know. You see, I don't know him so awfully well. We've only met walking back and forth from the bus. He sometimes comes on the same bus I do, though not every day. I have an idea he has a part-time job or something, but I don't know. He's never told me exactly. But he's always nice and friendly for the few steps we walk together. He has nice eyes and doesn't go around flirting like some of them. But you needn't worry. I haven't any silly notions about young men, mother, and you needn't go to thinking I'll go off my head at any moment, like Rex. I don't believe I shall *ever* marry. Certainly not till I grow up. I guess Rex has taught us all a good lesson."

The mother gave a wan smile.

"*Dear* child!" she said with a soft little sigh. "Dear *children!*" she added, and then after a second. "I don't want you to be morbid on the subject of course, and it's right that young people should have good times together, and get acquainted and all that, only I don't want you to make any terrible mistakes. I'm sure you won't do any wild things, nor run away and get married!"

She gave another wan little smile that was almost nothing but a sigh and turned away to hide the quick tears that wanted to fall.

"I should say *not!*" said Sylvia with her eyes snapping angrily. "I can't see how Rex *could!* I don't believe any of us will ever want to have anything to do with anybody who would marry us, just because of what we've been through today. Just to see you go through this! It's awful! That was the reason I didn't want to speak about this concert, and I wouldn't think of bringing Rance here now. If he were an old friend it would be sort of different. But he's pretty much of a stranger, and I don't want any of you thinking *I'm* up to any silly nonsense!"

"No, dear, we won't think that! Go tell this boy you'll go to the concert. I think it will be nice for you. It will take your mind off things."

"But suppose—he—they—should be just arriving when I had to leave!"

"That won't make any difference. You have a right to a previous engagement. Besides, they didn't stand on ceremony about their marriage. They can't expect formal consideration. Anyhow, if anything unforeseen occurs you can always explain to him of course. Go ahead and accept your invitation."

All the rest of that evening the stricken Garland family struggled to be brave and cheerful for one another's sake, watching to drive the shadow away from their mother's eyes, maintaining a kind of rigid cheerfulness, and they were all really glad when the time came to go to bed.

Mary Garland did not call her oldest son again. She reasoned that he probably wouldn't be back from Buffalo until very late that night, or maybe not till morning, and there would be another day's studies, maybe more examinations. She wouldn't disturb him now until his day's work was done. She had waited so long, she would wait until Rex had a chance to call her, or else to come in answer to her telegram.

It was not until ten o'clock the next morning that Rex called, and then he was in a tremendous hurry. By that time the children had departed for school again, in comparative contentment. Somehow the night's sleep seemed to have quieted their anxieties. The letter of yesterday morning that had caused such consternation seemed more like an ugly dream now, and after one quick reassuring look at their mother, they put on their accustomed smiles and ate their breakfast with a brisk cheerfulness that was almost normal.

Only Sylvia, as she left, whispered earnestly,

"Mother, if—if—anything unusual happens, or—they're coming quickly, or—something—you'll telephone me to come home, won't you?"

And Mary Garland gave her thoughtful girl a loving smile and promised.

It was a hard morning for the mother to go through, and she spent more time upon her knees than she had done for several years. So, when at last the telephone rang and she heard Rex's big boy-voice booming over the wire, her heart leaped up with quick response and the tears sprang to her eyes.

"Rex!" she said yearningly. "Oh Rex! Where have you been?"

"Been? Why, I've been to Buffalo! Didn't they tell you I was playing on the basketball team last night? I just got back. They promised to phone you. I didn't have a second. Just had time to throw my stuff in the bag and run. It was a swell game, moms, and *we won!* How's that fer just a soph? Now, say, what's the little old idea sending me that telegram, moms? You know I can't do that. Why, I have two exams to-day and another tarmorra morning. How d'ya think I can leave before vacation? These are important exams. Wha'dya mean?"

"I meant what I said, Rex. I want you to come home *at once!*"

"And flunk my exams? What's the idea, moms? You never talked that way before. You were always keen about my passing everything."

Mary Garland's voice was full of tears as she answered, firmly, determinedly:

"But things are different now, Rex. If what you wrote me in your last letter is true, then examinations have nothing to do with you any more."

"Aw, you don't understand, moms," said Rex impatiently. "They don't have any of those old-time straight-laced rules here any more. That's all right, moms, and besides, nobody knows—"

"Rex, I want you to come home *at once!* Don't even stop to pack. We can attend to that later. I want you *now!*"

"Aw, heck, moms! You just don't understand. And I haven't

got any time to argue. There goes the bell and I'm expected to be in my seat in three minutes! Goo'bye. moms! See you subse. Be home as planned heretofore, and *can't* come sooner! I'm as busy as a one-armed paper hanger with fleas! So long, moms!"

"But *Rex*—" He was gone!

4

SYLVIA was on the watch as the bus neared the corner where Rance Nelius usually boarded it. She wasn't sure whether this was one of his days to get on here or not. Still, it was nearing vacation time and there were no regular rules at such a time. But he was not in sight and she decided that probably his work up in this direction was over for the week.

She felt a distinct sense of disappointment as the bus started on again, wondering now where she would be able to see him that day. Would she have to call him up after all? She had a feeling that she would like to get it settled so that nothing could happen to prevent it.

Then the bus lurched to a sudden stop, and looking back to the corner she saw him running. That must have been his whistle she had heard a second before. The memory of it came back on the air now, like a living sound. A clear, sharp whistle! And the bus driver was watching him come with a look of interest on his face, as if Rance was one of his favorite travelers.

"Thanks awfully!" said Rance as he swung himself aboard, and dropped his fare into the hand of the driver. "I got held up, and I was afraid I was going to be late to my class."

The driver's eyes lighted up with the expression of admiration that a bus driver sometimes wears for daily passengers, and Rance smiled his nice friendly smile as he turned to hunt a seat. Then he saw Sylvia.

Sylvia's eyes were alight with friendliness, too, and she slid over to the corner of the seat and made room for him, for the bus was rather full, and there were only two or three other places at the back.

Rance came over and sat down beside her with alacrity.

"I thought I was going to be left behind," he explained smiling, as he settled his pile of books in his lap, and looked at her with that intimate friendliness that he had shown yesterday. "You see, I'm coaching a kid to pass some examinations for next semester in high school, and this morning he had a lot of questions to ask me at the last minute, so I got behind. It was nice of the driver to wait. He's an accommodating bird."

"Yes, he is," said Sylvia looking up with a bright smile. Then his eyes met hers, and for an instant she had a feeling as if they had just really noticed each other, and weren't strangers any longer.

"Well," he said as he studied her face keenly, "what do you know? Anything happened that is going to make it possible for you to take in the concert Saturday night?"

Sylvia hadn't any idea what a flood of pleasure swept over her face as she answered. She was lovely like her lady-mother, but she had never taken much notice of it herself, so her loveliness was utterly unspoiled.

"Why, yes," she said. "I think I can go! I talked with mother about it and she didn't seem to think anything would interfere then. You see, we, I—" then she stopped in hopeless confusion. She didn't want to tell Rance Nelius that her young brother had gone and got married without their knowledge and was going to bring an unknown bride home, maybe that night.

Rance Nelius' face lighted up with gladness, as if she had

just promised something that he had wanted for a long time.

"Say, I'm glad!" he said. "You know I haven't had much time to make friends this winter, and it isn't much fun to go off on a bat all by yourself."

"No, I guess not," said Sylvia sympathetically. "I've never had to do that much. I've always had two big brothers, till they went away to college."

Nelius' glance kindled.

"That's nice," he said. "I'd like to know your brothers sometime. They would be worth knowing, I'm sure."

"I think they are," said Sylvia modestly, and then like a sharp thrust in her heart came the memory of what Rex had done. Was Rex worth knowing? Would she always have to think of Rex with a discount after this? Would this burden never lighten through the years? Her face grew suddenly sober at the thought.

But people all made mistakes, many of them sinned, and were forgiven, and the sin forgotten, the mistake mended. Only marriage was such a final thing! It just couldn't be mended or forgotten. One always carried the blight of a wrong marriage. And anyway doing it the way Rex had! Oh, of course there were people who thought a wrong marriage could be made right by divorce, but the Garlands were not brought up that way. In their minds that could never be a cure for what Rex had done!

Her thoughts went rambling off till suddenly she realized that Rance had asked her a question about her brothers.

"Will they be coming home for Christmas?"

"Oh yes," she said.

"Then perhaps I'll have a chance to see them."

"Yes," said Sylvia thoughtfully. "I'd like you to. I know they would like to know you. I'll arrange it when they get here and I see what their plans are to be. Are you to be in the city all during the holidays?"

"Yes," said the young man suddenly grave, "I have to. My mother died last summer, the last of our immediate family, and I'm on my own now. Oh, there are places I could go, relatives, but I'd rather just stay here. They don't really want me very badly, and I don't especially want them." He grinned.

She smiled understandingly.

"Oh, I'm sorry," she said. "Mothers would be hard to do without. Mine is wonderful. My father is gone, but we all depend so on mother. And mother will be glad to welcome you, I know. We usually have quite a crowd when we are all home and our friends come in."

"That must be wonderful," said the young man wistfully. "I always thought it would be great to belong to a large family. I've been keeping as busy as I could this last year so I wouldn't feel lonely, but I shall enjoy knowing some real people. That's one trouble with attending a city university and not living in the dormitory with the rest, you don't get to know many intimately. And to tell the truth those you do know are not always the kind you would select. Well, here we are again. It's seemed a shorter distance than usual. That's what it is to have company on the way," and he gave her a bright smile as they rose to get out of the bus.

"I'm so glad you are going to be able to go Saturday night," he said as they fell into step again entering the university grounds. "I hope you'll enjoy it as much as I'm going to. I was almost afraid I would have to take the poor old legendary musician as my companion," he twinkled musedly.

The look in his eyes stayed with Sylvia all the morning as she went about her work, and seemed to lighten her heart, and keep her mind away from the possibilities of the immediate future. Though whenever she thought of taking Rance Nelius home to meet them all at Christmas and what a happy thing it could be, there would be a sudden dashing of her hopes at the thought of Rex. Could she possibly be glad to introduce her handsome brother Rex to Rance? Could she ever explain his foolishness in marrying while he was still in college? And then her young heart would cry out quietly to God: "Oh God! Won't you please help us? Somehow save Rex from this awful thing that he has done! Somehow make it come out right for us all!" Again and again she found herself praying this, as she sat studying or while she was driving herself through the examination that filled the closing hours of the morning session.

Sylvia was a beautiful girl, perhaps after the old-fashioned idea of beauty more than the modern one. Her complexion was clear and healthy, with a lovely flush of her own that was not applied daily. Her eyes were wide and blue with dark lashes and delicate dark straight brows. They were eyes that looked at you levelly and unafraid. Her lips were their own natural color, curved often into merry smiles, and bringing along a dimple or two when her heart was glad. Her hair was golden brown and needed no permanent wave as one had come with her when she was born, and bright little tendrils of curls fluffed about her face making a soft setting for her every expression. Even her brothers were wont to think of her as beautiful, though Sylvia had no notion of it herself. She was not a girl who thought very much about herself. The most of her thoughts were for the others, her dear family; if they were happy it always made her as glad as if the happiness had been hers personally.

That morning as she sat at her work, there was something unusually lovely about her, as if a fairy gift had been given her. Sometimes she found herself wondering why she was so pleased that Rance was glad to have her go. At any rate little by little, she ceased to be worried about the situation at home, and what it might be when he came after her. She had a feeling of assurance that whatever happened Rance would understand, and take it all in good part. She did not know that more than once that morning Rance Nelius made an errand past the door of the room where she was, and turned his head to get a glimpse of her.

The last class in the afternoon was the one they had together, and when Sylvia gathered up her books and started toward the cloak room, her glance met his, and she was not surprised when she came out into the hall to find him standing by the outer door waiting for her.

"Do you mind if I walk a little way and find out where I am to come Saturday night?" he asked as they went down the walk to the entrance together.

"Mind?" said Sylvia. "Why, that would be delightful. Let's walk all the way! I feel as if I had been cramped up for a week! It will be nice to get some exercise. Unless that will keep you too long from something."

"No," he said happily, "I haven't anything to be kept from for a wonder. Just one more exam tomorrow afternoon, and I'm fairly sure of that. It's my major, so I'm not going to worry. How did it go with you this afternoon? Those questions weren't so bad, were they?"

"No," said Sylvia with a little laugh of relief. "I was surprised. I expected they would be terrible. I think perhaps I did fairly well, all but that second question. I wasn't at all sure of that. I suppose you knew it all and didn't have to hesitate."

"No," said Rance, "I wasn't sure of everything. That second question I thought was rather tricky."

And then they launched into a discussion of their studies, and Sylvia felt the thrill of being on a level with this young man who was considered bright; though he seemed utterly humble, and unconscious of his superior knowledge. So she chattered on just as she would have done with one of her brothers.

As they came to the corner where Sylvia usually met Stan and Fae she gave a quick look around. What would they think if they saw her coming with a strange young man? Would Stan be apt to frown and think she was starting something like Rex's affair?

But neither of the children were in sight, and then she remembered. The university class had been much longer than usual, and perhaps Stan and Fae had been dismissed early that afternoon, or more likely kept for some Christmas doings. Well, it was just as well. She didn't want things complicated.

They were getting very well acquainted on this walk. They liked many of the same things, had enjoyed the same books, and the same lectures, and they seemed to have made much the same judgments about their professors. They spoke the same language. Both of them were realizing that.

"This part of the city is beautiful, isn't it?" said Rance, looking around admiringly. "I haven't been out this way before."

"Why yes," said Sylvia, looking up half wonderingly, "I suppose it is. I never think about it much. We've lived here all our lives and got used to it, I guess. The houses are rather old-fashioned, but they are big and pleasant, and have ground around them. There are a few beautiful gardens. We all went to school first down that street, about three blocks away, and the high school was in the same direction. Yes, it's been nice here, and we love it. This is our house." Sylvia said, turning in at the big stone gateway. Then suddenly it came upon her what might have happened since she left that morning! Had Rex come home yet? Should she risk inviting Rance to come in? Yet it was so awkward not to do it. Rance walked with her up to the house, studying it, noting the homelikeness of the place, the tall stop-nets of the snow-bound tennis court, the outlines of the garden beds.

"It looks like such a pleasant home," he said with a wistfulness in his eyes and tone that was most appealing. She couldn't help inviting him in.

"You'll come in and meet mother?" she said, trying to speak in an easy manner. "I hope she's home this afternoon."

He smiled down at her.

"Not this afternoon," he said. "I'll save that pleasure for Saturday night if I may. I wanted to find out just where I was coming. Now I shall not miss my way. You have a lovely home," he added giving an admiring glance up at the house again. "I like it. It looks as if it fitted you!" His eyes met hers once more with a satisfied look that gave her a little breathless feeling. "Good-bye. I'll see you in the morning," he said, and with a wave of his hand he was gone. Sylvia stood still and watched him walk briskly down the drive and out the gate, thinking what a good time she had had for the last hour, in fact for the whole day, so far. Now, what would be coming next?

She walked slowly into the house, almost afraid to stop and listen. But when she got inside the hall there was no sound anywhere except the canary in the dining room yelling till it seemed he would fairly split his yellow throat.

She ran upstairs to her mother's room, but she was not there. She called, and looked about, but there came no answer. She could hear Selma down in the kitchen putting away pots and pans.

She went into her own room and there on her desk she found a little note.

Sylvia Dear:

No developments. I have gone to the church to help with the Christmas luncheon for the mothers of the mission primary class. Will be back about five. Get your Christmas things finished and don't worry.

Mother

She drew a deep breath of relief. Nothing happened yet! Perhaps after all there wasn't anything. Maybe it was just one of Rex's jokes. She hadn't been able to think that before, because Rex was too kind-hearted and loved mother too much to keep her in anxiety all this time. But surely he must have meant it for a joke, and was sure she would understand. Oh, if it could only be that!

So Sylvia got out her Christmas cards and went at addressing the ones she hadn't yet finished. One of them she lingered over, a charmingly artistic card, not very large, but lovely. It was a soft beautiful etching of the wise men following a star, and a brief text in script. "We have seen His star in the east and are come to worship Him." She had set it aside with Rance Nelius in mind, and now she addressed it to him with a pleasant sense that it was all right. Mother would approve, she was certain. Somehow that walk home had made her entirely sure of that.

Then she went happily to work on an unfinished bureau set she had been making for Fae's room. While she worked she kept thinking of things they had talked about on the way home. Rance was very nice. Oh, if only everything were all right so they could have the party of old friends they had planned, and she might invite Rance. She knew they would all like Rance. He would fit in perfectly. But now—!

Then her mind trailed off wondering if she could bring herself to tell Rance about Rex. Suppose he came here for her Saturday night and Rex and his new wife should walk in! Rex looking so young and boyish, and having a wife! She couldn't bear the thought of having to tell Rance Nelius that her brother had done such a wild thing as to get married that way. Oh, if it only didn't have to be!

Then she heard the children's voices, Fae's pitched high with excitement. She remembered that Fae's school was to have their Christmas play rehearsal that afternoon. That was why the house had been so empty.

She hurried to put away her work so that Fae wouldn't see it. She could finish it tonight after Fae had gone to bed.

The children hunted her up at once.

"Anything happened yet, Syl?" asked Stan.

"Not that I know of," said Sylvia. "There's mother's note I found when I got home. I haven't seen her yet, of course."

"Heck! How long's this thing going to last?" said Stan with a frown. "Seems like it wasn't worth while planning any fun or anything."

"It can't last much longer," said Sylvia. "Tomorrow's the last day of school. I should think they'd be coming home tomorrow night, or Saturday morning at the latest."

"Well, it's the limit to have our holidays spoiled this way," said Fae. "Other people are having good times, and we just have to hold our breaths all the time. I don't see why Rex didn't know what he'd done."

"Maybe he does," said Stan soberly. "Maybe he's sorry as the dickens by this time. Maybe he's sore at himself. I've felt that way myself when I knew I'd done something wrong. Say, I'm going down to get an apple. Who wants one?"

"I," said Fae.

"Bring me one, too, Stan," said Sylvia.

And presently Stan came back with a plate of shining red apples, and they all fell to enjoying them.

When they sighted their mother turning into the gateway, they all raced down the drive to meet her, even Sylvia. But they did not talk about their worries on the way to the house. They smiled and talked cheerfully, for they all saw their mother was very tired. Fae told about how the play was going, and that she had to make a presentation speech tomorrow for the teacher's present. It was a beautiful big photograph album of real leather, with the picture of the whole class pasted in the front. Fae was very much excited about it. And then Stan had to tell about the tree he had trimmed, and how Mary Elizabeth Remley had helped him. Fae chimed in again about how mean Betty Lou had been about wanting to wear her new pajamas, and how she stayed away from rehearsal, and how Miss Jenkins had made Fae take Betty Lou's part, and if Betty Lou didn't turn up and apologize she would be cut and Fae would have to keep it.

Mary Garland listened to them all, smiling, gentle, her tired eyes on first one and then the other. Then she looked at her eldest girl. Sylvia wasn't saying anything, but her face had happy curves, and the strained anxious look was gone. The mother sighed as she entered the house and looked anxiously on the hall table for a letter. But there was no letter. Too many things going on at college for Paul to think of writing, and of course she hadn't called him again. She was glad of that, for now she wouldn't have to worry about his trying to discipline Rex. Undoubtedly Rex needed discipline, but college was not the place to give it, under the circumstances, and Paul was not the one to administer it at present. She was, however, feeling the strain of Rex's silence greatly. It had seemed to her that the hours since Rex's letter had first arrived had been the longest she had ever experienced, the days interminable, and the nights a torture. There was a sad sweet strained look on her face that the children could readily read, and their resentment against their hitherto adored brother was growing day by day.

They ate their supper quietly. Mother was not eating much. They all noticed that, and they got up from the table with a kind of apathy toward the evening. Mary Garland saw that their nerves were getting raw too, and that she must rise to the occasion, so she rose. It was what she had been doing ever since their father had died, rising to occasions, and somehow doing that had the power to erase from her brow the new lines of care, and give her a kind of loving radiance that drew them all within its power.

"Now, boys and girls," she said playfully, "have any of you any home work that has to be done tonight?"

"Not a scratch," said Stan triumphantly.

"Oh no!" laughed Fae.

"I got it all done early this morning," said Sylvia.

"Very well, then, I want you all to come up in my room for a conference. I'm going to lie down a little while. My back is tired, and there are a few things we've got to settle. Stan, bring a pencil and a tablet and you be secretary. Sylvia, you and Fae get pencils too. We've got to get organized and be sure everything is in working order, if we are to have unexpected things sprung on us. We won't have brains to remember everything if it isn't all set down in black and white."

They all came with alacrity. Perhaps Sylvia suspected her mother's brave gesture, but she said nothing and came along joyously enough, as if it were a game.

"Now," said Mary Garland as she settled herself comfortably on her bed with the three young people around her, "we want to see if we are all ready. Suppose, Stan, you write down a list of all the names and then we'll check up and see if we all have our presents ready, wrapped and labeled, for each one. That includes the maids, and outsiders too. Then as you go along and something comes up that isn't done, Sylvia, you write it down, and suppose you undertake to remind the different ones, and see that the matter is attended to at once. And Fae, if anything occurs to you as we go along that needs attention, or investigation, suppose you write that down."

They spent an absorbed half hour doing this, and there was a practical result when the checking was done. Stan handed each one a bit of paper on which was written the number of things that still needed their attention.

"But what I'd like ta know," said Stan, "is, what are we gonta call that girl? That new girl of Rex's. We don't know her name. Or do we have to give her a present?"

They all looked appealingly at their mother. It was a question which she had already side-stepped in her own mind several times, but now she saw it had to be met.

"Why, if she comes for Christmas, yes, I suppose we must give her a present. It would not be courteous not to, and it would certainly hurt Rex deeply if he cares for her. I think it would hurt him anyway, even if he didn't, since he has chosen to make her his wife."

"Mother," said Fae looking up, with her chin in the air, "I think it is enough for us to *stand her,* without giving her presents that won't mean a thing. We give presents because we love people, don't we? Well, we don't love her! And I don't guess we ever will."

"Sometimes," said Mary Garland thoughtfully, "we give presents for the sake of other people. In this case we would be giving something for Rex's sake, at least until we have had time to know her and love her for her own sake."

"Well, I'll never *never* do that!" said Fae shutting her childish young lips firmly. "Taking my brother away, and letting him get married when he had no business to. No, I *won't* love her!"

"Well, I'm afraid you never will if you start out that way, Fae. I thought you went and asked God to make this thing right somehow, and to make you feel right, didn't you?"

"Well, I prayed *some* of those things," said Fae. "But I don't think it's right to love her. And I don't know as it's right to give things to her for Rex's sake either. He did wrong, didn't he? Well, ought he to have a lot of love spent on him when he did that?"

Mary Garland sighed.

"If God did that way with us, when we have done wrong, there are a good many gifts we wouldn't get from Him. I guess perhaps we all need to go and pray again."

"Well, moms, what would you think we could give to her? Would a box of candy be all right?"

"Yes, I should think so," said the mother.

"I have a pretty scarf I got for Cousin Euphrasia, and then I decided on a book instead. I could give that," said Sylvia.

Fae was very sober and thoughtful for a moment, and then she said:

"Well, I could give her a pretty handkerchief. I've got enough money left from my Christmas fund for that. Would that be all right, muvver?"

Mary Garland drew her youngest child within her arm and kissed her round pink cheek.

"Yes, dear. I think that would be nice."

They scattered presently to their rooms but their mother lay still a long time, thinking of her own problem. It hadn't been as simple as the children's. It wasn't just a matter of a present. It involved too many questions that might affect a whole lifetime if she went astray in her judgment.

She fell asleep at last, comforted by the thought that at least the strain of not knowing could not be much longer. Paul, anyway, would surely be coming home tomorrow night.

ABOUT two weeks before that letter came that so disturbed the Garland family, Rex stamped into the pieshop of the college town around ten o'clock one night, when most of the other students were attending a fraternity dance. It didn't happen to be Rex's fraternity, and anyway he didn't care much for dancing. Besides he was trying to study hard and make really good marks.

He had been working away in his room since dinner that night, and now he was suddenly hungry, so he had come down to the pieshop to get a bowl of soup.

It happened that there was no other customer in the shop but himself, and a blond waitress was the only attendant that night. One got extra pay for evening work, and she was buying an expensive suit on the installment plan. Another installment was due in a few days now, so she had offered to work that evening.

The waitress was seated behind the counter on a high stool reading a movie magazine when Rex came in, but she cast the magazine aside and came forward with alacrity. This was Rex Garland, already famous as a probable athletic star. He had dark, crisply curly, well-cut hair and eyes that were deep blue, darkly fringed.

"Ice cream?" she said cordially. "We have fresh strawberry, vanilla, chocolate, caramel-custard —"

But he held up his hand to check her list.

"I want something real," he said. "I'm hungry. I want a bowl of soup. We had a rank supper tonight at college. Sauerkraut, and I never could abide it."

"Is that so?" smiled the girl indulgently. "Well, I don't like it either. I don't think it's fit to put in a human stomach. What kind of soup do you want? Tomato or mushroom?"

"Haven't you got plain vegetable soup?" he asked eagerly. "The kind they make at home? I'm hungry for my mother's cooking!"

"Isn't that the truth!" sympathized the girl. "Does your mother cook? Most ladies don't have time for that nowadays, what with all the bridge parties and clubs and things."

"Oh, my mother doesn't go to clubs much, and she doesn't play bridge. Yes, she can cook, though she doesn't do much of it any more, but she's taught the servants to cook as well as she ever could."

All the time this idle conversation was going on the girl was working rapidly, manipulating a can of soup and a bright kettle on the gas hotplate, and now she set the bowl of steaming soup before him, brought a plate of crackers, and a glass of ice water.

"Do you have many servants?" she asked casually.

"Only three now, a cook and a waitress and a gardener."

"You're lucky to have a home like that!" said the girl with a wistful sigh. "Take me, now, I haven't got any mother, nor any home either," and she sighed deeply.

"Say, now, that's hard luck!" said Rex pleasantly. "It doesn't seem as if one could half live without a mother."

"Ain't it the truth!" said the girl.

"Has your mother been dead long?" asked Rex, because she still lingered around and it didn't seem kind not to say something.

"Yeah. She's been dead since I was a little kid. My aunt

brought me up, and she wasn't very motherly. We lived in one room, and she went to work in a department store every day, so you see I really never had a home at all."

"That's bad!" said Rex between hot mouthfuls of soup. "Your father dead, too?"

"I don't know," said the girl shyly, wiping a furtive tear. "He went away when my mother was very sick and we never heard from him again. I don't suppose he was worth much. He was the son of a rich man, but it just about killed my mother, having him go off like that."

"Well, that must have been pretty terrible," said Rex, reaching for another handful of crackers. "Haven't you ever heard from him?"

"No," said the girl sadly. "Well, only just once after he went away, he sent me a little locket and chain, but that's all. And we don't even know he sent that. It was after my mother died, and we weren't sure it was his handwriting. But there wasn't anybody else who could have sent it, so we gave him the credit of it. But after my aunt died that was the end, I guess. He probably thought I'd try to get supported by him. But you know, it's awfully hard. Being all alone in the world that way, and having to earn my living."

"It must be," said Rex sympathetically. "I think you deserve a great deal of credit the way you've got along. I guess they think a lot of you here."

"Oh, well, it's not so hot here, you know," said the girl with a toss of her head and a contemptuous look on her very red lips. "You know in a place like this where so many men come in you have to watch your step. They aren't always so respectful as they might be, either, and a girl has to run all sorts of risks to keep on going from day to day. There's a fellow now that's got me on the spot. He's been trying to make me go with him, but I don't like him, and anyhow he's already married. At least I *think* he is, and he gets so mad when I won't accept his invitations. He's got so now he watches for me when I go home at night, and three times already I've had to change my rooming-house because he follows me, and just hounds me to go to dances and things with him, and I'm afraid to stir anywhere for fear I'll meet him. He carries a gun too. He told me that, and sometimes he gets it out and fools around with it, and scares me out of my life."

"Who is this fellow? Does he live around here?" Rex asked angrily.

"He says his name is Rehobeth. Harry Rehobeth, but I'm not at all sure that's right. I think he just changes his name on occasion, if you know what I mean. And he might be hiding from justice for all I know. The first time he came in here to get something to eat was way late at night. They had asked me to keep open here till midnight, that night, and when he came in he was tight, if you know what I mean, really tight! And when I brought him his order he just reached over and caught my wrists and kissed me, just like that! Well, I wasn't used to that sort of thing and I told him so, and I shied off him and kept in the background. But the next day he came in again and said he was going to take me to a night club in the city, and he wouldn't take no for an answer. And he got furious when I wouldn't promise to go. A few nights after that he met me half-way home and grabbed me and tried to make love to me, but I screamed, and we heard a policeman coming so he beat it. But I've been deathly afraid of him ever since. He declares he's going to get me yet. And I've always been respectable, even if I was poor and alone."

By this time the girl was crying. Great crystal tears like beads rolling down her cheeks. She put up her hand and tried to wipe them off, and turned her head away to hide them from him.

"Say!" said Rex, "that's pretty tough! Is there anything I could do for you? If we knew where to find him I could get a bunch of the fellas together and we'd whale him within an inch of his life, and make him lay off you!"

The girl buried her face in her hands for a minute while her slender shoulders shook with sobs, and then she turned a teary smile on Rex.

"You're sweet!" she said under her breath. "But I wouldn't want to make you all that trouble."

"Why, that's no trouble at all," said Rex. "The fellows would just love to fight a guy like that and scare him to death. Tell me where you think we could find him. Do you think he'll be around tonight?"

"Oh, I'm afraid so," said the girl shivering fearfully, "but he wouldn't show himself of course if there were college boys around. Besides, you mustn't think of doing any such thing! You'd get in bad at the college, you know, and it would get in the papers and all. Why, he might even shoot you, and I'd never forgive myself if he did."

"Oh, I'd risk that!" said Rex gallantly. "Suppose you get me a cup of coffee and some of those cinnamon buns, and we'll make a plan to catch that guy and bring him to justice."

The girl cast a look of deep admiration at him that made him feel a real hero, and then her eyes grew frightened again.

"No!" she said. "No, I couldn't let you do that! I really couldn't! But there's one thing you could do for me if you don't mind. Wait! I'll get your coffee and then I'll tell you."

Rex watched her as she flew around getting his cinnamon buns, pouring his coffee, and thought how pretty she looked in that blue print dress that fitted her so well, and made her look so frail and delicate! What a shame any fellow was bad enough to torment a poor girl like that, just because she was alone in the world with nobody to protect her. What a rotter her father must be that he didn't hunt her up and look out for her!

The girl was back in a moment with the food, telling him again how grateful she was for his kind thought of her.

"You don't know what it means," she said with an adorable expression in her wide gray eyes, "to have someone offer to do a thing like that. After all these days and years of fending for myself, to have someone actually sorry for me! I just can't thank you enough."

"Oh, forget it!" said Rex royally. "*Any*body that was half-way decent would do the same. Forget it, and tell me what it was you were going to ask me to do for you."

"Oh, but I can't ever forget it," she said softly, "you're so good! But what I was going to ask you was, would you mind so very much walking home with me tonight? I'm just scared to death, I really am! And if I could be walking with some man I know he wouldn't dare touch me. Not tonight. And maybe by tomorrow I could find me another room, and then I'd be free from him for a while, and he'd get tired trailing me."

"Sure, I'll walk home with you! What time do you leave here?" He gave a quick look toward the clock. He was supposed to be in bed by a certain time since he was in training, but perhaps he could do it without being caught, and if he were he could explain that it was a matter of life and death, something he had to do for a lady.

"Sure," he said again. "When do we leave? Do you have to stay here late?"

The girl cast a look at the clock.

"Why I'm expecting the proprietor here any minute now. He's always in by quarter past eleven. He knows I want to go home by that time at the latest tonight. And if you would be so good as just to hang around till he comes—? Then you could pay your check sort of as if you were through here, and go outside, and in a minute or two I could get away. I'd meet you up at the corner by the drugstore. Would that be all right with you?"

"Sure!" said Rex again, feeling very gallant and generous, and thinking how pretty the girl looked when she smiled. What pretty little white teeth she had. He certainly would enjoy teaching that hound a lesson if they should chance to meet him.

So, presently, when the proprietor came in with another man, Rex paid his check and left, and in almost no time at all the girl stood beside him on the dark side of the drugstore.

"Come up this way," she said softly. "I think I see some college boys coming down the street, and you don't want them to see you going out with a waitress."

"What do you think I am?" growled Rex. "High hat?" But he turned his steps into the street where she led him and they walked away into the darkness side by side, she accommodating her steps gracefully to his longer stride.

But she kept looking back fearfully, and catching her breath. Once she started and clutched at his sleeve.

"Oh!" she said, "I thought I saw him coming!"

"Say, look here, you don't need to be scared. I'm here to protect you. What's the idea? Can't you trust me?"

He drew her arm within his own and looked down at her as if she had been a little child, and she edged closer to him and clung to his arm confidingly.

"You're so good to me!" she whispered. "And I should feel so perfectly terrible if anything happened to you on my account."

"Nonsense!" he said and tried to laugh it off. But, every now and then as they turned into far and darker streets, her body would quiver, and she would draw closer to him in another spasm of fright, till Rex, as if she were a frightened hysterical child, put his arm about her to steady her, and she drew still closer, and hid her face against his shoulder.

She was weeping there, her whole body quivering against him, her slender hands creeping into his. He wasn't just sure whether that was his fault or hers, but it seemed the right thing to do. He had to protect her, and comfort her, didn't he? And there she was in the darkness against him, and his whole body thrilled with the contact. His heart suddenly went out to her, such a sweet little frightened thing, her tears falling hot on his hands, and filling him with tenderness!

Suddenly he drew her closer into his arms and bent his head down to her face. And she lifted her sweet white face there in the darkness, her wet cheeks against his lips, her slender body creeping closer within his arms, her lips raised close to his. Then without warning even to himself, he kissed her, a long kiss, her lips clinging even after his astonished ones had ceased.

"Oh, you're *won*derful!" she murmured. "You're *dar*ling!" and clung the closer.

Then his whole body thrilled again, with an exaltation he had never known before. He had not been a boy who spent much thought on girls, or love. Heretofore girls had been merely good pals, or else flat tires. But this girl was different. This was a little spirit who had been shut into sorrow all her life, imprisoned by fear and desolation, and she had turned to him in her distress. She was pouring out her young soul to his, and it filled him with a great and reverent joy.

That was the beginning of it all. Yet Rex felt as if a new world had opened before him and life had taken on a different meaning from what he had ever dreamed it would have.

He didn't see her often, of course, for he was bound by college duties, and strict rules, rules which he had been brought up to respect and obey, and to count among first obligations. But the girl managed to impress him with her importance even amidst these. She claimed all possible moments when she was free herself from a job on which depended her bread and butter, and more important still, the smart garments she considered necessary to her outfitting under the circumstances.

For a day or two after that first night Rex went about in a daze of ecstatic joy, his mind on new matters that had never concerned him before. But gradually the exhilaration cleared somewhat and his mind settled down to sanity again, enough at least for him to keep up with his studies, and to keep fit athletically. By that time the thought of the girl only appeared on the horizon, at intervals, like the memory of a pleasant dream—until she herself took a hand in things and wrote him cryptic notes that were most intriguing. Not long letters, only a word or two that revived the memory of her, the wonder and the charm that she had brought; now and again she demanded his presence at some late hour, in a lonely meeting place where danger, she said, lurked for her. And then he would be recalled.

It was on one of these nights that she wept and pleaded that he would put her at once safely under his guardianship by marriage. If she were married, she told him, the man would cease to torment her. They needn't necessarily tell everybody. The college needn't know it, but she should be able to tell people who were intriguing against her, that she would send for her husband at once if they dared trouble her any more.

Rex didn't quite see this. He couldn't understand her line of reasoning. He was ready to come out in the open and fight her enemy, but he told her that he was in no position to marry anybody yet, he had to finish college or he never could be a man and take his rightful position in the world. He tried out all the traditions of his upbringing on her, but somehow they didn't seem to register with her. She was like a child, it seemed, when it came to reasoning. She said she never would feel safe again unless he would marry her. She was willing to go on working, and keep still about it for a time, at least until he was through his examinations, but to go back to desolation of loneliness with nothing sure ahead but his promises was beyond her. She could not endure it.

She wept and clung to him, till her very nearness and abandon of utter love for him, wore down his good sense, and reduced him to desperation.

He had half a mind to go home and tell his mother all about it. Ask his mother to take the girl home with her, and take care of her until he was able to look after her aright, but when he suggested this to the girl she went wild. She would never go to his mother unwed. What had his mother to do with it, anyway? She would kill herself before she would ever go and stay with his mother. Besides, that would not make her safe from the man she professed to fear. He would find out where she was. He had the most uncanny way of discovering things. He would find out and come to her, and perhaps make it uncomfortable for his mother; he would tell lies about herself, claim that she belonged to him, make Rex's mother think horrible things about her! And then she would go into despairing tears again, until Rex was at his wits' end, and at last he gave in and went with her to get a license.

The week-end that followed he had set aside for some gravely important study which meant a good deal in his course, but that was the time that she had chosen for their wedding. Rex looked troubled but her radiant face when he finally said yes seemed for the time being to repay him, filled him again with that ecstasy that had overwhelmed him the first night he had known her.

"Do you, Rex, take Florimel—?"

Florimel! That was her name. And somehow it seemed to him most euphonious and lovely, expressing what she really was, just a lovely flower that had been unfortunate and almost got crushed and trampled in the mire. Now she was his and he meant to cherish her and bring her into loveliness. He looked down at his little bride as they came away from the very common place where she had suggested it wouldn't cost much to be married. Her face was shining in triumph like the face of a sweet child who had just gotten what she wanted most of all in life, and he felt a sudden thrill that she was his. Why, he hadn't known that a man would feel that way when he had taken a bride. For a few minutes at least he was glad that he had done it. Lessons, and college, and the future, what were they? This was here and now, and he was finding out what real life meant. Why had he been afraid to go ahead when she first asked him? Why hadn't he known it would be like this? He looked down at her and saw beauty in her where it did not exist, because his eyes were full of glamour.

Florimel was exquisitely garbed, according to the taste of this world. She had just the right amount of make-up to give her wistful girlish appeal. Her hair had received distinctive attention and she was wearing the new black suit with the gray karakul bands. She really looked very smart. Her gray eyes as she looked up adoringly to his, seemed almost jade green in color; her hair had glints of gold and copper in the sun; and she had brought with her a shining gray suitcase filled with delightful garments that she had been preparing for several days, whenever she could get time off to visit the store where they sold goods on the installment plan. Of course Rex knew nothing about that part. He could only look in wonder that she could be so beautiful, and look so altogether properly clad on the very small earnings she must receive for her job in the pieshop. He was infatuated, perhaps not so much with the look of this girl, but with her utter dependence upon himself, and her great abandoning love for him. It had never occurred to Rex that anybody would ever care for him that way, and his senses were all stirred by her, till he was scarcely responsible for the time being.

She had not revealed to him until they were out and away from the place where they had been married, that now she was expecting a honeymoon. But she made it plain almost at once.

He looked at her gravely, sadly, when she suggested it, asking him naively where he was taking her.

"I'm sorry," he said. "I didn't know you were counting on going somewhere. I've got to go right back to college and do some tall studying. I'll have to study half the night to make up for being away as long as I have been this afternoon." He tried to smile apologetically, tenderly, to make up for the hard facts, but her childlike radiance vanished at once and she pouted.

"You don't mean that you are going off to leave me! Now, when we have just been married!"

She looked up into his eyes with sudden large tears in her own, that gave them the appearance of strange sinister jewels, and gripped his heart with quick reproach.

"But I told you," said Rex, "I told you we oughtn't to get married now. I told you I had to graduate first. And you said you were quite willing to wait for all the nice things I could get you till later, and to get along as best we could now."

"But I never thought you would be so hard-hearted as to grudge me a little honeymoon! Just a couple of days! That is all I asked. When you consented to get married I supposed of course that you understood that at least a honeymoon went with getting married! And I got time off from my job. I don't have to be back till Monday morning! And now it's all for nothing!"

Rex looked down at her in troubled perplexity. This was something he had not counted on.

"You don't really love me!" said Florimel sadly, and one big tear rolled down and made a little wet path on her cheek before it dropped on her black wool coat and sank into its texture.

"Florimel! Don't say that!"

"Well, you don't!" said the girl. "You think more of your old studies and your college than you do of me!"

"Now you know that isn't right," he declared. "You know I *have* to care about my college, because if I don't graduate I'll never get to a place where I can support you."

"Well, but surely two days won't make any difference!"

The tears were rolling down thick and fast, and people passing were looking curiously at the lovely girl who so evidently was being persecuted by the young man with her. Rex was suddenly very sensitive to the public gaze, and annoyed beyond measure. If his sister had ever carried on this way on the public street he certainly would have told her where to get off in short order. But Florimel was his bride, and he was responsible! He must do something about it!

"Two days makes a good deal of difference if it's two days before examination," said Rex sharply. "I really don't know what to do, Florrie! I didn't dream you counted on going away somewhere. And there's another reason, too, why we can't. It takes money to go away. I haven't but fifteen dollars in my pocket, and I owe that to somebody I promised to pay today!"

"Oh, *that!*" said Florimel laughing lightly. "You should worry about what you *owe!* You can pay him again some day. Tell him you forgot it, or you didn't have it, or you'll pay him next week. Don't let a little thing like that worry you! Besides, I've got a little money myself! I can lend you, and put your fifteen with it. I'm sure we can get quite a honeymoon out of it. I know a good cheap place to go." She launched into a description of its qualities, and her face lit up with anticipation as she talked, until Rex, watching her eagerness, stirred by her little hand in his, her confiding young body hugged close to his side, little by little yielded.

"We don't get married but once, you know!" she pleaded with a tender look, and Rex, with a despairing thought of the studying he had meant to do, yielded.

"All right!" he said and sighed deeply, his eyes full of trouble. "Come on! Where is this place we're going?"

She explained volubly, but his own mind was leaping ahead, trying to plan.

"If I'd only brought a couple of books along," he said meditatively. "I could snatch a bit of study while you're resting or something."

"Well, I like *that!*" said Florimel plaintively. "If you're going to divide up even this little time we have together I might as well go back to the pieshop and begin to serve again, and pretend we didn't get married at all."

In the end he had to soothe her and do as she wanted him to, there seemed no alternative, and of course, one only got married once, as she said. She must have what she wanted.

So they went to a sordid forlorn hotel that was really nothing more than a cheap roadhouse on a back country road, and Florimel showered endearments upon him, and smiles on the way, till she brought him back to think of her again, and how good it was going to be to make her happy.

But after they had dined he stood by the window gazing out at a bleak countryside, then turned with disgust from the noisy room with its blatant radio and its cheap assembly of unpleasant uncongenial people.

"This is a lousy place!" he said. "I wish we hadn't come here. This is no place for a honeymoon!"

"Oh, but you mustn't say that!" protested the girl. "This is *our* honeymoon. Forget the things you don't like, and let's have the time of our life! Let's go in the other room and dance!"

Then she exerted herself to make him think of nothing but herself, and for a little while succeeded. But the place, and the time that was not his to spend this way, kept intruding into his thoughts. Then Florimel would fling her lithe young body against his, slide her warm little hand possessively into his hand, lay her soft red mouth against his lips in a brief moment of privacy, and he would forget everything except his wonderful glamour-girl who loved him, and who was worthy of a far better honeymoon than the one he was trying to let her have these two days.

That was the way it all happened, so that afterward that honeymoon became a dream memory, full of strange sweet incidents, with a background of worry, like lovely poison that came to him with sinister menace as they made their way back to the college town very late Sunday night, at an hour that most people would have called Monday morning.

Back in his college room he flung himself down on his bed unwilling to waken his roommate who was sleeping, and then what he had done rushed upon him like a fierce tribunal, and put him through the ordeal of a regular trial, wherein he found himself deeply guilty.

It was that day, later on, being unable to get away from the sense of guilt, now that Florimel was not about to dull his mind with her glamour, that he wrote to his mother and told the truth.

Always, as a little boy, when he had done wrong he was

uneasy until he had told his mother. His brother Paul used to say about him that Rex always felt if he could just tell his mother he didn't have to be sorry for what he had done any more. Perhaps that feeling still lingered with him. For at least he seemed beset behind and before with the thought of his family and what they would say when they found out what he had done. He could not settle down to think or study until his mother knew. After the letter was written and mailed he plunged into his college work with all his might to make up for lost time, and seemed to cast the whole thing from him.

He had a feeling that now that his mother knew—that is when she got his letter—she would somehow help him to make all things right. He would take Florimel home for Christmas, and she would become one of them all, and then his way would go on happily.

Fortunately for his own peace of mind he had very little opportunity to see his new wife all the rest of that week, that is, to see her alone. The basketball games and his examinations filled up all the hours. And when he did hurry down to the pieshop for a few minutes, frequently Florimel was so busy she had only time to cast a quick smile in his direction.

But when the examinations were all out of the way, and he got a moment alone with Florimel, he found her strangely reluctant to go to his home with him. She put it on the ground of shyness. She wanted to be perfectly sure what his mother thought of their hasty marriage before she went there. And so from day to day and then from hour to hour he was not just sure how his affairs were going to come out, for Florimel did not give in easily. If they could possibly have got together money enough for a "real holiday" as she called it, she would have insisted that they go to the shore, or some winter resort, for she was eager to see life, and she had understood that she had married a young man who was fairly well off, and would be more so some day. Not that Rex had told her much except that until his majority he had only an allowance which was mostly all spent just now and he didn't expect more till after the holidays. But now she began to urge him to borrow money enough for them to have a good time. He wouldn't, of course. He had been well drilled on things like borrowing money before ever his mother sent him away to college, but Florimel couldn't understand why he wouldn't. Now that he had told his mother they were married, she ought to make everything right for them, and Florimel fought hard against going there to spend Christmas. So they argued and argued, and Rex compromised, first on one small thing and then another, that took almost the last cent Rex had.

And still he thought he was very much in love with his bride.

6

PAUL barged into the house while they were at dinner Friday evening, excited, eager, overwhelmingly glad to get home, greeting them all almost boisterously. And that wasn't like Paul, for it was natural for him to be rather grave and serious. But he hadn't been home but once since he left in the fall, and he had been working very hard.

"It's great to be here again," he exclaimed, after he had paid his taxi and set down his baggage.

He enfolded his mother in a close embrace, and kissed her on both cheeks, and the pretty color came into Mary Garland's face, making her look almost like a young girl. What a relief it was to have Paul at last. She felt that the worst of the strain was almost over.

Paul kissed his sisters, in his old teasing way, clapped Stan on his shoulder, and told him he heard he had been holding his own as man of the house in a swell way, and then he went back and kissed his mother again.

"Gee, mom, I've missed you like everything!" he said.

A minute later Mary Garland remembered.

"But, Paul, where is Rex?" She looked beyond him and toward the door. One of her white hands flew to her throat, and a ghastly worry came into her eyes.

"Why, isn't Rex here yet? I thought he would be here before me, but I suppose he got delayed. You see he left a note on my desk this morning saying he had a chance to drive up with somebody and he thought he might beat me to it. You never can tell, however, when you are dependent on somebody else, how may places they may want to stop over, or how many flat tires they may get on the way. Don't look so worried, mother, there's nothing to be alarmed about. He'll come barging in pretty soon, I'm sure."

But the entire family continued to look at him in that frightened, startled way, as if something terrible had happened.

"Then—you don't know yet—what's happened!" said Stan in a dignified elderly way, as if his position as man of the house made it necessary for him to take the responsibility of explaining.

"Don't know what?" said Paul, speaking sharply, impatiently, an apprehensive look coming into his eyes. He looked from Stan to his mother and back to his brother.

"Then you don't know Rex is *married!*" blurted out Stan with a choke in his voice.

"Married!" laughed Paul. "You're crazy! Where did you get that idea? I never heard such nonsense. Where did you get such folly, I say?"

"Mother had a letter," said Stan, and Paul's eyes, wide with unbelief and disgust, turned toward his mother.

"Yes," she said. "It's true, Paul!" and she broke down weeping. "Go get the letter, Sylvia. It's under my little jewel tray in my upper bureau drawer." Then her self-control gave way, and she covered her face with her hands, her shoulders shaking with her emotion.

Paul gathered her into his arms and tried to soothe her, patting her shoulders and smoothing her hair.

"But it can't be true, muzzie. You know I've seen Rex practically every day, and he's always going along fine. I haven't seen him around with girls much either. You know we don't go to the dances. It isn't in our line."

Sylvia was back in a moment with the letter, handing it out with the air of one who bore the weapon that had just killed a beloved one, and retired solemnly to her chair.

Paul took the letter with the air of handling a joke which he was about to explain away, and they waited breathless while he read it. His arm was still about his mother, her head on his shoulder. His dark brows were drawn in a frown as he read.

"But mother, I can't see how this can *possibly* be so!" he said in a puzzled voice. "He *couldn't* have got married and nobody else know. I tell you he hasn't been around with girls, and he hasn't been off visiting week-ends, or anything like that. I've made it my business to watch out for him, you know."

He looked down at his mother's sad face, and noted the drooping weariness of her body, then drew her over to the couch, and sat down beside her, one arm still about her.

"I can't understand it," he said, "unless this is his idea of a joke! But Rex was never like that."

"No," said his mother eagerly, *"never* like that!"

"But—mother, what have you done? Why didn't you get in touch with me at once?"

He looked at the date of the letter.

"Why, you've known this for several days! And you didn't *do* anything? You should have called me at once!"

"I did call Rex, right away, but they couldn't find him. They said he was in class, first, and then they said he wasn't. I didn't want to disturb you in the midst of an examination perhaps, so I tried to get Rex. I kept on calling him, every little while, and finally I sent him a telegram to come home at once. But before it could have got there the college called me and said he was just running for a train to Buffalo, that he was playing on the basketball team there, and he couldn't stop to come to the phone. He would call me up when he got back in the morning. So then I *did* try to call you, Paul, and word came back that *you* had gone to Buffalo to the game too."

"That's right," said Paul with distress in his eyes. "I went to the game. Almost everybody went. It was a great game and meant a lot to the college. I wanted to see how my kid brother did, you know, the first big game he's had. And he was swell, mother, simply *swell!* He shot several beautiful goals. But mother, I don't see why they didn't tell me when I got back that night that you had called."

"Well, I didn't try you again. I thought you would have been up late, and there were more examinations that next day, and besides I had sent Rex that telegram and thought he would surely call up pretty soon, and I wouldn't need to bother you until I knew more about it. But when he called he hardly had time to talk. He said he had important classes, and wanted to know what I meant by ordering him home before the term was over. I told him that if what he had said in that letter was true, that examinations and classes didn't make any difference now, and I wanted him to come right home. But all he said was 'Aw, you don't understand. I've got to hurry. Good-bye, I'll see you soon,' and that's the last I've heard from him."

Mary Garland tried to stop the tears which were again in full force, and Paul drew her close to him and put his lips down to her tear-drenched face trying to comfort her.

"There, there, mother! I'm sure there must be some mistake about this! Don't worry! Rex will surely be here soon, and he'll explain it all. You know, mother, he's a *good* kid!"

Her heart leaped up at that. It was what had made this whole thing so bitter to understand how Rex could have done this thing to her. Although she was not one who thought a great deal of herself, yet she knew that Rex loved her deeply, and how could he help but know what pain he had given? If he was suddenly in love with somebody, surely he could have waited a little. Surely he could have given them some warning, and they could have arranged a quiet little wedding, if they insisted on it so soon, even though he was so young!

They talked it over gravely, carefully, considering every phase of every possibility. And in the midst of it all they awoke to the fact that Paul had had no dinner. They summoned Selma, who adored "Mr. Paul," and with smiles produced plenty to eat, good and hot.

"I was keepin' it warm for ye," she acknowledged with a shy smile.

So while Paul ate they sat around and talked it over. And suddenly the question of the girl came to the front as she had not done before.

"But Paul, haven't you any idea who the girl could be?" asked his mother.

"Not in the least!" said Paul decidedly. "There aren't any girls at all around the college, that is, girls that would be at all in his class. The waiters at the college are all fellows who are earning part of their way in college. The telephone operator in the college happens to be an oldish woman. She used to be a teacher in the town, and she had a fall that left her lame, so the college gave her this position to help her out. Her family were somehow connected with the college."

"Aren't there any girls in the village?"

"Why, there isn't any village, much, you know. Just a few stores, a couple of restaurants. Of course they have waitresses in the restaurants, and there are girls in the telephone office. There's one in the pieshop, rather startlingly attractive, with platinum blond hair, or maybe that isn't it. It's more like the color of nasturtiums. Anyway, it isn't natural. They call her Florimel. But I'm quite sure Rex wouldn't have anything to do with her. I will say she has a 'come-hither' in her big gray eyes, but she's away and above older than Rex, and anyway, you know he has some sense, mother."

"I've heard that common-sense doesn't count for much when people think they are in love."

"*In love!*" snorted Paul. "*Rex* in *love!* That's ridiculous!"

But his mother sat there and sighed and tried to check the slow tears that kept stealing out upon her face, trickling gently down to her chin, and dripping off, until the children's hearts were wrung. Mother had been so brave and cheerful all these awful days, and now here that Paul had come to help she had gone to pieces! They didn't realize that she had been relying on Paul to dispel the trouble in some unexpected way, and Paul hadn't been able to do it. He had tried, he didn't believe it was true, he said, but he wasn't in the least convincing. And now there had taken form a very definite girl. She might not be the one, of course, but her frilly name, Florimel, expressed all the fear and dread of her that had been forming during their anxiety.

Paul swallowed the last bite of pie that Selma had brought, glanced at his watch, and then announced:

"I'm going to call up the college. It's time that kid was here, and if he doesn't come pretty soon, and I can't find out any good reason for his delay, I sure will wallop him when he does get here." So he strode across the hall to the telephone.

The family slipped one by one into the living room and waited for him.

It took a long time, but Mary Garland understood that. She had had experience of how unsatisfactory it was to call that college, especially out of hours when the regular operator was not supposed to be on duty. So they sat patiently, like those who wait for life and death crises at the hospital where dear friends are in critical situations. But at last Paul came into the room.

"I can't get much satisfaction there," he announced with an artificial gaiety which did not deceive his mother. "Almost everybody has gone home for Christmas, or else doesn't know anything. At last I got the office boy and he says Rex left early this morning in a car. He says he's sure. He says he saw him, and he was with another fellow, one of the college boys, he thinks, but he didn't look very closely, and they were some distance away, so he couldn't be sure which boy."

Mary Garland gave him a hopeless look, and remained pitifully silent.

"Well," said Stan with a note of relief in his voice, "if he didn't see any girl around then that settles that, somewhat, doesn't it?"

"He might have picked her up later," said Fae keenly.

A look flashed over Paul's face.

"I'll try something else," he said, and went back to the telephone. But he didn't tell them he had called up the pieshop and asked for Florimel, neither did he tell them that the owner of the pieshop had told him that Florimel was off for the holidays. They said she drove off that morning in a hired car with a couple of college boys. But Paul didn't come right back to the living room after he heard that. He called up two or three other fellows whom he knew were staying at college and asked them if they had seen Rex, and one of them said Rex told him that morning he was off for home. He hadn't seen him around since, so he guessed he was gone. Then Paul tried several other calls, but got no satisfaction, and presently he came back and told them that everybody agreed that Rex was gone home, so it was probably true that he had started off with somebody in a car, and very likely the other guy had sidetracked him for a while, and he had to wait to be brought on, or maybe the other fellow wasn't coming all the way and Rex had to wait for a train. Or they'd had a flat tire or something. And why didn't mother go to bed now? He was here and could keep watch for his brother. But he said not one word about Florimel.

But no, Mary Garland would not go to bed. She wanted to sit up and wait. Surely Rex would come pretty soon. And anyhow, Paul was here, after the long months without him, and she wanted to be with him and hear all about everything.

So Paul talked. He told them all about his examinations. He described his teachers, and some of his classmates, and made a pretty good job of keeping the atmosphere lively, as if nothing had happened and they were just waiting for

Rex to come, sure that he would come pretty soon.

But by this time Paul wasn't at all easy in his mind. He was trying to rack his memory and think if he had ever seen Rex with Florimel, but try as hard as he would he couldn't remember.

He wouldn't ever have connected Rex with Florimel in any way. He wouldn't have thought she was his type. In fact, Rex had never been a lady's man. But somehow he didn't trust a girl like Florimel. His impression of her was, from the few times he had noticed her, that she was ready with her smiles, and her sly eyes, to make up to any lad who would notice her. He hadn't liked her type and he had never joked with her when she waited upon him at the pieshop as some of the rest of the fellows did. But surely, *surely,* Rex, with his fine upbringing, and his high ideals, and his love for mother and sisters, would never get in the toils of a girl like that! It couldn't be.

But yet as he talked on, making time, trying in some other way to account for Rex's strange behavior, the idea of Florimel kept gnawing like some little beast of prey in the back of his mind, and worrying him to the last degree. Florimel and Rex! What an impossible combination! How were they ever to endure it if it was true?

The hour was growing late, and Fae, curled up on the floor beside her mother's couch, was almost asleep. Sylvia, under the big lamp was hemstitching a handkerchief that was to be one of her Christmas gifts for an aunt up in New York. She wore a dejected look. Stan was sitting over by the front window where he could watch the drive and see the first minute a car turned into it. Stan was looking suddenly grown-up and as if he were carrying great burdens. He hadn't even brightened up much at the very elaborate account of the basketball game up in Buffalo, in which Rex had starred so wonderfully. Paul had made the account last as long as possible, but he realized as he went on that perhaps he was only succeeding in making them see Rex in all his best lights, and filling them with terror at the thought of what he had done.

And then as he paused, trying to get a different topic, thinking perhaps he would tell them about his own successes, and turn their thoughts away from Rex a little while, the mother spoke out of a great sorrowful silence.

"What kind of a girl is this Florimel? You didn't mean she was not respectable did you, Paul?"

Paul turned and realized that his mother had not been blinded by his silence. Her mind had caught the worst possible construction and turned it over in her thoughts.

"Mother!" he said distractedly. "You mustn't get such ideas. I just spoke of that girl because I wanted to show you there wasn't anyone there that Rex could possibly get entangled with. No girls except visiting ones at dances. No, I don't think she is not respectable. Just silly, perhaps. She may not even be that. I truly don't know much about her. It isn't of course a nice position for a girl in a college town, to be a waitress in a pieshop where the fellows go, but for all I know she's perfectly respectable. Mother, you simply must forget about her. If this is true about Rex, which I'm not at all sure it is, then it's probably something perfectly all right. That is, as right as it could be to marry *any*one at his age. So please try not to think it out and torture yourself any more. Now, why won't you all go to bed and rest? Rex ought to be here in a very short time now, that is, if he isn't held up by a flat tire or something like that. Or, it may be he finds it necessary to stay all night with the fellow who brought him."

"In which case of course he ought to telephone me," said Mary Garland sadly. "No, Paul, I've had three days to think this thing over carefully, and I'm satisfied there is something absolutely wrong about it all. Something that perhaps Rex is ashamed of, and he is afraid to come home after what I said to him about his classes not being important now. I'm afraid I let him see too clearly how I felt about what he had done. Perhaps he has decided not to come home at all."

"Nonsense!" said Paul sharply. "How *could* he? Mother, he hasn't got any money to hang around anywhere. I know that for a fact because Rex borrowed ten dollars from me before he started for Buffalo, so he can't be very flush. He wanted more, but I couldn't spare it."

"Oh!" moaned the mother and lay very still with her hand shading her trembling lips and her tortured eyes.

"Say, mother," said Paul, jumping up and walking over to the couch, "would you feel better if I took the midnight train and went back to college and scouted around to see if I can locate Rex? Or to find out just when and how he left the town? I *can,* you know. There *is* a midnight train, and," he glanced at his watch. "I've just about time to catch it. Then when I get there if I find out anything I can telephone you at once, and ease your mind a little. Wouldn't you like me to do that?"

The room was very still while Mary Garland turned that over in her mind. Then she shook her head.

"No, Paul, you'd better stay here. I need you. If Rex is really married it would make him very angry to know that you had gone hunting him. And as you say, he may be staying over night with whoever is bringing him, although I can't think he wouldn't telephone if he could. But I guess we've got to be patient and wait. He'll likely come later, or at least in the morning. If he doesn't, we can think what to do then. But you had better stay here. I'm glad you have come, son."

Paul stooped down and kissed her.

"Dear brave little moms!" he breathed gently. "I'll do whatever you want."

She smiled sadly.

"Yes, I know, and I'm glad to have you here. It's a comfort."

In a moment she looked up again and about upon them all, and then she sat up.

"Children," she said, and her voice was very gentle. "I think perhaps we need to ask God to help us. I think perhaps we've drifted a long way from our Heavenly Father since your earthly father went away, and it's my fault. Suppose we just bow our heads right here and ask our Father to help us. There really isn't anything we can do to help ourselves tonight, that I see. We don't want to call in the police to help us search. Our Father knows all about it. Let us pray to Him about it."

And then Mary Garland bowed her head in her hands and began haltingly, almost shyly, to pray, pleading her own weakness and failure and inablility, pleading His love for all His redeemed ones.

"And Thou knowest, dear Lord, that we have been redeemed by Thine atoning sacrifice," she said. "Oh, we haven't walked with Thee as we should, and we have no right in ourselves to ask this great thing of Thee in our distress, but because Thou art our Saviour and lovest us, we have confidence that Thou wilt forgive our wanderings, and hear our prayer now for our dear Rex, wherever he may be. Thou knowest where he is. Wilt Thou care for him. Wilt Thou help us to find him. Wilt Thou relieve our distress. And whatever our Rex may have done, no matter how wrong, wilt Thou forgive him, and open up a way for him to be a man after Thy plan, a man who will be pleasing unto Thee. We ask it in the name of the Lord Jesus."

It was very still for an instant after she had finished, and no one was expecting any more, they all were bowing there before God with uplifted hearts. Then suddenly Paul's voice, strong, solemn, clear, broke the silence.

"Heavenly Father, I haven't been following You the way I meant to when I went to college, but I did mean it when I accepted You as my Saviour, and I'm asking You now to forgive me, and help me to be what I ought to be. Help me to be a help to my brother. O Lord, pity him, and save him from what he seems to have done to his life! Somehow help him to get back to You, even if it is through a hard way. And help me to know what I ought to do to find Rex and help mother!"

Paul's voice was very solemn as he finished. Then Sylvia very softly breathed a few words, almost inaudibly, and then Stan spoke, as if God were right there beside him.

"O Lord, I haven't been much of a Christian, but after this I'm going to try to be different, and won't You please bring our Rex home, no matter how foolish he has been?"

Fae, her voice drowned in tears, murmured:

"Dear God, please bring Rex home."

They looked at one another shyly after that experience. It was something they never would forget. It was more tremendous than even the sorrow which had brought it about.

Stan got up silently and went about locking the doors for the night as he had been doing since his brothers went away to college, just as if he were the head of the house. Then they all kissed their mother good night, and Paul escorted her upstairs, with Fae just behind patting his arm, and saying, "I'm glad you're home again, Paul." He smiled at her and answered, "And I'm glad to be here, little sister!"

When they were all lying in their beds, their doors open into the wide hall, they thought about that prayer time. It was as it used to be when father was alive, and they were little children and had worship every night and morning. It was beautiful. It was a bond between them all, like no other bond that had ever been. They would never forget their mother's prayer, with tears in her voice, nor Paul's clear petition that was a confession and a testimony, nor the others' halting sentences. It was as if God had come into the house to be with them and help them.

They did not listen for taxi wheels that night, nor footsteps on the drive. They had put the whole matter into stronger hands than theirs, and they could rest and trust. It was a new feeling and they liked it.

The mother fell asleep with peace in her soul, such peace as she had not had for years. Trouble might come back on the morrow. She was reasonably sure that it would. But she did not have to bear it alone now. God would somehow help them through.

Sylvia, as she drifted off to sleep, had a passing thought of Rance Nelius; he would have fitted into the prayer time too, if he had been there. She didn't know why she felt he would, but she did, and she was glad.

The night came deeper, blacker, with no stars above. No Christmas stars! But Christmas was not many days off, even if trouble *was* all about.

Silently, stealthily, down through the darkness, came flakes of snow, thicker and faster they came, whirling this way and that, hurrying down to cover the ground, and the dead grass, and the place where flowers had been, and where flowers would be again in the spring. But now they were spreading a Christmas robe upon the earth to surprise the sleepers in the morning.

And out in the world, somewhere, beyond that white blanket of snow, was Rex, out in the world! But God knew where he was.

7

NEXT morning there was still no word from Rex.

Paul spent a good deal of time at the telephone doing some wise detective work, and finding out very little. But he found enough to convince him that there would be no real use in going back to college now to search for Rex, for some of his faithful friends had made sure that Rex was not in or about the college anywhere, and now there was more testimony to make sure that Rex had driven away in a car, with another young man. And if there had been a girl along also, the fact was still shrouded in mystery.

About mid-morning Sylvia went to her mother when she knew she was alone in her room, and her eyes were very sad and anxious.

"Mother, what do you think I ought to do about the concert tonight? It doesn't seem right for me to go off and have a pleasant time when all this is going on at home. I don't believe I could really enjoy a concert unless Rex is home."

"I don't see why you shouldn't go, dear," said Mary Garland. "You won't be helping anybody at home by staying here and sorrowing. And you owe it to your escort to go now. He will be disappointed. He has been counting on your going. Better just leave it in God's hands, and go on, Sylvia dear."

It was just then while they were talking that the maid brought a florist's box upstairs.

"It's for you, Miss Sylvia," she said.

Sylvia took it to her mother's room.

"Mother! See! Flowers for me! I expect Rance has sent them."

She opened the box and found a lovely corsage of talisman roses.

"Oh, mother, I wish we hadn't any sorrow so I could enjoy these beautiful roses!"

Her mother smiled sweetly.

"There is always sorrow in the world somewhere," she said, "but God sent those roses to you to enjoy. It is right for you to enjoy them. The sorrow and the joy is always mixed up down here on earth, and we have to take the joy and thank God for it, and trust Him with the sorrow."

Sylvia gave her mother a warm sweet look.

"You're wonderful, mother!" she said softly. "To hear you talk one would think the trouble was all mine and none of it yours. I wonder if I can ever get where I'll be brave like you, and trustful."

So Sylvia got ready her prettiest garments, her dark wine-colored taffeta, her string of pearls and her pearl clip that she only wore on special occasions. They were not real pearls, of course, but a very nice imitation, simple and girlish. She got out the little chic new hat that matched her dress, with its tiny ostrich tip at one side, and then she thought of the roses, how well they would look against the wine color.

Fae was watching her happily.

"You're going to look wonderful, Syl," she said admiringly. "I'm so glad mother thought it was all right for you to go. And your gray squirrel coat is going to be swell with the other things. Have you got gloves to match?"

Sylvia smiled.

"Yes, open the top drawer and you'll see them. You're a dear generous sister to be glad that I'm going to have a nice time, even though you may be at home with unpleasant things happening."

Fae took out the gloves from their tissue paper wrapping and put an admiring finger on the white stitching on the back, that stood out so crisply against the wine-colored kid.

"Oh, what pretty, pretty gloves!" said Fae. "I like that stitching, don't you? And the scallops on the cape-edge, bound with white kid. They are sweet. Oh, I'm glad you are going to have a good time. No matter what is going on here I'm going to think about you a lot, and how you are sitting in the front row of the first balcony. I've always thought that would be the most marvelous place to sit where you could see everybody, and really hear so much better too, I should think. If things get bad here I'll just try to pretend I'm there sitting beside you hearing it all. And when you come back you'll slip into my room, even if it is late and I'm asleep, and tell me about it. You'll wake me up and tell me, won't you?"

"I certainly will, you precious," and Sylvia stooped and kissed her sister gently, more stirred than she had the courage to show.

"Well, and I'm glad, too, that you've got such a nice young man to go with," said Fae with an adoring smile. "Selma saw him when you came home the other night. He only came to the door, but Selma was up at the front window and watched him walk down the drive. She says he has a nice walk, kind of strong and sure, as if he was never ashamed. Like our Paul. And she says he's very good looking, too. I'm glad of that. I shouldn't like to have you go with Henry Parsons. He's too awkward and bushy. His hair is too long, and I just hate that little funny mustache he wears. Why do men wear things like that on their lips? I think it makes them look funny, don't you? And your young man has a nice name.

Rance Nelius, isn't that it? I asked mother. It doesn't sound sissy and yet it isn't just like every other person."

The day went on with still no sign from Rex.

Paul and his mother went into conference early in the afternoon, and Paul did a good deal more telephoning, but got no new light on the matter.

"I am afraid," said Mary Garland with a troubled look, when Paul came back to her after another siege at the telephone and acknowledged that he could not think of anyone else to call. "I'm afraid that I hurt his feelings when he called up. I was so insistent that he come home at once without waiting for his classes. Perhaps he doesn't mean to come home at all. You know I've never really answered his letter, saying whether he may bring his wife home for Christmas. I am afraid he is hurt at me!"

A cloud of displeasure darkened Paul's pleasant face.

"If he is hurt, mother, he certainly deserves to be. He must know he has done wrong. And he knows you love him and were terribly hurt at his letter. I suppose he really doesn't deserve to come home at all. But somehow I think he won't stay away entirely. And where can he go? I tell you he hasn't but a very little money. Unless he borrowed some of someone else, and you know there's no college fellow that has any surplus of money, especially around Christmas time. No, mother, he's bound to come home sometime. And it's better for him not to know just how you are going to receive him. I'm only afraid that when you see him you'll turn softhearted, and not make him understand what he has done. He's used to counting on you. He thinks he can wind you around his finger. Of course he loves you, and all, but I guess maybe we've spoiled him. He knows we're all just nuts about him."

"He's pretty stubborn though," sighed his mother. "If he gets an idea in his head he sticks to it a long time, you know."

"Yes," said Paul, setting his lips in a troubled determined way. "Yes, and I suspect if dad had lived he would have thrashed that out of him somehow. I guess we've been too easy on him."

"There's another side to it, too, you know, son. Rex is very tender-hearted. I got to thinking about his letter in the night, how he said she was a nice girl, and we would like her, that she was all alone in the world. I'm just afraid he was sorry for her, and married her to protect her. And now, of course, he'll stand by what he's done, even though it may have been done impulsively, and he'll try to carry it off the best way he can. He won't give in. You know Rex."

"Yes, mother, I know Rex, but I thought *you knew God!* Mother, didn't you put this whole matter into God's hands and say you would trust Him?"

"Oh, yes," quivered Mary Garland, trying to smile through the quick tears that had come. "Yes, I do trust Him, and I'll try. I will put away my fears. Perhaps this is something I needed, a disciplining to teach me something I wouldn't learn in any other way."

Paul stooped and kissed her tenderly.

"Dear little mother! You're a great little brave woman. I don't believe you ever needed any disciplining. Not since *I've* known you, anyway."

"Oh, yes, I have, many a time," smiled the mother.

"Well, we won't discuss that, because we should never agree about it, I'm sure. But mother, now honestly, wouldn't you like me to get a car somewhere, and drive back to college and hunt around to see if I can find out anything about this, and if I can possibly trace Rex—or both of them, if they are together, and I suppose they must be. Wouldn't you like that? I could even get hold of a detective to help trace them if necessary, and I'd bring them back, or at any rate bring Rex back, I'd promise you that. I can't see having you put through any more torture."

Mary Garland shook her head decidedly.

"No, Paul," she said. "That would make the future impossible. It would make a breach that would not easily be healed, perhaps forever. No. We will wait. He is married. He probably feels that he is independent. Eventually Rex will discover he has done wrong, and will come. I am sure he will come. And it will be better for him to come, than for you to run after him. He must not feel he is in leading strings. He would never forgive you. Certainly his wife would not, if she has any spirit at all. We can't have a break like that in our family, our loving family! We can't, Paul!"

"I know," said Paul huskily, looking very sad.

"No, Paul," went on Mary Garland. "God isn't dead, and I've promised to trust Him. We'll wait."

"All right!" said Paul, sinking down in a big chair and burying his face in his hands.

After a little his mother rose.

"Come, Paul. Come and help me. I'm going to put up the best curtains in the guest room for them. I wasn't going to, after I got Rex's letter, but now I've decided to. I always put them up for gay times and holidays, you know."

"I didn't think you considered this a gay time," said Paul grimly, with a wry smile, "but whatever you say goes! By the way, where are you going to park them—if they come?"

They were standing now in the doorway of the great beautiful guest room, looking around, the place where they had always enjoyed putting beloved guests. Great wide windows looking out upon the snow-clad lawn, lovely simple old furniture, a few rare pictures.

Mary Garland did not answer for a minute, as she looked about on the place she had so enjoyed planning in every detail. Then with a look of renunciation in her eyes and decision in her tone she said:

"Here, I think! Rex's room is scarcely large enough for two, and has only a single bed. We'll just leave Rex's room the way it has always been, and then if he wants to get away by himself among his own things, he can. But we'll get this room ready and make it festive. After all, he is my son!"

"So!" said Paul with a comical twinkle. "The fatted calf, is it? Well, I'll try not to act the part of the elder son. I'll do my best not to be hostile, if you say that's the proper way. I'm not sure it is, but I won't hinder you."

"Oh, Paul, that's good! I was afraid you might make trouble. I know he deserves it, but we must remember he belongs to us, even if he has done wrong."

"Well, after all, mother, you've got to remember that I love Rex too. He's my brother, and we've been wonderful pals. Maybe it was somehow my fault that this happened. If we had been rooming together as we did his first year at college it wouldn't have happened, I'm positive. Just because it was the custom for the seniors to room in the new building I thought I had to pull out and go with them, and in some ways I've been sorry ever since that I did. Now I guess I've got to bear with the consequences too. Mother, all last night I've been blaming myself. I got interested in my fraternity, and what the other fellows were doing, and I didn't follow up my brother. Of course that is no excuse for him, but I know what I should have done, and I'm never going to forgive myself for it. Rex is a social lad, and can't bear to be alone. I guess he missed me. We've always been so much to each other!"

"Perhaps," said the mother sadly. "But Paul, you mustn't blame yourself too much. We must go from day to day and do the right that we see. Perhaps this is going to prove a good thing for us all in more ways than one — as suffering always is, I guess."

They went to work then at the curtains, filmy things of exquisite texture, edged with delicate hand-wrought lace, and then draperies of heavy silk, gracefully rose-flowered. It was lovely when it was done, and Mary Garland brought out the little trifling oraments, rosy satin pillows, beautifully costly accessories in silver and crystal and enamel, for the bureau and dressing table with its draperies matching the windows.

It was a fitting place to which to bring a bride, and Mary Garland stood back and definitely began to visualize the girl who was to occupy it. Would she be worth it? The mother felt as if she were bringing of her most cherished possessions to sacrifice at the altar of this unknown daughter whom Rex had thrust upon her.

Paul watched her for a moment and turned away struggling with his own feelings. Then he said:

"I doubt if she's worth it, mother. I doubt if any girl is. But it's beautiful of you to do it. She may not appreciate what it costs you, and I doubt if even Rex does now, but *I* do, and someday I'll see that Rex understands that you gave of the best you had."

And then as if he were leaving a holy place Paul went out. She heard the front door open and close, and glancing out of her window Mary Garland saw her eldest son go down the drive with quick brisk steps. She was not afraid for him, as she might have been yesterday, not since she heard his humble prayer. Not since she heard his words to her just now. Paul was growing in his spirit, and she was proud of him. He was going to be a help to her and not a hinderance in this trial that was ahead of them all.

A few minutes later Paul came back with a florist's box in his hand. He took off his coat and hat and put them away, and then he tramped upstairs with the box and a clear crystal vase in his hand, a vase he had always liked because he said it fitted flowers, having no frills whatever to mar its clearness. He came to her door.

"Here, mater," he said, "see if these'll do. I thought they matched. But you'll have to fix them, I don't know how."

Her eyes met his and she understood. He wanted to have some part in this. She smiled. Her face was filled with a kind of radiant glory, and a soft glow was reflected in the boy's eyes.

He filled the vase with water, and handed out the pale pink

rosebuds, one at a time, watching her while she arranged them, and she could see he was enjoying this little incident too. If the bride didn't know enough to appreciate what they had done it would not matter, for they would always have this memory of each other doing this together.

8

DINNER was early that night. Mary Garland understood that Sylvia would be excited, and it was as well to have plenty of time. Besides, the young escort was to be introduced to her. So she put on one of her most becoming gowns, just a simple plain one in deep purple like ripe grapes, with a bit of hand braiding on it, and a touch of lace at the throat and wrists. Paul told her she looked like a queen, and defied his sister Sylvia to rival her, even if she did have talisman roses to wear with her new garnet dress.

They had a gay little meal, each trying to smile his brightest, all realizing that they were coming nearer and nearer to the crucial time when something had to happen. The recalcitrant bride and groom might walk in upon them at any moment now and they were trying to strengthen one another for the time of trial.

"Mother," whispered Sylvia, as they met on the stairs on the way down to dinner, "what should I do in case Rex and—and—that *girl* would turn up just when Rance gets here? Should I introduce them, or what? And how would I know what to call her?"

"Certainly, if they come they'll have to be introduced," said

Mary Garland. "Just say 'this is my brother Rex and his wife,' and leave it at that."

"But mother, I'm afraid he'll notice how young Rex looks and think it's awfully queer. I'm afraid, too, that everybody will act kind of stiff, and he won't know what to make of it. Do you think, mother, that it would be the wrong thing for me to tell him about it this evening, sort of explain that it was something we didn't know about, or something like that?"

"Why, no, he's a friend of yours, and if you continue to see him occasionally he will undoubtedly have to know the facts. I wouldn't force them on him, however, unless you feel it is necessary. You could say it has caused us anxiety because he was married so suddenly, and without our knowledge. Oh, I don't know, Sylvia, whatever you want to do. Just follow your own good sense. Remember Rex is your brother, and don't say hard things, but don't talk a lot about it. Just say we don't know her at all, and are worried. Or you can say *you* are. But follow the counsel of your own heart, dear, and don't let this matter get on your nerves. Enjoy your concert with all your heart. These things of life will work out. They may bring a lot of sorrow with them, but that we can't help. Now let's get the dinner out of the way."

"But suppose Rex comes while we are at dinner?"

"Never mind. They didn't let us know when they were coming and they'll have to take what they find. There will be plenty to eat, however, no matter what time they come. Now forget it all. If there is anything you have to explain, do so briefly when the time comes, but don't consider it beforehand, for the time may not come. Just don't worry about it."

"Oh, mother, but you look lovely!" cried Fae as they came down the stairs, "and Sylvia looks like a dream! See, Stan. Aren't they both wonderful?"

"Swell!" said Stan looking solemnly at his mother and sister.

"Why all the glad rags?" asked Paul as Sylvia came into the dining room. "Is this in honor of the bride, or are you trying to outshine her?"

Sylvia looked up and smiled, realizing that no one had told Paul she was going out that night.

"No," she said earnestly, "I've been invited to hear The Messiah tonight at the Academy of Music. Do you think I'm dreadful to go away when Rex may arrive any minute?"

"I certainly do *not!*" said Paul. "Why should we sit around and wait on his highness till he gets ready to arrive? I'm thinking of going out myself a little while, that is, if mother can spare me. Mother, I thought I'd run over and see Marcia Merrill a little while. Is that all right with you? You could phone me over there and I'd come right over in case Rex arrives. The Merrills are good enough friends to understand in case I have to run away early. Stan, you going to be here? You'll call me the first thing if Rex comes, won't you? Can I depend on you?"

"Sure!" said Stan loftily.

So immediately after dinner Paul vanished.

Sylvia was a bit disappointed. She wanted Paul to meet Rance. But she reflected that perhaps it was just as well, for mother would have more chance to talk with him.

And almost at once Rance arrived.

She met him with quick color in her cheeks that rivaled the depths of the tailsman roses, and they had one minute of meeting that made both of them very happy. Rance looked down at her as though she were something utterly new and wonderful in this world of human beings. As if she were a thousand times more lovely than he had thought her.

Sylvia was shy and grave and sweet. For the moment she had forgotten that Rex and his bride might at any moment arrive and spring a disagreeable impression. Then she heard Fae and Stan talking in the library and she called them.

"I want you to meet my youngest brother and my little

sister," she said. "This is Fae and this is Stan. The older boys aren't here just now."

Fae smiled shyly, and Stan gravely shook his hand and said he was glad to know him. Then he stood there a moment deferentially, till Sylvia sent Fae after her mother.

"I suppose that tennis court out there smothered in snow belongs to you," said Rance to Stan in a friendly tone.

"Well, it's partly mine," said Stan. "We all play a lot when the weather is right. You'll have to come over and try it when spring comes, that is, if you play."

"Sure, I play," said Rance. "Love it. I'd be delighted to come. Right now I challenge you to a set as soon as the weather permits."

Stan grinned.

"It's okay with me," he said. "Our court is supposed to be good when it's in shape."

"All right, that's a date," said Rance Nelius. "Put that down on your calendar, and let me know when the court is ready."

"Okay."

And then Mary Garland came in and greeted the young man and they all sat down, while Sylvia slipped away to get her hat and coat on, and fit on those new garnet gloves most carefully.

Fae had slipped to the sofa beside her mother, nestling down with her mother's arm about her. Stan knew his presence would not be required, but he liked "this new guy," so he stayed to see how he tried out. Not if he could help it were there going to be any more mistakes in this girl-and-boy business in his family! If this man wasn't right for his sister he wanted to find it out before anything serious could happen. At least until Paul got back from college to stay, he, Stan, was head of the family, and it was up to him to be sure about people. That's what Paul ought to have done in college and then they wouldn't have had all this trouble about Rex. But of course nobody ever thought Rex would do a thing like that.

So Stan sat and listened, gravely, grinning now and then at the visitor when he cast a pleasant glance his way, or told a funny story.

Mary Garland talked with the young man graciously about the concert they were about to attend, told about the first time she had heard that oratorio given, back in the days when Walter Damrosch was a very young man conducting the orchestra and choral society for the first time, and what a wonderful impression it had made upon her. She spoke of her own vision of a green valley beside the still sparkling water that had come when she heard the tender words. "He shall feed His flock like a shepherd," and how it had always stayed with her when she read the shepherd psalm.

"People don't go to these things as much as they used to do when I was young," she said. "I think it is a great loss for the young people. Sylvia has never heard many great concerts, and I am afraid that is my fault. I've had so very many things to attend to. She has never heard The Messiah. I'm so glad you are taking her to her hear it tonight. It is so much a part of the Christmas time that I used to think one ought never to miss it."

She asked a few questions about where his home had been, and whether he was far from his family this holiday time, and he told her briefly how his family was gone, and he was far away even from his lifetime acquaintances. They had lived in the west till his mother died, and then when it was all over and he found himself on his own he had come east because there were some things he wanted to study that he thought could be better done in this university than any other he knew.

It was just then that Sylvia came downstairs ready, looking fairly regal in her fur coat with the gorgeous roses glimpsing out on her shoulder, and the little feather nodding over one ear. Mary Garland looked up and rejoiced in the sweet young beauty of her daughter, and Fae, and even Stan, looked at her adoringly.

Then they could hear a taxi come throbbing up to the door and stop, and for an instant Stan thought that must be Rex. Sylvia held her breath, till Rance Nelius glanced at his watch and looked toward the window.

"I guess that must be our taxi," he said. "I told them to be here on time."

"Oh, you shouldn't have bothered to get a taxi," smiled Sylvia. "It's a lovely night, even if it is snowing a little. We could have gone in the bus."

"It is snowing pretty hard, lady," said Rance, "and a bus is a sordid equipage for a festive occasion." Then he turned to Mary Garland and said: "I'm so glad to have met you. It's been nice having this little talk with a real mother again." And he spoke to Stan and Fae as if they were real people and not just children. Then they went out to the taxi. Sylvia drew a breath of relief, as the taxi rolled down the drive and turned into the street. They were out and away, and Rex and his girl hadn't come to spoil it all. Sylvia was very happy. Now for this evening she would try to forget the blight that had fallen upon their home.

"You have a lovely mother," said the young man. "She makes me think a little of my mother."

"That's nice," said Sylvia. "Yes, she is a lovely mother! She's been just like one of us, as if she were a girl herself with us all. She likes to laugh and she used to play games with us, and even tennis now and then. Yet she's very brave and strong when anything comes along to worry her. She's been a father and a mother both since father died."

"My mother had to be that to me nearly all my life, for my father was killed in an accident when I was a mere baby. It makes a difference in people when they go through hard things. It gives them courage and strength, and power. My mother was like that. But I can see now why you are different from a lot of the girls I see everywhere today. With a home like that and a mother like that, it's bound to tell in the children. You're like your mother, do you know it?"

"I'd rather be like my mother than anyone else I know," said Sylvia earnestly. "She's been a wonderful mother."

"I'm eager to meet your older brothers," said Rance. "When do they get home? I'm sure they must be worth meeting."

Sylvia flushed in the darkness of the cab, and hesitated.

"Why, my oldest brother is home now. He came last night at dinner time and we certainly were glad to see him. I wanted you to meet him, but he had gone out for a few minutes to see an old friend. Rex, my second brother, hasn't come yet. We've been expecting him all day, and I think mother is worrying a little about him. You see he drove home with somebody, and we don't know but they may have stopped off somewhere on the way, but we hope he is coming tonight."

Sylvia paused. Was this the time she should tell him about Rex, and his getting married? Should she, or should she not?

And then suddenly they were in the city, turning in among the heavy traffic and bright lights of the broad avenue that led to the Academy. People in gay garments were hurrying to the side doors of the Academy, where already there was a long line waiting to go to the top gallery, standing there with the snow coming down thick and fast. Oh, it was lovely! The snow with all the bright lights and the Christmas decorations everywhere, the avenues lit as for a procession. Sylvia hadn't thought much about the snow on the way down, only that it had seemed to shut them in and make it cosy as they rode along and talked. But now it seemed like a lovely drapery, a fleecy curtain between the cars and cabs, lighted up with scarlet and green and gold and silver lights. It seemed a fairy world.

On the opposite side of the street was a great stone church lit up for service, and a chime of bells was singing out the old, old story, "Hark the Herald Angels Sing," "Joy to the World, the Lord Is Come!" It was very solemn and sweet, and Rance Nelius said:

"It's very wonderful when you think of it, that something that happened more than two thousand years ago is being talked of and thought about over the whole civilized world today, isn't it?"

Sylvia's heart gave a glad little thrill to hear him say that, for she had been wondering whether he was a Christian, but she had been too shy to ask. She had been afraid that he might think her a fanatic if she did. But now he was talking about it, and she answered eagerly.

"Oh, yes, isn't it wonderful! I was thinking how pretty it is tonight and how it doesn't look as if there was any sin or wrong anywhere. It seems as if all the world was rejoicing in the Lord. But of course they aren't. Of course there is a lot of sin going on, after all these years, as there was before the angels sang 'joy to the world.' "

"Yes," said Rance, "I'm afraid there is. But there's a lot of people loving and serving Him too, don't you think? And even the world has to pause and listen when His story is sung, as we are going to hear it tonight. Isn't that something?"

"Yes, it is," said Sylvia. And then suddenly the taxi lurched across the street, drew up near the entrance to the Academy, and they got out.

It seemed a new world they had entered as they settled themselves in front gallery seats and looked about on that great hall, with its crimson cushions, and curtains, and its tiers of galleries above them all the way to the far ceiling. It was fascinating to see it rapidly filling up now, a face at every seat.

Sylvia wasn't a little girl; she was nineteen, but she had a little girl's genuine delight in the scene, for she had not been often to such affairs. Her life had centered around home and school so long that she did not bring a jaded mind to this pleasure tonight. She had never been a part of fashion in the great world either. Home and school and church. That had been the round, especially since her father had died.

Rance watched her admiringly and saw her delight, thrilled to think she was like that, and that he had been able to give her this pleasure and witness her joy in it.

Then the great crimson curtain went up, the music began, and they sat entranced.

It was on their way home that it all came back to Sylvia again about Rex and his wife, and her heart almost stood still as it forgot its ecstasy of the evening and remembered possibilities.

As if she had spoken her thoughts aloud, suddenly Rance said, "I hope your brothers will be there by the time we get back. I know it's late, but I would like to meet them, if only for a minute."

Sylvia was very still for a minute. She could hear the big flakes of snow still splashing on the window as they drove along. Then she lifted her head and looked toward her escort.

"I think there is something I ought to tell you," she said in a low voice. "I don't like to, because it's something that breaks my heart, but I guess you should know, especially if there is a likelihood that you will meet them."

"Don't tell me anything that gives you distress," said Rance. "We've had such a happy evening, let it go at that."

"No," said Sylvia. "I think I'd better tell you now that I have said so much, and I think perhaps I'd like you to understand. You see, we've been very much worried for three days, ever since mother had a letter from my brother Rex saying that he had been married, and wanted to bring his wife home. My older brother did not know anything about it till he got home last night, and he's been trying ever since to get in touch with him. Rex is only eighteen, and just in the middle of his college course. We don't understand it. He never was silly like that. And we don't know anything about the girl either. But we suppose they are coming home tonight or tomorrow, and I thought if they should be there when we go in I'd like you to understand the situation. Rex is so young to be married—but he's a dear."

"Oh, you poor child!" said the young man gently. "And you had to go out this evening and try to enjoy a good time with that hanging over you! I'm sorry I caused you that strain."

"Oh, but it was a good thing," said Sylvia, "and I'm so glad I went. It was almost as if God was there. I seemed to get a broader view of the universe, and to feel that there is a time surely coming when even such hard troubles as this won't matter any more, because God is going to wipe all tears away. No, I'm glad I went. But I wanted you to understand if Rex is there."

"Perhaps you'd rather I didn't come in tonight."

"No. I want you to meet my older brother. And mother will want you to come in, I know."

"Well, I thank you for trusting me with your confidence. I certainly will pray about it tonight, and will hope that somehow God will work this out gloriously for you all. I only wish that there were something else that I could do, some way that I could help."

"Thank you," said Sylvia, "you've helped a lot already, taking me away from the thought of it. And there is no help like praying. I'm glad you know how to do that. That will help more than anything else. Rex is a Christian, but I guess somehow he's got away from the Lord, or he wouldn't have done a thing like this to mother, or to himself either."

"Well, I'm glad you counted me enough of a friend to tell me, and of course it will go no further. I'd like to be a friend you can call upon for help at any time. May I?"

"Why, yes, that will be wonderful," she said softly.

And then the taxi drew up at the Garland home, and their talk was over, but Sylvia was glad that she had told him.

So they went into the house, not knowing what to expect.

9

THERE was a light in the big pleasant living room when
they entered the door, and they could see Mary Garland sitting there before the open fire with a book in her lap. But
she was not reading. Her face had a faraway look as if she
were pondering great matters. Even the children were up,
idly working at a picture puzzle with the air of killing time
till something important would happen.

And then Paul got up from the other side of the fireplace
and came out in the hall, and looked at them.

"Well, if that isn't Rance Nelius!" he said, his big hearty
voice booming out joyously as he came forward to meet the
guest. "Upon my word, how did you get away off here? I
thought you lived out in the wild and wooly west! And how
did you get to know my sister? Say, this is great! I didn't know
you were within a thousand miles of here and I wasn't sure
I would ever see you again. *Man,* this is great!"

"Why, Paul, how did you know Rance Nelius?" asked Sylvia, wide-eyed at the revelation. "I didn't know any of my
family knew him till he came after me tonight and met
mother and the children."

"Why, a couple of years ago, Syl, when I was football manager, Rance's team came out to play our college. We had a great game, and then when it came time for their team to leave, they found there had been a wreck on the railroad, that would make them miss their connections for their train home, so they decided to stay over till morning. We parked the team around among our men and Rance fell to my lot. We were just starting to get acquainted when he had to leave. I've tried to trace him since, hunted among the football news, even wrote out to your college, Rance, but they told me you had moved away, and they didn't have your address. What became of you, man? My, I'm glad you've turned up at last!"

Rance smiled.

"Why, you see, my whole life was upset shortly after I was with you. My mother was taken quite ill, and we had to go farther west for her sake. And when even that didn't do any good, we went to California for a time. I left college of course, indefinitely, to be with her during her last days. And after she was gone I came east. I've been here in your university for the past year. I graduate in the spring, two years later than I would if I had gone on from the time you knew me. That explains how I came to know your sister," and a pleasant glance passed between him and Sylvia, almost as if they had been friends of long standing. "But I certainly am glad to see you. I didn't know a soul around here. I never connected you with this city. I thought of you as living somewhere near that college where we met. Of course I've been rather busy, taking a heavy schedule, and doing a little coaching besides."

"Football?" asked Paul. "I don't see why I didn't hear of you."

"No, not football," laughed Rance. "I've grown up since I saw you. I haven't any time for that now, though I used to love it. No, I've been using my brains instead of my brawn lately. But say, I'm glad I've found you! I've often thought of you, but couldn't for the life of me remember your name. No wonder Garland sounded so familiar and pleasant to me when I met your sister! Say, this is great!"

"Where are you living?" asked Paul. "You and I have got to have a good talk. I always felt that one night we had wasn't half long enough. You're in the university dorm, I suppose."

"No," said Rance, "I'm on my own. I have a room in an apartment house, and that reminds me that I ought to hurry. I'm supposed to be child's nurse to a reluctant furnace for the next three nights while the janitor is away getting a holiday at his married daughter's, and I'm under oath to see that the apartments are all comfortably warm both night and day."

"But say, that's no work for you! That furnace won't go out if you stay a little while longer, will it? It's not awfully late. Come on in and sit down. I want mother to know you."

"I met your mother, when I came for your sister earlier this evening. She's worth knowing. And I'm coming to see her again if I may."

By this time Fae and Stan were clustered around with shining eyes, and their mother had come to the door.

"Of course you may come whenever you like," said Mary Garland. "You will be twice welcome since you are Paul's friend as well as Sylvia's. And I was just wondering. Couldn't you take Christmas dinner with us? I know we would all enjoy it very much. Unless, of course, you have other plans."

Sylvia gasped in pleased surprise and Rance looked eager.

"No, I haven't any other plans except to take dinner in a restaurant and try to forget that it is Christmas."

"Good!" said Paul. "Then you'll come with us! That will be swell. And by the way, mother, I asked Marcia Merrill to come over to dinner, too. I told her you would call her and let her know about the time. Her father and mother have gone down to Florida for a couple of months, and she is staying with the housekeeper and a couple of teachers who are there for company. But they are going to a shindig some of their friends are having, and she was going to be alone, so I asked her. I knew you would, mother, if you knew."

Mary Garland could always be counted on for a thing like that and now her eyes lit up pleasantly.

"Why, of course! How nice that will be! We'll have a real house party, and I'm so glad your friend Mr. Nelius is free—"

Rance looked troubled. He couldn't help seeing the half-frightened glances Fae gave to Stan, and the sudden lighting of Stan's face as they both gave Sylvia a quick look. He remembered what Sylvia had told him on the way home and realized there were complications which might make his staying hard for these dear people.

"Your house will be full," he said. "Hadn't I better come some other day than Christmas? I don't want to barge in on your family gathering." His eyes sought Sylvia's for understanding, and she smiled, trying to let him know it would be all right.

"No," said Mary Garland earnestly, "you're not to make that excuse. We want you. We'll love to have you. Now come in and sit down by the fire just a few minutes before you go, and let's get the hour settled. Christmas is the time to have a big gathering of dear friends."

Then Paul joined in and urged, and Fae clapped her hands and said, "Yes, that would be wonderful! And I'm glad Marcia is coming too. She's nice. She always fits in."

For the moment the coming of Rex and his problematic bride was in the background.

They were still standing in the wide hall, Mary Garland just within the living room doorway. Only Stan's alert boy senses heard the soft creak of wheels in the snow outside as a taxi drew up. Stan gave a startled glance toward his mother, darted a warning at Sylvia and Paul, even with that pleased look of eagerness still on his lips.

Simultaneously with the dim slam of the taxi door came the sound of feet stamping snow outside the door, then the rattle and click of a key in the lock.

Paul looked up, startled out of his cheerfulness, and Rance

glanced toward the door, giving Sylvia a quick look. Her eyes were toward the door too, and now she gave Rance a fleeting smile as if to signal him that the time she had been telling him about had come. Then, the door swung wide letting in a gust of wild snowy air, and two figures, one tall, one small and slight.

"That will be Rex," thought Rance, and tried to adjust his attitude so that he should not be taken unaware.

Rex lifted a long arm, plucked off his cap, gave it a flirt that flicked the snow from it in a shower, tossed back his handsome head and shook it a little to fling the snow from his crisp dark curly hair, and then cast a quick keen glance over the group at the door. His eyes first lingered on his brother Paul's face, appraising it, then traveled on to the stranger hostilely. Who was this guy barging in on a family scene? It was going to be hard enough without strangers.

But Paul spoke out genially.

"Hello, Rex, you got here at last, didn't you? Took your time I should say! Mother has been awfully anxious." And then without change of tone, "Rance, this is my brother Rex. You've heard me speak of him. Rex, this is Rance Nelius. I guess you've heard of him before."

Rex was utterly taken off his guard.

"Rance Nelius!" he exclaimed with a sudden flash of interest. "You don't say! Glad to meet you, Mr. Nelius. Paul has had me about worshiping you ever since you played football at the college once." Rex stretched out a long arm, and grasped Rance Nelius' hand warmly. "I certainly didn't know we were to have this pleasure!"

Behind Paul Stan's tense face relaxed, though his watchful eyes were still on the alert. Rance could hear Sylvia draw a quick little catch of a breath, as if she were somehow relieved, but he saw that Mary Garland's eyes were still anxious, and went beyond the easy figure of her second son, to the girl who stood behind him, watchful and belligerent. Rance saw Fae's young hands clutch the pleats in her dress skirt and give a long unloving look toward the alien girl. Poor little girl! Poor mother! Poor all of them!

The only one who didn't look concerned in the whole group was the alien girl, and she looked angry. She was being ignored but she didn't intend to stand it long. She stepped up beside Rex and looked at him.

She was very smart-looking. They could see that at a glance. And almost pretty, though not according to their standards. Her lips were too red, and her cheeks were not a natural color. Her eyebrows were slender and too high, her hair was in a long bob, like a page boy of King Arthur's time. It was a sickly gold dashed with a queer red like nasturtiums, as Paul had said, that gave a weird effect to the whole picture. Her lashes were long and much the same color. She certainly was startling.

She was dressed in a heavy black winter suit, slim skirt and trig jacket, banded with gray karakul. Her hat was a curious little pillbox affair, a black crown with a band of the karakul facing the straight-up brim, and a two-inch strap of the karakul around the back of the head over the gold hair holding on the hat. There were gloves too, quite unusual ones done in black and white with a gauntlet effect. But her eyes were the principle thing. They were long and gray and cold with flecks of steel in their make-up, and when she stepped up and looked at Rex he seemed almost to wither. Rex! Withering! He didn't seem the type to wither!

"Oh—ah!" he said, stepping back imperceptibly. "Meet my wife—Florimel—everybody!"

Rance Nelius admired the way that Mary Garland arose to the occasion, though he pitied her from the heart. Gently, like a lady born, as she was, she stepped forward to the girl's side.

"Oh," said said sympathetically. "You must be very cold traveling in this awful storm. They tell me it is below zero. And you have no heavy coat! I should think you would have frozen!"

Florimel laughed an ugly little laugh.

"Spare your sympathy," she clamored out. "We've been in the movies all the evening. I'm not cold. And my coat is outside with the baggage. I didn't think it was worth while to bother putting it on; this jacket is warm. But good-*night*, I'm thirsty! Haven't you got something to drink?"

Stan departed kitchenward solemnly, but everybody else was looking in astonishment at the new daughter-in-law.

She was very slim. Even in the thick cloth jacket she seemed to be but a sliver. And her face wore the expression of a naughty child. Rex stood there helplessly looking at her, unable to cope with the situation. He scowled at his new wife as if he didn't quite know what to do with her. As if he had suddenly discovered that she didn't belong in this environment where he had brought her, and he was atonished. He had thought that home was a panacea for all that was wrong, and now he found that it wasn't.

But before anybody could say anything more, and while Rance Nelius was trying to think whether he could help more by staying or going, Stan appeared in the hall with a great crystal goblet, one of the very best set of company goblets, full of clear cold water. He stood stiffly like a butler, before his new sister-in-law, offering it to her.

She turned and looked at it, and then at the boy curiously.

"What do you want?" she asked, with a hint of annoyance in her voice.

"You said you were thirsty. You said you wanted a drink, and I've brought it," said Stan.

The girl looked at Stan as if she could not believe her senses, and then she burst into uncontrollable laughter.

"And you thought I wanted *water*, you poor boob, did you? Well, if that isn't the very limit for a child your size!" and she went into more uncontrollable peals of laughter.

But nobody else was laughing. They were all very grave. Even Rex was grave and angry-looking. His face was red in a great wave.

It was then that Mary Garland stepped quietly up to Stan as he stood there white with anger, wishing with all his heart he dared to throw the contents of that goblet full into the hateful face of Rex's new wife. She put out her hand to take the goblet from him.

"I'll take the water, please, Stan," she said sweetly. "I've been very thirsty for some time."

They stood there while she drank it, every drop, and then handing Stan the goblet, she thanked him again, and turned to Sylvia.

"Dear, suppose you take Florimel upstairs to her room. I'm sure she must be very tired."

"Thanks, no!" said Florimel decidedly. "I'll stay down till Rex is ready to go up."

"Oh, very well," said Mary Garland coolly. "Then will you come in and sit down, or would you rather take off your hat first? Sylvia, will you ask Selma to bring some coffee and cakes? I'm sure Mr. Nelius might like some, and I think we all could enjoy them. Rex, find your wife the chair you think she would like. Mr. Nelius, sit there by Paul. I can see he wants to talk to you. Fae, you might run out and help Selma bring in the tray. Stan, pull out the coffee table."

Mary Garland had a way of taking an uncomfortable situation and making it bearable, no matter how twisted it was. Rance Nelius wondered at her calmness. Her children were wondering at her too. Not that they had ever seen reason to doubt their mother's ability to solve any of their problems, but this was different, and she was managing it with the ease of an angel. Even Rex was impressed, and humbled by it. He had come home hoping to show them what a sweet lovely smart wife he had found, and lo she was no longer sweet nor lovely, and her smartness seemed somehow not to fit into this home environment. He couldn't understand it, and he sat there dumb. He seemed to have stepped off with the wrong foot, when he had been so anxious to have everything all right!

The new member of the family fussed petulantly with her anxious husband about which chair she would occupy, and at last settled down in a straight backed chair at the far end of the room from all the rest, and sat there staring first at one, then at the other, finally letting her glance rest speculatively on the guest, Rance Nelius. Just who was he and what relation had he to the rest? There was something about him that made her desire to dominate him, and yet she could see she was not making her usual impression. She was used to making an impression. Rance Nelius' glances were all for Sylvia, and her mother, and his understanding smiles went toward everyone but herself.

Finally she turned deliberately and studied Sylvia. Sylvia with no make-up, in a simple dark silk with those gorgeous roses nestling on her shoulder. She decided she was the ingénue type, and turned up her nose accordingly. Rex had spoken of Sylvia with great fondness and admiration and Florimel was not prepared to like her.

She turned her attention back to Rance. He looked a cold sort of party, although he was good-looking of course. It might be interesting to win him away from Sylvia for a few days if she was compelled to stay around that long. He wouldn't be hard to seize, she thought. It would make Rex jealous, perhaps, and keep him more thoroughly under her thumb. Maybe she would try it if she got bored.

She didn't look toward Paul. She knew him from her pieshop days, and felt it would be wasted time. Paul was indifferent. Probably had some girl he was dead in love with, and was too aristocratic to look at a girl who had been a waitress in a restaurant.

But she was no longer a waitress in a restaurant, and she intended to make everyone understand that from now on. She was the wife of a young man who would soon inherit a small fortune. This family probably thought they were something, but she intended to show them that *she* was *more* than something. Yet here she sat in the heart of the family, just arrived, a bride, and nobody was paying the slightest attention to her! Even the children were seated near this outsider named Nelius, listening open-mouthed to every word he uttered, and her own new husband was eagerly engaged in conversation with him.

And of all things, there were discussing *music,* apparently. Talking in terms that were to her a foreign tongue. Sylvia with kindling eagerness in her eyes was describing a lovely pastoral they had heard that evening, and doing it with ease, the kind of ease that Florimel did not understand. Bluntness and impudence had always been her forte. She had been trained in the school of the modern world, and not a very cultured one at that. She resented all these people because they did not talk her language. Because they were not blasé and ill-mannered like the young people she admired so much in the movies and dance halls which she had frequented as often as she could inveigle anyone into taking her there. Of course Rex himself was a little soft too, but she had felt that she could train Rex, and he would soon be able to hold his own in her world. But a long stay here wasn't going to help toward her training of him. She meant to get him away just as soon as she could make him pry enough money from this tight-fisted family to finance them. Then she could begin. But it was going to be a terrible bore to stay here even a few days.

She didn't pull off her gloves at once. She didn't want them to see that she was sporting no diamond ring on the third finger of her left hand, just a plain little cheap gold band like his mother's wedding ring. He had bought it at a little hick town on the way, and insisted on her wearing it for the time being, at least till he could afford to get her another. By the way, she must keep that in mind, in Rex's mind, and have him get her some good rings the first thing after Christmas!

Her thoughts were rambling on in this wise, as she idly

studied the room, taking in the old-fashioned furniture, not even knowing enough to recognize that some of it was so old it was almost priceless.

Then the trays were brought in, the coffee was passed, and the talk became a little more general.

Mary Garland tried to draw her daughter-in-law into the conversation with little pleasant nothings, but Florimel remained rudely hostile.

"No, we didn't have a hard drive," she said definitely. "We started yesterday morning. We stopped several places on the way, places where I had friends. I had another place I wanted to stay over Sunday, but Rex was determined to get here, so we finally came on."

She spoke as if it were entirely Mary Garland's fault that Rex would come on. She didn't mention the fact that they hadn't money to stop anywhere else, or do any more celebrating than they had done. She didn't say that it took the last cent they had to get into the movie that Florimel had insisted upon before she came on to this that she considered an ordeal.

Mary Garland reflected that perhaps the least she said to this girl before she had a thorough understanding with Rex, the better, so she made no reply to this statement, and the conversation presently languished. But she kept her seat near by, and, not to seem utterly silent, took advantage of a lull in the conversation across the room, to speak to Sylvia.

"Sylvia, tell us more about the concert tonight. I'm sure from your face that you enjoyed it."

"Oh, mother! It was marvelous!" said Sylvia, her face lighting up in a wonderful way that caused the new sister-in-law to reverse her decision somewhat. She decided that Sylvia wasn't so shy and backward as she had thought at first. Instead there was a loveliness about her, a marvelous quality that she didn't understand. And when Sylvia began to talk about the oratorio, and discuss the skill and technique of the musicians and singers, she realized that the girl knew what she was talking about, and that she was far above Florimel's head, away beyond her education or comprehension. Was this just a patter that people used, to show they understood classical music, or was it real?

Then Rance Nelius was drawn into the conversation and added his impression of the soloists, and Florimel simply sat and stared.

"That's one thing I've missed at college, music," declared Paul. "You know we scarcely ever had any concerts up in that direction that are worth hearing, except by way of radio. I always have the symphony orchestra on Saturday night of course. But we're too far from any big city to get the best things, and it takes too long to run back home for an evening. I didn't even take my violin up with me this winter. And Rex didn't have his 'cello along, either. By the way, Sylvia, we must have some good workouts this holiday. I suppose Rex and I are both out of practice, but we can make a stab at it, with you at the piano."

"Oh, I've been working too hard myself in the university to do anything at practicing either, except a few minutes now and then," said Sylvia.

"Well, that settles what we'll do part of the time on Christmas Day," said Rance Nelius. "I shall be audience and shall simply clamor for music."

Florimel favored him with an angry scowl. Not if she could prevent it, he almost felt she was saying. This was the first she knew about Rex playing the 'cello. She turned and glared at him. 'Cello! Sissy instrument, wasn't it? No music for a man, an *athlete!* Well, she'd see that he soon got over that!

But now suddenly Rance realized that it was getting late and took his leave. Paul and Rex immediately followed him to the front door and stepped outside to bring in Rex's baggage, but they didn't come back at once. They stayed for last words. Mary Garland excused herself to go to the kitchen a moment and see if Selma understood about breakfast. Stan strolled outside to be "with the men," and the atmosphere of silence grew tense.

Sylvia unpinned her flowers and released their stems from the confining wires.

"Fae, dear, will you go and get the cut glass celery dish with some water in it for my flowers?" she said.

"Sure!" said Fae, glad to get away for a moment, and was back again with the dish and a pitcher of water.

Sylvia arranged her flowers, and then turned brightly toward her new sister-in-law.

"Don't you want to take your hat off, and your jacket? It's pretty warm in this room."

"No!" said Florimel shortly. "Why on earth don't they come in? What do they find to talk about, anyway?"

She got up and stalked over to the window, but the shades were down, and when she snapped one up to the top of the window she couldn't see the young men very well, as they were standing at the other side of the front door.

"Oh heck!" she said furiously, and flounced over to Sylvia. "Where's my room? I can't stand around here waiting for Rex any longer!"

"Why, of course," said Sylvia brightly, "I'll take you right upstairs. You must be very tired of course."

But the visitor said nothing until they had reached the top of the stairs, and then she spoke as to an inferior: "I wish you'd get me a glass of wine, or brandy or something. I don't feel very well!"

Sylvia stared at her an instant, and then she said, "I'm sorry you don't feel well, but I can't get you anything like that. We haven't any in the house. I could get you some aromatic ammonia. Mother always uses that in place of liquor when people feel faint."

"Aromatic ammonia!" sneered the bride. "Oh heck! Gosh! What are you anyway? A bunch of lilies?"

Sylvia looked at her aghast for an instant, and then with a kind of dignity that Florimel didn't understand, Sylvia said:

"I'm sorry!" and turning went downstairs, leaving Florimel standing in the doorway of the big beautiful guest room, a more beautiful room, perhaps, then Forimel had ever entered before.

Rex was on his way upstairs with his bags and suitcases, and Florimel's heavy coat with its silver fox collar dragging behind him. He gave his sister a shy, wistful, half apologetic smile, as if he would plead with her not to judge him too harshly, and kept on up the stairs.

It keenly reminded Sylvia of the day in their very early youth. Their mother had made a rule that if they left their things around out of place they would be carried up to the back attic, a sort of lumber room over the kitchen, which was approached by steep stairs, and was dark and dusty. It was a hard jaunt up there to find lost articles. One day she, a little girl, only a year older than Rex, had come down the hall and had seen Rex ascending those back attic stairs. He had given her a quick furtive look, and she had lingered about. He came down a few minutes later with perspiration dropping from his brow, carrying his ball, his bat, his cap and a handful of his handkerchiefs crumpled in his hands, grinning shamedly. Sylvia, being nearest his age, had been Rex's confidante in times of stress, and his eyes had a trick of telling her the truth, and knowing that she would sympathize.

As he went upstairs now, he gave her one of those pleading, understanding looks. Could it be that Rex was a little ashamed of what he had done?

They had all long ago been broken of their habit of leaving their possessions about. But could it be that there were still as deep-seated faults that Rex must be disciplined for? Oh, must he suffer for having left his emotions about? Poor Rex! So generous and warm hearted! So impulsive and eager! Oh, to see Rex chained to that creature upstairs was going to be rare and exquisite torture for mother and them all to endure! How was it going to be bearable? She seemed to be worse than even their most dreaded fears. Poor mother! How terrible it was going to be for her! And yet how royally she had entered into the punishment!

Should she tell her mother what Florimel had just said?

No! Not at present anyway. She would see enough herself. Why give her more to worry about?

So in due time the household settled to quiet, though few of them to real rest, perhaps, except it were given them from above.

THERE were crisp brown hot sausages and buckwheat cakes with maple syrup for breakfast; fried potatoes, too, with brown edges, and tasty dashes of pepper, just the way they all liked them. Apple sauce, and amber coffee, and a great pitcher of milk for those who preferred it. A real old-fashioned breakfast. Just the thing for a cold winter morning on the day before Christmas.

Mary Garland had ordered the hour to be a little later than usual, because they had all been up late the night before, and she wanted the air of good cheer to prevail. It was going to be a hard day, of course, both for the family, and for the new member of it who seemed to have entered with such a belligerent spirit.

"You'd think *we* were the ones who were forcing ourselves in where we have no right to be, instead of the bride," remarked Paul, as they waited around at the door of the dining room for Rex and Florimel to appear. But he said it in a low tone with a comical grin. He had no intention of making any more trouble than they had already.

"Perhaps she thinks we ought to hand over Rex root and

branch to her, and keep out of their affairs," suggested Sylvia with a wry smile.

"There, now, children!" said Mary Garland. "Don't foster such thoughts."

Then they heard Rex open the door upstairs, and come out and shut it with a slam. Paul gave a glance up and saw he was coming alone.

"Ah ha!" said Paul comically in a whisper to Sylvia. "The bride is not going to favor us with her presence!"

"Hush up!" said the sister. "You don't want to hurt Rex's feelings."

"Don't I?" growled Paul. "Well, mebbe not, but that's not saying he doesn't deserve it!"

Mary Garland was at the foot of the stairs now, looking up toward her son, as Rex came slowly down, his brows in a heavy frown, a hunted, terribly worried, half-frightened look upon him.

Mary Garland's eyes searched her son's keenly. She didn't ask the question "Where is your wife?" but her eyes demanded kindly to understand her absence.

"Florimel doesn't want to come down," he said, haltingly, "I guess she's pretty well all in."

"Yes?" said his mother. "That's too bad. Could I do anything for her? Does she want a doctor?"

"Oh my no!" said Rex in alarm. "She'll be all right. She just wants to lie still awhile. I just thought I'd take her up a cup of coffee if you don't mind."

"Why of course!" she said. "Sylvia go and get a tray with some breakfast for Rex to take up."

"Just coffee would do, I guess," said Rex with a worried look.

"You fix a nice tray, Sylvia."

Sylvia vanished, and was back in an astonishingly short time with a well-laden tray. They all felt deep and humble relief that the stranger was not coming down to breakfast. Rex, too, looked relieved.

He took the tray and hurried up the stairs, calling back, "I'll be right with you!"

So they all sat down at once, to make him feel more at his ease, and he was soon back. Luckily the walls of the old house were thick, and they could not hear the words that passed between Rex and Florimel when she heard he was leaving her to eat her breakfast by herself.

"You think you have to dance attendance on the whole crew of them, don't you? You're terribly afraid of them, aren't you?" were the final words, fairly shrieked in Florimel's most carrying tones, after Rex had opened the hall door to go back to breakfast. But he shut it quickly behind him and hurried down the stairs, thereby gaining the admiration of his older sister, who had been reckoning that he would stay upstairs with his bride.

Rex took his old seat at the table with an air of relaxing, and one of his old-time smiles beamed out on his lips.

"I'll say this breakfast smells good!" he declared, accepting his plate from his mother. "Buckwheat cakes! That's great! We don't have anything like that at college! And Selma's fried potatoes! Oh *boy!*"

He applied himself to his breakfast and his mother noted with tender concern that his old boyish attitude was upon him for the moment. Poor boy! How he had messed up his life with a girl who didn't know how to help him, and wouldn't have been so inclined if she had known how!

As they rose from the table at last she said in a low tone to Rex:

"I suppose Florimel won't feel like going to church this morning, will she?"

"Church?" said Rex and his face grew suddenly blank. "Oh, *church!* Why, I forgot it was Sunday. There'll be church of course. No, mother, I don't believe she'd want to go this morning. Of course I forgot to say anything about it, but I'm quite sure she wouldn't want to go today!"

"Well, then, Rex, after the rest are gone, I would like to have a little talk with you. Perhaps you'll come down in the living room. We can shut the dining room door and there'll be no one about to disturb us."

"Okay, mother! I'll be down!"

Rex departed half reluctantly, his mother thought, and presently came down with the empty tray. Florimel had devoured every crumb! Unless she had flung them out of the window. Fae stole over and looked out on the lawn below the guest room window, but the snow was too deep to tell any tales.

Rex did not go back upstairs immediately. He lingered with the others, half shyly, as if he were not quite sure of his standing with them. And when they gathered around Sylvia at the piano and began to sing, he joined the circle and let his voice blend with the others as they sang:

> *This is the day the Lord hath made,*
> *He calls the house His own,*
> *Let Heaven rejoice, and earth be glad,*
> *And praise surround the throne.*

They sang the verses through. They did not need a book. They knew the hymn book from cover to cover. It had been a part of their daily life while they were growing up, and their voices drifted in beautiful harmony up to the guest room above. Rex was singing as hard as any of them, and was thrilled with the thought of being back among them all again. It did not occur to him to wonder what his angry wife would be thinking of it all. It might later, but not at once.

Then Sylvia's fingers drifted into another song, and they followed:

> *Safely through another week*
> *God has brought us on our way.*
> *Let us now a blessing seek,*
> *Waiting in His courts today.*

As the last note died away Mary Garland spoke:

"Fae has been learning some verses this morning. Repeat them now, dear, will you?"

Fae looked up surprised, a shy flush coming over her face, but she began to recite the Christmas story from Luke till she came to the verse:

> *And the shepherds returned, glorifying and praising God, for all the things that they had heard and seen.*

"That's as far as I've learned, mother," she said.

"All right," said Mary Garland with a smile, "that's far enough for now. That's lesson enough for today. Now, Paul, will you pray?"

Paul looked up startled. She hadn't prepared him for this. But if she had he might have felt more embarrassed. This hadn't been a habit of the family, not since their father died. What would Rex think of it?

But Paul's face grew grave and humble, and at once he knelt there beside the piano where he had been standing and began to pray. All of them followed his lead, Sylvia slipping down from the piano stool and bowing her head.

It wasn't a long prayer, just a bit of rejoicing that they were all together again after the separation, just a humble confession of sin, asking for blessing, pleading that they might so live as to help one another to serve their Lord better.

When they rose even Rex's lashes were wet, and there was a subdued expression on his face. No one had rebuked him, but he felt rebuked, perhaps by the Lord, rebuked with tenderness.

Sylvia slipped to the stool again and touched the keys, and again a song came back through the years from old habit to their lips:

> *My God, is any hour so sweet,*
> *From flush of morn to evening star,*

As that which calls me to Thy feet—
The hour of prayer?

Then is my strength by Thee renewed;
Then are my sins by Thee forgiven;
Then dost Thou cheer my solitude,
With hopes of heaven.

And when they had finished the hymn Mary Garland looked at the clock.

"It's time you went to church, children," she said in the old sweet tone, with the old phrase she had used through the years. And while they hadn't all contemplated going to church perhaps, they turned with a smile and went to get ready.

Rex, greatly stirred, went upstairs. He went to his own old room first, and locked the door.

Presently when he came out he went gravely into the guest room where his wife lay staring unhappily at the wide white distant landscape. She was not one who was fond of pastoral scenes, either in summer or winter, and her thoughts were only of plotting what she might do to get herself out of this place as quickly as possible without offending her young husband beyond reparation. Already he had hardened beyond her faintest expectation. Already he had answered her coldly, and criticized severely the way she had behaved the night before. But she didn't intend to let him think he could tell her what to do. She would show him who was the ruler in this combination. Not for nothing had she married him. She had planned that he was young enough for her to train her own way, and she didn't intend to weaken now at this stage of the game. Now was the time to conquer. Now while he was amongst this precious family of his. Let him find out, and they too, that she was boss now. They were *done!* They needn't think they could control him any longer.

So now when he came into the room she lay with cold

hard eyes staring off into a landscape that, though it was lovely, she did not see.

"Well," she said in anything but the honeyed tones wherewith she had at first won his interest, "where have you been? Did it take all this time to take a tray downstairs? And by the way, why did you have to carry it up? Are there no servants in this house? It seems rather insulting in them to ask *you* to wait on me."

And when he did not answer, just stood there leaning against the door sadly contemplating her, perhaps wondering why he had ever thought her lovely, she burst out upon him in contempt.

"What on earth has been going on downstairs anyway?" she asked, her face expressing scorn. "Of all the holy howlings I ever heard, that was the limit. Sob stuff, I call it! What is this, anyway? A camp meeting revival, or a funeral, I'd like to know? I suppose your mother thinks she'll convert me or something, and that stuffed shirt of a brother of yours is about as bad. If you get like that I'll get a divorce mighty quick, I can tell you!"

"Florimel!"

"Yes, Florimel! I'm right here listening, and I *mean* it! I never could bear pious youths. That other man that was here last night was just as bad if not worse!"

"Florimel, don't talk that way! You're not yourself!"

"Oh, *yeah?* A lot you know what myself is! And if I had ever though you would turn pious on me I certainly wouldn't have come off here with you!"

"Don't talk that way. I can't bear to see you so transformed!"

"Oh, and you think I like to see you knuckling down to those poor simps downstairs? You think I enjoy seeing you trying to pretend you are a saint, the way they do? Well, I don't and that's the truth. And this is the worst dump I was ever in. An old-fashioned house with not a modern stick in it. Victorian, that's what it is. A bunch of junk, the furniture is, and the house must have veen designed by Adam or Noah or some other Bible saint. As for that dough-faced sister of yours, I'd like to throw some of her aromatic ammonia in her eyes and hear her howl. I wished I had a lot of rotten eggs last night to douse her with. She is the most sanctimonious piece I ever came across, and that kid brother isn't much better. You needn't tell me he didn't know what he was doing last night when he brought me that glass of water when I had asked for liquor in perfectly plain language that anybody would use out in the real world. Your people are all a lot of flat tires, and I've had enough of them! If you don't take me out somewhere this afternoon I shall do something awful, and just show you what I think of them all!"

"Florimel! Cut this out! You are beside yourself! For heaven's sake, get calm. Until you do I'd rather not talk any more about it," and Rex walked with dignity from the room and closed the door behind him.

He went slowly downstairs, feeling as if he had had a great shock. He felt a good deal as he had done the first time he played football and was knocked cold. He was dazed that his beautiful girl whom he had thought so sweet and lovely had turned hard and bitter-tongued, fairly coarse and insolent.

He walked into the empty living room. He had heard them all go out to church. Even his mother wasn't here.

He went over to the window and stood staring out at the scene that had been familiar to him all his life. He had come to this dearly beloved place, and everything seemed changed. He had thought home would be a blessed refuge for Florimel. Florimel who had told him she had no home and no mother. He had thought she would be so happy here, as he had always been happy, and now she seemed to be an utterly different person from the young woman he had brought. He was stunned! He didn't know what to say or think. He did not know what to do!

He passed his hand heavily over his forehead and realized that his head ached.

He was standing right by the piano, in the spot where he had knelt when Paul prayed. It seemed a sacred spot. That had been a beautiful time. Why had they done that? It had seemed to him a tender welcome for himself and Florimel until now since she had talked that way. It was as if she had befouled and besmirched all their lovely sacrament of tenderness that morning.

What was the matter? He hadn't realized that Florimel would feel that way about religion, or that she would demand liquor. He had never seen her drink, though she had often laughed about drinking. But she had seemed so fragile and gentle and lovely that he hadn't thought of her as having coarse unholy thoughts such as she had just expressed. Surely, surely he had not heard her aright! It must be that he had hurt her in some way, angered her without knowing. Oh, he should have been so careful bringing her into a strange environment! He hadn't realized how different her upbringing must have been.

Suddenly the qualms of conscience he had had now and then blazed into a real questioning of his action in marrying Florimel. He had realized all along of course that his mother would have been disappointed if she knew all about that hasty courtship, but until this morning, he had had no real question in his mind but that everything was coming out all right. Even yet he assured his startled heart that Florimel would soon see how wrong she was, and would ask his forgiveness for these hard things she had said about his family.

Just at that moment he heard his mother's step behind him, and he turned and met her loving questioning smile.

She came over to him and taking hold of his hand drew him down on the couch beside her. She had come from her knees, and her eyes were very sweet, as she looked at him tenderly, searchingly.

"Rex," she said in a low tone, "suppose you tell me all about it. Tell me how all this happened!"

And then, although he had been rehearsing in his mind

for the last three days just what he would say to his mother when the time came, how he would bring her to see he was right, and it had been the grandest thing that could have come into his life, now all those flowery phrases deserted him. He dropped his face into his hands and groaned aloud, and then said:

"Oh, I don't know, mother!"

It was the last thing he had meant to say! He was horrified at himself now it was said, and he sat there with his head bowed in his hands, his elbows on his knees.

"Oh, mother, mother, *mother,* I didn't mean to bring you all this sorrow!" he moaned.

Mary Garland put out her hand and laid it on her son's head and he understood that for the moment she was weeping and could not speak. Then she suddenly roused and spoke out in a steady tender voice.

"Rex, why didn't you tell me about this when you were home a few weeks ago? You never even spoke of her. Why didn't you tell me all about it then and let us talk it over together, son?"

Rex quivered all over at her gentle touch upon his hair.

"I—didn't *know* her then, mother!"

"You—didn't *know* her then?" said Mary Garland. "But Rex, that was only five weeks ago. I mean when you came home to have that dental work done."

He was still for a long time, and the great significance of her words dawned upon him.

"Yes, I know," he said at last. "I really haven't known her very long. Not more than three weeks. Of course I'd seen her more or less all the fall, but I hadn't spoken to her then. But mother, she was very sweet. I'm sure when you know her better you will find out."

He was coming back to his first convictions now. He had forgotten for the moment the harsh bitter words upstairs a few minutes before. He remembered only her enchantment.

"She's had a very hard life, mother. Her mother died when

she was very young, and her father ran away and left her with strangers, and she was utterly alone and needed protection. I was sure you would think it was right that I should protect her. She was in danger from a scoundrel who used to know her father, and she was afraid. She needed protection at once, and there wasn't time to come home and talk it over with you, I figured that you had taught me to be a gentleman—and—mother, I *loved* her. I felt that if I didn't marry her, and any harm or trouble came to her because she had no one who had a right to protect her, I should never forgive myself."

It was very still in the room, so still that when a stick in the fireplace burned deep with a rosy light, gray ashes fringing its edges, then suddenly burned in two and fell apart, it was a startling sound like the crack of a whip. Rex shivered, and drew a deep sigh.

"I suppose perhaps it would have been better to tell you about it, and bring her here to you, let her be protected here. But you see, mother, I was right in the midst of the most important examinations of the whole year, and I couldn't stop then to do anything about it. And there was that basketball game, and others, and they were making a lot of me. I knew it would mean a great deal next year in college—"

He paused as his mother suddenly sat up and looked at him in astonishment.

"But my son! Why should examinations and basketball games and the like have anything to do with your decision, after you had taken a step like that! After you were *married!* You certainly knew that you could not go back to that college after you had done a thing like that! You knew that they have a rule that if any students marry during their college years they are automatically dropped. You knew that and yet you thought it important to take examinations! I don't understand it!"

"Oh, mother, you don't understand," said Rex wearily. "Nobody out there knows we're married, and I thought I'd put her in some nice place where I could go and see her week-ends and she would be safe. Then I could go on and finish my college course. You see, don't you, mother?"

"No, son, I'm sorry, but I'm afraid I don't see how you figured that way. Just what were you planning to support your wife on all this time while you were getting an education? Even if your father's son would do a dishonorable thing like that to the college. Even if you could bring your conscience to do a thing like that, just what were you planning to support a wife on?"

"Why, *moms!*" said Rex, aghast, "what do you mean? Haven't I got money? You always made it seem that I had. I don't know that I ever paid much attention to business, but I've always been under the impression that I would have money to start with in the world, that dad left it that way for each one of us."

There was a grieved dignity about him now that almost broke his mother's heart, but she had prayed about this for hours, and she knew she must not weaken. She longed to stretch out her arms to him and tell him that of course she would see him through, but she knew that she must not do that unless she wanted to ruin him for life.

"Yes, Rex," she said sadly, "you will have money, but not for several years yet. Your father arranged it so on purpose. He wanted to safeguard you from being a spoiled boy. You are only eighteen you know, now, and there is only a small amount which was distinctly designated for your education. Even your monthly allowance for incidentals was not to be used for anything else whatever. Then a larger sum, at my discretion, is to come to you when you are twenty-one, under certain restrictions. You can find out about all that by going to our lawyer. And when you are twenty-five, another larger sum is to be yours. But you see there are many years to wait for any substantial amount, and you are not educated yet, therefore not fully fitted to cope with the world, and support a wife."

Rex lifted stricken eyes to her face and was speechless.

"You see, Rex," went on Mary Garland. "You aren't grown up yet. But you have chosen to skip about three or four years, two at least, out of your life and preparation for living, and therefore it is up to you to take the consequences. You have chosen to take upon you the support of a wife, so I don't see that there is anything for you to do but to give up your college course, and a get a job. Of course, while you are finding a job — and I know it isn't an easy thing to find a job in these days, especially for a young untrained boy — but while you are finding one, of course you and your wife can stay here, so you are not like many a young couple in your circumstances. You are not actually out in the cold. I am your mother, and I will gladly share with you until you get a job."

"Not on your life, you won't!" said a sharp voice from the hall, as Florimel sauntered in arrayed in a flaming pajama suit of bright orange with fierce dragons of blue and black embroidered all over her. "I wouldn't stay in this dump for any money! If you want to be mean, all right, but you can't put *that* over on us, anyway! I have a lawyer friend that'll help us if I ask him. He's smart, and there isn't anything in the lawline he can't do. He has more tricks up his sleeve than you'd believe, and he'll find a way to break that old will. If Rex's father didn't have any more feeling for him than to fix up a rule like that that would send him off to some menial job while he waits for his money, then we'll get that lawyer and do the trick. And you can't stop us either! And of course, there are always other colleges that will take Rex if that's what he wants, though I don't see any sense in his having any more education than he's got, myself. He's plenty educated to suit me. But if he's got to have it, I've got a job myself of course that I can work at, so you haven't got much on us that way! And you might as well hang up your fiddle and get down off your high horse. I'm not going to be managed by *you,* and I'm not going to live in your house! Not while we're hanging around waiting for the money that is Rex's by right!"

"Florimel!" said Rex severely. "Don't say any more! You don't realize what you are doing! And you certainly will *never* attempt to break my father's will for I won't allow it! Of course I didn't understand or I wouldn't have been so rash as to get you into something like this. But it's done now and we've got to stand by it. Of course I'll quit college and get a job. I'm not afraid of work, and I'll take care of you."

Mary Garland's heart, even in the midst of her perturbation, had a quick throb of pride in her son. He was standing true to the Garland form, being as game as his father would have been. Perhaps he had not understood how things were. Very likely he had not counted on her doing a thing like this. He had always expected her to stand by him. But he was not whining and crying, neither was he arguing nor angry. Dismayed he was, of course, but not conquered. Perhaps after all this was one way in which this terrible act of his was to bring out the best that was in him. Nevertheless it made it all the harder for her to go on and not relent about her decision. Rex seemed all the more lovable to her now that he was taking this so rightly.

But not so with his young wife. She curled her lip contemptuously and lifted her well-modeled chin.

"Not me!" she said with a toss of her arrogant head. "I'm not going to stand for a skin game like that. Send a guy to college and frill him up with all the accessories of a millionaire's son, and then when a girl has lost her head over him, and given up all she had in life for him, tell him he hasn't a cent! That's what I call a dirty lousy deal, and there are lawyers to look after people like that! In smart society they call those people good little Christians, but in my world they call them low-down liars and thieves!"

Florimel finished with a flourish, and suddenly without warning she stuffed her hand in her pajama pocket and brought out a little gold cigarette case with a flash of near-jewels, took out a cigarette, lighted it with a tricky little lighter, and took a puff or two at it, her eyes down on the cigarette.

Rex looked at her in astonishment and horror.

"That'll be about all, Florimel!" he said severely. "Mother, if you'll excuse us we'll go up to our room!" And taking his recalcitrant wife by the orange satin arm, he marched her across the room, out the door, and up the stairs into the guest room, shutting and locking the door behind him.

WALKING home from the pleasant Christmas service in the big old stone church that had been their place of worship ever since they were born, Sylvia and Paul, with Fae and Stan just ahead of them, drifted into talk about old times.

"Marcia Merrill looks wonderful, doesn't she?" said Paul thoughtfully, showing where his thoughts had been during at least part of the morning service, for Marcia Merrill had sat across the aisle just two seats ahead of them, and Paul could easily have watched her all the time.

Sylvia flashed a look of agreement at her brother.

"Yes, doesn't she? I'm so glad you asked her for Christmas dinner. It will seem like old times having you all together. Only—" and then she paused in dismay.

Paul gave her a quick look.

"Yes, *only!*" he said with emphasis. "I wonder how anything is going to work out with this new element Rex has chosen to collect. But I suppose we've got to go through with it. I blame myself a lot. If I only hadn't gone off to the senior dorm this fall I don't believe this could have happened. Heavens! I didn't think our Rex could be a fool like that!"

"No, nor I," said Sylvia. "Do you think he knows her really

well? It doesn't seem as though he *could* care for a girl like that. Not if he realized what she was!"

"I don't know," said Paul with troubled eyes. "He hadn't any chance to get acquainted with her unless he took her off somewhere. Of course she's capable of making a dead set for him, but how Rex could be fooled by her is more than I can understand. When I think of all the friends he's had. Natalie Sargent for instance. There isn't a finer girl anywhere. I can't understand it. He must be crazy. Honestly, I get so hot under the collar when I get to thinking about this little yellow rat he's brought home and foisted on you and mother, that I could thrash him within an inch of his life. And then it all comes over me that it must have been entirely my fault. I just got to thinking about my own advantages, getting in the new dorm, and being around with my classmates all the time. I ought to have stuck by Rex!"

"Don't blame yourself, Paul," said his sister. "Rex isn't a baby. He knew better than to get married in a hurry, no matter how crazy he was. And it's likely that girl hasn't ever showed her unpleasant side to him. He couldn't admire that. Rex has good taste and refinement."

"Well," said Paul, "it's too late to talk about that! He did it, *whatever* made him do it, and we've got to stand it."

"Oh, but *he's* got to stand it too, remember," said Sylvia shaking her head sadly. "Do you realize what it's going to be for him when he goes out with Florimel, and meets all his old friends? You know, last week before his letter came I almost wrote a note to Natalie asking her to come over to a party we were going to have during Christmas week. My, I'm glad I didn't! Imagine what that would have been! Natalie's wide brown eyes looking in unbelievable horror at Florimel! Florimel's hard gray slits leering in contempt at Natalie. I'm quite sure Florimel wouldn't hesitate to tell her just where to get off. If she had the least suspicion that Rex used to be fond of Natalie she certainly would."

"Well, we'd better take care that she doesn't then. Fae! Stan!

Hear that? Look out that you don't mention Natalie Sargent before our new sister-in-law."

"Whaddaya think we are, brothah?" flashed back Stan contemptuously. "Dontcha think we have any sense at all?"

"Well, yes, I've always supposed you had a lot," responded the older brother, "but then I used to think Rex had, too, and look what he's done."

"That's right, too!" said Stan with a grave sad look in his eyes. "I suppose you can't be sure what any of us will do now."

"Oh, dear!" sighed Fae with big tears suddenly darting out and rolling down her cheeks. "Won't we ever get over this awful thing?"

"Hi, there, kid!" cautioned Paul, "no sob-stuff! Besides, there come the Hartleys. You don't want them to see you bawling."

Fae broke into a nervous little giggle and quickly dashed the tears away.

"I guess," said Sylvia thoughtfully, "I shouldn't have brought Rance Nelius into the picture at this time."

"Why not?" asked Paul quickly. "I thought that was the best thing that happened. It put Rex right at his ease, and filled in the awful space when they first arrived. Rance is a prince, Syl. He has what you call understanding. Don't worry about Rance. He's a thoroughbred!"

"Yes, I thought he was," said Sylvia, her cheeks a sudden pink, "but somehow I was afraid afterward it only made you all feel more conscious. And it certainly was terrible that he had to hear everything."

"Oh, you don't have to worry about that. I'll tell him a word or two that'll make him understand."

"I did," said Sylvia in a worried tone. "I was afraid they would get there just when we came in, and so I told him my brother Rex had just got married, and we were all worried because he was so young, and we didn't know the girl."

"Well, that was the right thing to do of course. Rance

would understand. Say, Syl, where did you pick him up? I certainly admire your choice."

"Why, he's in one of my classes, you know. We just naturally drifted together now and then. I really don't know him awfully well. This was the first time I ever went out with him, but he seemed very nice, and mother said it was all right for me to go."

"You couldn't make a mistake going with the guy. He's A-number-one!" said Paul enthusiastically.

"Well, I certainly was glad you knew him. I was just scared when I heard that taxi drive in, and knew they must be coming. But Paul, how do you figure out we're going to get through Christmas with that Florimel?"

"Well, I don't figure it," said Paul with puckered brows. "I reckon that's something God will have to work out for us. And we've got to walk mighty carefully and not give way to our feelings. Poor mother! It's going to be hard on her. I wonder how she made out this morning."

"Mother's simply great!" said Sylvia. "If anybody can take the wind out of that girl's sails she can, but I'm afraid it will make mother sick. We've got to help her every way we can. Only I can't quite figure out how that's to be. I'm afraid tomorrow is going to be an awful Christmas! If it had been any other time than Christmas! I always thought that Chirstmas was the best day there was!"

"It *is!*" said Paul thoughtfully. "But at that maybe it won't be so bad. You know Rance and Marcia will understand, and they've both got a heap of sense. In a way it will be better than if we were alone. It *may* hold Florimel somewhat in check."

"Oh yeah?" said Stan suddenly under his breath. "If anything'll hold that baby in check, lead me to it!"

"Stan, I'm surprised that you'll speak of your sister-in-law in that disrespectful way," grinned Paul. "But, no kidding, topper, we've got to watch our words and our steps or we're going to hurt old Rex beyond reparation."

"I know!" sighed Stan, and kicked a chunk of snow ahead of him viciously.

"Do you 'spose we'll ever be happy again?" asked Fae wistfully, lifting eyes that were very near to tears again.

"Why, sure thing, kiddie," said Paul with sudden compunction. "Most hard things pass sometime. But you know you've got to be strong and brave and go through them, not around them, Faerie child!" The brother spoke with a courageous attempt at a merry smile. The little sister answered it with a trembling teary one and assented. Then they turned into the driveway and walked solemnly up to the house, half afraid to go in, fearful, hopeful, wholly embarrassed.

Inside the hall it seemed very still except for a loud murmur of voices up in the region of the guest room. A petulant angry voice, rising, complaining, casting contempt. A deep, rumbling voice of protest, command, argument, sometimes almost pleading, broken in upon with another tirade from that high querulous tone.

They drifted into the living room, but even there the voices could be heard distantly, a rumble of discord in the house that had hitherto been such a haven of peace to them all.

Paul sat down for a moment and put his head back on the chair, closing his eyes wearily. He had been working very hard in college the last three weeks, and had counted so much on the rest and joy of home. Now to find it all tumult and discord was such a disappointment!

Sylvia stood in the doorway a moment, glancing up the stairs and dreading to go up lest she should hear words that were not meant for her ears, dreading to stamp indelibly on her memory anything that would leave a mark of sorrow for the future. Poor Rex! Poor, *poor* Rex!

She went over to the piano and sat down, removing her hat and coat, and flinging them on a chair. As she laid her hands gently on the piano keys, very softly a melody stole out. A sweet old sacred classic, so quietly played that it scarcely seemed it could possibly reach to the floor above, yet it served to drown the loud angry voices.

And presently Mary Garland came downstairs with a troubled look in her eyes. Paul sprang to his feet at once and went over to his mother, putting an arm around her and drawing her gently over to the couch by the piano.

"Sit here and rest with us, mother," he said tenderly, for the haggard look in her eyes went to his heart. He had been the one of all the children who had most comforted his mother after their father died, and now he was back again in his role of tender comforter.

"Don't worry so, mother," he said in a very low tone. "It'll all come out somehow. I'm sure it will."

"Yes," she breathed softly, "it will come out in God's time. I've been telling myself that. I came down to talk to all of you a minute. There's something I want to tell you while we have the chance alone."

Low as she spoke, Sylvia caught the words and whirled about on the piano stool, her fingers holding the last notes, as a sort of sound-screen in case anyone should come into the room.

Mary Garland lifted her hand with a motion, and Stan and Fae drew near, Stan sitting on the arm of the couch on the other side of his mother, and Fae dropping down at her feet with her chin resting on her mother's knee.

"I want to ask you *all,*" she said in her low clear voice, "to be on your guard every minute!"

"Oh yes!" assented the four pairs of eyes that were watching her lovingly.

"I am afraid that there are going to be many things that will be very trying for you all, and sometimes make you very angry. You will be tempted to judge this stranger very harshly, and perhaps attempt to set her right."

The four pairs of eyes promised instant allegiance to her, but Mary Garland went on.

"I know you all understand, and will want to guard your lips and your tongue and even the glances in your eyes. But you know we are all human, and the old human nature can't stand much, even when it tries hard. You can't do it alone. I've found that out myself in the last twenty-four hours."

The eyes searched her face anxiously and wondered what had happened while they were at church, but they found only that lovely chastened humble look that Mary Garland wore like a crown.

"So," she said tenderly, "I want to ask you one thing. I want to ask every one of you to do one thing when you feel yourself tempted to be angry, or if you find unwise words springing to your lips, or even when you just see something coming that *will* make you feel so. I want to ask that you will quite quietly and quickly get out of the room, go up to your own room, lock your door and *pray!* You can carry that appalled angry feeling to the Lord, and He will show you how to deal with it, and get your own spirit utterly under His control. That is the only possible way we can hope to conquer."

"But mother, suppose there is something that ought to be said! Suppose, like last night, questions are asked and have to be answered, just for courtesy?" Stan asked with troubled brow. "Do you mean we must keep our mouths shut and not answer?"

"Oh, no," said Mary Garland. "I mean that if you make a habitual practice of running to God for strength, and the time should come when you *have* to answer something, your lips will be under God's control so utterly that you will answer only the words which He gives you, and not the words your wishes prompt you to give—your angry wishes, you know."

"Oh!" said Stan, with eyes down. He was still feeling the weight of his responsibility as man of the house which he had borne while his two brothers were away at college. He was thinking back into last night. And his mother seemed to read his thoughts.

"Like last night, Stan," said his mother gently. "God taught you just what to say and do when you brought that goblet of water," and she smiled understandingly. "You knew just what she meant, I think, didn't you?"

"Sure!" said Stan with downcast eyes.

"Well, that's what I mean. Keep on God's side of all questions and if the time should come for rebuke or setting right, God will surely teach you how. But not if you do not keep in constant touch with Him. Now, are you all willing to do that?"

"Sure," said Stan, and they all assented.

"That's all, then. I just felt that if you would all do that I had done all the warning and cautioning I could. If you do that then I can be sure that nothing that happens will be our fault. And you know, Rex is *our own,* and we must try to make everything right for Rex. He must realize that we love him and he can depend on us to be loyal to him whatever comes!"

"Oh, *sure!*" they breathed it almost in a chorus.

Mary Garland smiled.

"Then God bless you all and give you a real Christmas, dear children!" she said, and her eyes were dewy with unshed tears.

Mary Garland left them presently and went to the kitchen for a consultation with Selma about arranging the supper trays in the refrigerator before she went out in the afternoon. Her children sat thoughtfully quiet in the living room, hearing the distant rise and fall of the discussion that was raging upstairs and troubling their young souls. Then suddenly Paul got up and went over to his violin.

"Have we got any strings, Syl?" he asked taking out the instrument and twanging the one remaining string.

"Oh, yes," said Sylvia springing up. "Mother had me get a lot of them last week. She's been counting on hearing you and Rex play. They've over here in the drawer of the music cabinet. Some for the 'cello too."

Paul busied himself for a few minutes with putting on some new strings, and Sylvia, as the voices grew stormier upstairs, began to play again. At last Paul had his strings on.

"Give me an A," he demanded, and twanged away for a few minutes getting in tune.

"You know Stan and Fae are doing pretty well on their instruments, too," said Sylvia. "Go get your horns, kids! Let Paul hear how well you can do!"

"Aw, he won't think it's anything!" said Stan with a studied indifference.

"Oh, yes he will," said their sister. "They've both been playing in the school orchestra, you know, and I think they've improved a lot."

"Great news!" said Paul. "Bring on your music boxes and let's make the house ring. What's your best number?"

"Christmas carols!" said Fae proudly as she hurried to get her cornet. "Any one!" she announced proudly. "I know them all."

"Great work!" said Paul. "How about 'It Came Upon the Midnight Clear'? That ought to sound well on trumpets."

And so, suddenly the rumbling sound of voices above was drowned out by the sweet clear tones of the old carol, as the children stood together, heads up, shoulders in good form, trumpets lined up. Paul played too, as he watched the two, his look commending them.

"That's great!" he said as they finished. "Let's try another. Say, folks, we'll have a real orchestra by and by. Let's have a try at 'Joy To the World.' "

12

UPSTAIRS Rex had caught his breath in the midst of an angry pleading word, and looked rebukingly at his bride of a week, then lowering his tone almost reverently he finished his sentence.

"I never thought that you would say such things to me. I never expected you to take a dislike to my wonderful mother, and say such awful things to her. I didn't suppose you could speak like that! I thought you were like an angel!"

The bride of a week looked him in the eye with her slow sullen battleship-gray eyes, and gave contempt from her too-red lips that were made up fuller than they should have been even for smartness.

"Oh, you little tin god!" she hissed furiously. "You thought I was an angel! You thought I would stand anything you chose to put over on me, didn't you? You thought I'd be so glad to get away from that miserable little hash-house that I'd just smile and take any old thing you handed me! And you never thought how you were deceiving me! Taking me out of a good job where I had my freedom, and played around wherever I liked. Where I was independent, with nobody telling me what I should wear and how I was to act, and whether I could smoke or drink or not."

"Florimel! You never either smoked or drank in my presence! I thought you were different from other girls. I thought you were good and pure and well brought up. You gave me the impression that you disliked such things. You didn't even wear make-up the way you've got it on now. I thought you didn't do things like that! I thought you were a dear little lonely girl, with no mother and no home and—"

"Oh, yeah?" mocked Florimel, "and what did you look like yourself? A million dollars! Ready to give all that you had to make me happy! Ready to take me on and take care of me! Ready to spend plenty on me! You wore good clothes, and took me to see shows, and let on you were no end wealthy. You—"

"Florimel! Look here, did I ever say I was wealthy? Did I ever talk about money?"

"*Sure* you did!" The battleship-gray eyes were flashing now like hot metal, the lips curling wide, the teeth with a snarl in their tiny white points. "You told me to wait till you got me and you'd see that I never wanted for anything! You told me you had an allowance, and we'd never need worry. You said you would always want me to have the best. And when I asked you, you said, yes, your father had been well off, and you'd have plenty! You said some day I should have a limousine, and diamonds."

Rex's dark eyes were wide with amazement.

"Why, Florimel! We were only kidding that night. I thought you knew I was only telling you what I would do in the future years. I thought you loved me, Florrie! I didn't know you thought so much about money and automobiles and jewels and things. I was only trying to tell you what I meant to do for you in the future years. Oh, Florrie, don't talk that way! Don't spoil all our dreams!"

"Dreams, bah! It's you that's spoiling our dreams. You make me think you're rolling in wealth and I was going to live in a palace on Easy Street, and then you bring me to a dump like this, with queer old sticks of furniture that must have come out of the ark. Look at that bed. Did you ever see a bed like that in any of the big department furniture stores?"

Rex cast a glance at the rare old colonial furniture with which the room was filled.

"What do you mean, Florimel? Don't you know that's a very rare specimen of antique mahogany? That's fairly priceless. It belonged to my great great grandmother."

"I should think it did!" Florimel burst into loud ridiculing laughter. "That's just what I'm saying. Putting your wife into a room where the furniture came practically out of the ark. Antique-your-grandmother! Not for *me!* I want everything up to date. I just adore modern things. I like those modern beds that practically don't have any legs at all and are set up on a platform. Dais, they call it. They have them in the movies. I like the mirrors done in sort of steps up, and when I plan a bathroom it's going to be all done in black and red! The bath and washstand black, you know, and the trimming and walls red, with mirrors set in. This room is what they call 'Victorian,' all little bunches of pale pink flowers and washed out colors. It makes me sick! I just screamed to myself when I saw it. There seems to have been practically nothing done to it for thousands of years. Everything old style! Gosh, I'd go mad if I had to stay here!"

Rex gave a hurt look around the room that had always seemed to him the height of refinement and perfection.

Then he turned back and looked at the sharp, petulant little face of his furious wife, and suddenly she seemed a great deal older to him than she had ever looked before. It came to him in a flash of wonder how he had ever thought her sweet and pitiful. How had he ever supposed her gentle and refined? Just because she had told him her pitiful story, and seemed to dread an evil man, he had thought her so superior to everybody else. He had supposed she would be one who could appreciate his lovely home and mother, and all that they as a family held dear.

And now, how was he ever to get over this thing that had happened this morning? Those things she had done and said? How could his sweet mother ever take her in and make her a real daughter as he had hoped? Oh, surely, *surely* this was some horrible mistake. *Some*how Florimel had misinterpreted the family and the lovely way they had treated her. She thought she ought to resent everything. If only he could get her calmed down and quieted, and make her understand that the things she was raving about were fine and precious. Poor child, she just hadn't been taught right in the first place! She hadn't had proper friends and companions!

Still, that didn't excuse her present garb. Wherever did she get those awful garish pajamas? And how did she dare to wear them downstairs before his lady-mother! Nor did it excuse her insolent remarks to his mother.

His thoughts were interrupted by the distant tinkle of a silver bell. He was alert at once, rising from the chair where in his feeling of helplessness he had dropped down a moment. He assumed an attitude of command.

"There!" he said, "there goes the dinner bell, and you aren't ready! Hurry, Florimel, and take off those outlandish clothes. Put on something decent if you have such a thing!"

"There you go! Criticizing my clothes! When I spent almost a whole month's salary on these perfectly spiffy lounging pajamas, just to please you."

"Well, you needn't bother wasting money on togs like that to please me!" said Rex thoroughly disgusted. "It wouldn't be so bad if you wore them when it was just you and I, though I think a perfectly simple plain nightgown would be much more attractive on *any*body. But when it comes to putting on clothes that were meant for night wear and going into the family circle with 'em, I draw the line at that! Get up and get something decent on right away! And make it snappy! I don't like this business of your not being down to meals on time. You can't ever win over my family acting like that!"

"Oh, you and your *family!*" sniffed Florimel. "If I ever saw such misplaced devotion! I ought to have known better than to come here with you! I told you we'd better keep this thing quiet for a year or two, and now look what a mess you've got me into! But you just might as well understand now as later that I don't intend to be ordered around and made to go in a certain pattern. I'm coming to meals when I like, or have them sent to my room if I choose! And *you're* not going to bring them, either. Those lazy servants will have to do it. And as for my clothes, I'll wear what I like! What do *you* know about what a young woman should wear anyway? I suppose your ideal is that dowdy Sylvia. My, I wouldn't look the way she does for a million dollars!"

"Suppose we leave my sister's looks out of the conversation!" said Rex severely. "Get up and get dressed this minute! And another thing, if you ever smoke again in this house you'll have me to settle with! You never smoked before in my presence. What do you mean by doing it? Was that just a gesture you had planned today to annoy my mother, and mortify me?"

"Oh, didn't I?" laughed Florimel. "Well, I've smoked for years, so you don't need to get on edge about that. Every woman that is a woman smokes nowadays."

"My mother doesn't, and my sister doesn't, and the girls I have known all my life don't."

"Oh, they don't don't they? Well why didn't you marry one of them instead of roping me into an outfit like this?"

A stern look came into Rex's face that made him seem a great deal older than he really was, a dawning disillusionment that was to him scarcely credible.

"You have a strange way of looking at things," he said grimly. "It wasn't my remembrance that I roped you in. You represented to me that you were in a terrible situation and needed protection! However, if that was your understand-

ing of the matter, never mind. We won't talk about it now.
The important thing is that we have to go down to dinner,
and you are not dressed! You can't possibly go down to dinner in that rig!"

"*Why* can't I?" demanded Florimel angrily, her eyes snapping. "You'll see if I can't!" She flounced up from the bed
where she had thrown herself and marched toward the door
defiantly.

Rex whirled upon her and took her by the arm firmly.

"Because, however it came about, *you* happen to be *my wife*,
and I *won't stand for it!* You've got to treat my family with de-
cency! Whether you like them or not, you've married into
a family that has always been considered respectable, and we
don't go around the house in night clothes!"

"Night clothes!" she burst into mocking laughter. "These
are not night clothes. They are very expensive, awfully smart
garments for high teas and that sort of thing. In fact I consider this about the best outfit in my wardrobe. I put it on
in honor of your precious family that you are so afraid of,
and I don't intend to change it."

"Then you won't come down to dinner!" said the young
husband firmly. "And I'm not bringing you anything up either. You're perfectly able to come down."

"Oh, well, I'm not hungry anyway. When I get hungry
I'll call down to Selma to bring me what I want."

"No, you won't do that either!" said Rex, his eyes growing stormy. She hadn't known he could look fierce and angry like that. "You'll get dressed and come down right away
and not keep them waiting any longer, that is, if you want
anything before supper time. And *I mean it!* I'm not waiting
for you, either, any more," and Rex stalked out of the door
and shut it hard behind him.

Rex, heretofore, had been most courteous to her. She had
felt that she had him pretty well in hand and could venture
to show her power, for to tell the truth it irked her sorely to

pose as a sweet virtuous young woman who needed protection. It wasn't in the least in her line.

She could hear his footsteps going downstairs briskly, almost hurriedly as he neared the hall below. She could vision the family waiting for him at the foot of the stairs, and she grinned to herself triumphantly and waited. They would probably send him back to say they would wait for her.

But instead she heard them all go into the dining room, and presently the quiet tinkle of silver and glass betokened that they were seated around the table beginning their meal, without further delay. Her eyes grew angry, her whole body trembled with her young fury. Her hands were clenched, and she set her sharp little white teeth together with rage. Once she even stamped her foot. But the sound was instantly muted by the heavy velvet rug, and the quiet pleasant voices coming up distantly from below were uninterrupted. She hadn't made the slightest impression. She had expected to hear Rex come flying up the stairs when she stamped her foot, but if he had heard her he was ignoring it. Her turbulent spirit resented his indifference.

Very cautiously she went over to the door, turned the knob silently and opened the door a crack, putting her ear close. But the sounds from below were quite calm and normal. They were talking together as if nothing at all had happened. Yes, and Rex was talking too! Then he laughed, just a quick casual laugh, but it didn't sound in the least as if he were all stirred up about her. It sounded rather as if he was relieved that she was not present. He was having a good time enjoying his dinner and his family.

Her brow darkened.

Yes, his words came clearly.

"Mom, could I have another slice of that roast beef? I haven't tasted roast beef like that since I went away to college. They don't furnish dinners like this in an institution of learning."

"I should say not!" said Paul. "Sometimes I just get so hungry for a piece of home-grown bread and butter I don't know what to do."

"Here too!" growled Rex, like a little boy, and then a ripple of laughter went around the table.

"Poor undernourished little boys!" mocked Sylvia.

"Well, I'm glad you appreciate your home!" said Mary Garland.

"I should say we do!" said Paul warmly.

It was a pleasant sound of comfort and friendliness that came to the angry girl upstairs, and something else came up. The appetizing odor of well-cooked food. Florimel was hungry, in spite of her anger. She was baffled too. She wasn't gaining the dominance she had expected over this family. All her daring had but served to alienate Rex from her, to cool his devotion, which had really been lovely when they started out on this trip, and which had been the only reason she had consented to come to his home.

But now suddenly a look of determination went over her hard young face. She closed the door, marched over to the closet where she had hung her gaudy wardrobe the night before, and surveyed the lot. What should she put on?

She decided on a frilly negligee of pale blue chiffon with long ruffles of white and blue falling back from almost bare arms. No stockings, and barefoot sandals of silver with blue satin straps. It was most effective, and had the added advantage of taking only a jiffy to don. She gave a glance of self-approval as she passed the mirror, putting up one of the rampant fat yellow curls of hair in the bunch just over her forehead. Then she swung out the door and downstairs.

She had the satisfaction of hearing a stir of surprise from the dining room. As she arrived in the room the three boys arose politely, with a suddenly assumed formality, and she fancied, quick annoyance.

"Oh!" said Mary Garland, lifting serious eyes to greet her. "You are feeling better? That's good! I'm glad you came be-

fore everything got cold. I never care for warmed up food.
Selma, you needn't take the meat out yet. Perhaps you'll need
to bring some more hot vegetables!"

Rex drew Florimel's chair out for her and seated her coldly.
It was then that her costume dawned upon the family.

"Oh!" said Fae involuntarily, and then gasped, giggled and
went into a fit of choking that covered up the episode for
an instant. The others gave one quick look and then with
averted eyes went on talking. But the happy home atmosphere had chilled. They were all on their good behavior
at once of course, but the cheerful clatter of familiar home
life was stilled.

Not that Florimel minded that. It was not her home, nor
her atmosphere, and the quicker she could spoil the pleasure
of the rest of them the better for her purposes. This mother
had got to understand that she couldn't expect to have peace
and happiness as long as she continued that tight-fisted program she had outlined for Rex. She had got to understand
that she and Rex wouldn't stand for her treating them that
way. She had to fork over their fortune or expect to have un-
pleasantness.

But Florimel was hungry, and the plate of food set before
her was exceedingly appetizing, so she silently fell to eating.
But there was no smile on her face, and her eyes did not meet
theirs with friendliness. For all that she did she might have
been a young tramp they had brought in to sit down with
the family. She made no response to any questions addressed
to her, except yes and no, and ate with her eyes on her plate.

Presently the family regained their composure, and began to talk again, quietly, about indifferent matters.

"Have you see Phipps Seymour lately?" Rex asked Paul.

"No, he's gone on that archaeological expedition that the
university was sending out."

"Oh, has he? Say, that's great! I knew he was interested but
I thought they had enough men."

"One of their men broke his leg in an automobile smashup

and of course couldn't go, so they took Phipps."

"Say, that's fine! I always hoped something good would come to him, he had to work so hard when he was a kid."

"Yes, I guess he was happy about it. His sister went as a missionary to Africa, you know, so that left him pretty much alone in the world."

"I heard a letter from her read in missionary meeting," said Sylvia.

"I always liked that guy. Even when he was teaching in high school I thought he was a good scout," said Rex. "I'm glad he's got a good berth. Who had charge of that expedition? Rathbone?"

"Yes."

They said nothing in which Florimel could possibly be interested. Girls didn't go to Africa as missionaries in her world, nor young men aspire to a place in archaeological expeditions.

The conversation droned on and nobody looked at Florimel except as there was something to pass. Mary Garland tried to include her in the conversation but for the life of her could think of nothing to say except to ask her if she would have more bread, or another piece of meat. Florimel answered her questions in short sharp monosyllables. Stan and Fae were entirely silent and Florimel looked at them in wonder pondering how two modern youngsters knew how to keep so still. Yet with it all, the new member of the family could not help but be impressed with their pleasant unity, though their interest was in people and things that seemed to her utterly stupid. Occasionally she cast a quick furtive look toward Rex; he seemed somehow to be a stranger to her, as in fact he was in spite of the bond of marriage. As she ate her dinner in almost utter silence she wondered whether perhaps she had not overstepped herself by marrying him after all. Perhaps he had more ability to dominate her than she had counted on. She recalled his authoritative tones upstairs, and realized that she had finally succumbed to his orders and changed her garments to come downstairs. She wouldn't have believed that of herself twenty-four hours ago. And now that her hunger was appeased she wished she had not done it. The next time she would starve herself awhile, and let them worry. It never paid to give in to people. Especially not to a husband whom she expected fully to dominate in a very short time now. Tomorrow she would go out and buy a few cakes and candies and nuts and keep them hidden to help her through a time of famine in case she found she had to work a hunger strike on this family she had acquired unawares. Candy would help out wonderfully. She had a few dollars stowed away in a safe place where Rex would never see it, against a time of need, and she would manage to have something eatable on hand another time.

So she kept her chin up and held her head proudly while she devoured the excellent dinner, even to the last crumb of crisp piecrust from the delectable lemon pie. Then she sat back and drooped in what she thought was a becoming manner in her chiffon robes, and stared with wonder at them all. Mary Garland gave the signal to rise from the table, and Paul, looking affectionately at his brothers said "Well, I thought I'd walk around and see old Uncle Fremley. You know he always likes to have us drop in on him when we're home from college. Want to go, boys?"

"Sure!" said Rex, brightening at the affectionate tone. "Yes, I guess poor old Uncle Fremley finds time hangs heavy on his hands since he's all crippled up with arthritis and can't look forward to working in our garden next year. Come on, Stan!" and he clapped his younger brother heartily on the shoulder.

Stan, much pleased, marched after them, and they seized their coats and hats from the hall closet and were off before Florimel realized that they were going.

She looked up blankly.

"Where've they gone?" she demanded, looking stormily at Mary Garland's sweet serene face.

Mary Garland looked up and smiled.

"Oh, they've just gone for a few minutes to see our old gardener who has been with us ever since they were babies. He adores them, and they were always very fond of him. It's not far, about three quarters of a mile."

"Gone to see a *servant!*" exclaimed Florimel, forgetting entirely the station from which her marriage with Rex had just rescued her. "Well, I like that! I certainly don't think Rex is treating me very well, walking off like that and leaving me all by myself!"

Her chin went up in the air and her eyes snapped angrily. Mild yellow-lashed eyes like that snapping fire! It was a curious combination.

"Oh," said Mary Garland pleasantly, "I think Rex thought it might be a nice time for you and me to have a little talk together and get acquainted."

"I don't know why I should have to talk to you!" said Florimel. "I never was very much interested in old people anyway, and we're not likely to have much to do with each other, as I don't intend to stay here. I don't see why we have to get acquainted, do you? You're only my mother-in-law. I didn't marry *you*, you know."

Mary Garland looked at the girl in sheer amazement, but gathered her composure instantly, and said in a pleasant voice:

"Well, then that's all the more reason why we need to have a little talk and understand each other. Suppose we go up in my room. That'll be cosy, and since you're wearing a negligee it will be just as well to be out of the living room. You know, some of our old friends might drop in for a few minutes to see the boys, and you wouldn't want to be caught dressed like that. It might be embarrassing. We'll just go upstairs!"

"Embarrassing!" jeered Florimel. "*I* embarrassed? Well, I like that! Besides, this isn't a negligee. It's a tea gown for a high tea, and it's meant to receive people in."

But Mary Garland had led the way up the stairs with swift quiet feet. There was no one to hear Florimel's jeers, for Fae had disappeared kitchenward. And if she wished to continue the conversation she must perforce follow. She gave one disgusted look around through the empty rooms, and then went tearing up the stairs, arriving almost as soon as the despised mother-in-law.

"Come right in here," said Mary Garland, gently, yet with a quality in her voice that held authority, as she led the way through her own door, and drew forward a comfortable chair for the girl.

13

THE three brothers walked into the wintry afternoon with zest. It was good to them to be together again, and they felt a fellowship which even Rex's sudden marriage could not quite dim. In fact since they had seen Florimel it seemed somehow that there was a new bond of fellowship between them, in that they were sorry for him, tied to a girl like that, so obviously not of his kind! Oh, they still blamed him of course, that he had got himself into a strait like this, but they pitied him more than they blamed.

Their talk fell to old times, recalling incidents of their childhood and school days, and Paul even gathered up a handful of snow, casually crushing it into a half-formed ball, and doused Stan with it, who laughingly brushed the snow out of his collar and gave him back as good as he had taken.

So they walked down the familiar streets to the little cottage in a quiet section where the old gardener lived. They burst in upon him like rays of unexpected sunshine, and rollicked and kidded him the way they used to do when they were young. And how he loved it! How he made them stand up in a row to measure their heights! How he asked them if they remembered this and that incident of their childhood in which he had been connected. How he delighted in them!

They had brought him gifts for Christmas, a subscription to a magazine he liked that had beautiful pictures of gardens in it, a big box of candy that he could share with his friends who dropped in to see him, a warm sweater from their mother, woolen socks and a pair of comfortable slippers. The old man's eyes were bright with happy tears as he opened the packages and said how much he needed this and that and how he was going to enjoy them, and think of the givers during the long lonely nights when he couldn't sleep. What wonderful people they were, *"his"* people, *"his* family," he called them.

When they went away their hearts were warmed with the quaint words of their old friend, and their own tears were somewhere in their throats, very near the surface.

"He's a great old Uncle Fremley!" said Paul meditatively, his eyes reminiscent of other days. "And wasn't he pleased, Stan, that you had sent that little tree up for him? Fancy his wanting all his presents hung on it, just like a child!"

"Yes," said Rex thoughtfully, his mind on the fact that he was going back to the house and would presently have to settle with his angry wife, and explain why he had gone on this expedition. "I'm *glad* we went! We mustn't ever let the old man down. He was always good to us, when we were kids, and we often must have been a perfect pest when he was trying to work conscientiously."

"You're right," said Paul.

But Paul's eyes were on ahead, for he had sighted a couple of girls in the distance who would be meeting them presently. One was Marcia Merrill. He always recognized her at a glance, no matter how far away she was. But the other girl he wasn't quite sure of. Was that Natalie Sargent? Yes, it was. And how was it going to be for Rex, meeting her? She was Rex's old girl. For years they had gone together as children, playing tennis, boating, skating. Rex was married now! Did Natalie know it, and would that be something to explain? Had those two been keeping up a correspondence since Rex went to college? Probably not, or perhaps Rex would never have married Florimel. But what ought he to do about this meeting? Should he forewarn Rex?

Suddenly Stan looked up.

"There come Marcia Merrill and Natalie Sargent," Stan said in a low tone and gave a quick look at Paul, a look that almost seemed an echo to his brother's thoughts. Had Stan been thinking the same things? Paul wondered. He was only a kid. Would he be keen enough to realize the situation?

But Rex looked up instantly with a startled glance and recognized the two girls. There was a quick light of pleasure in his eyes almost instantly followed by one of dismay. He frowned in a troubled way and dropped his glance to the pavement, saying slowly:

"I thought Natalie went abroad. The last letter she wrote me she said the whole family were going abroad."

Ah! Then they had been corresponding! Why had they stopped, Paul wondered. Had there been a quarrel, or was it just indifference? Had that anything to do with Rex's marriage?

But it was Stan who spoke next.

"Yes, they were going abroad, but Nat's dad got sick, and then something went wrong with the business and they couldn't go. Her dad's about well now, but the business is still on the blink, so Natalie stopped university and got a job. She's a secretary or typist or something with a publisher in the city."

"You don't mean it!" said Rex in a tone of consternation, almost as if it might have been his fault. "Why didn't anybody ever tell me?"

"Why, we all thought you knew it of course, Rex," said Paul. "I don't know why we never mentioned it. I guess there's a whole lot more to that girl than we ever suspected," he added quite casually, as if she had been just any girl out of their past instead of the only one who in former days had seemed to be Rex's special companion whenever they were having good times together.

"Yes!" flashed back Rex sharply, "I always knew there was a lot to her. She was a peach. She was the real thing!"

He said it so earnestly that Paul could scarcely refrain from answering, "Then why in thunder, kid, did you ever mess your life up with the girl you've married?" But he walked on silently beside Rex, thinking it over and over until if there was anything at all in thought transference Rex must have understood it, for there was a downcast droop about him that made Paul's heart ache for his brother.

In another minute the girls were upon them.

They had had time of course to realize who they were meeting and were on their guard. Paul remembered with relief that he had told Marcia yesterday about Rex's marriage. Marcia would likely have told Natalie, and maybe they wouldn't have to explain.

Then they heard Marcia's gay voice.

"Well, if here aren't the wanderers! Welcome home, strangers!"

And then Natalie's voice, a little too gay perhaps, and just a shade too formal in tone:

"It's grand to see you both again. I hear you're married, Rex? Congratulations! You certainly gave us all a surprise!"

Rex looked down on her and grew red and embarrassed.

"Does look a little that way, doesn't it?" he hedged. "Perhaps it was a little irregular. Perhaps I should have had a high-hat affair with the doo-dabs and invited all my girlfriends to be ushers, had two stringed bands and a procession."

He tried to grin with his old happy-go-lucky manner, but somehow couldn't make it, and stood there like an awkward boy grinding his heel in the snow, and floundering about among the words of his vocabulary to find suitable expression for his embarrassed thoughts. When he lifted his eyes to look into the big brown eyes of his former playmate he found a wide sad look in them as they searched him keenly for just that fleeting instant. Somehow for the fraction of a second their glances got tangled, trying to fathom one another; then they drew away.

"We must hurry on," said Natalie formally. "Marcia and I are on an errand of mercy to take a Christmas gift to a poor little sick kiddie in my Sunday School class, and I have to get back early to read to daddy. See you again, boys!" she managed a quick almost brilliantly gay little smile at Rex. "And of course I want to meet your wife, Rex," she added politely. Then she turned with Marcia and went on down the street. She didn't look back or even seem to hear when Rex murmured a belated, "Why, yes, come and see—" he paused and saw himself trying to explain to Florimel who Natalie was. But by that time the two girls were walking briskly away and the rest of his inarticulate sentence did not register.

"Nice girls!" commented Paul quite unnecessarily, merely because he couldn't endure the silence that there would have been if he had said nothing.

"Certainly!" said Rex with unusual dignity.

"I think they're both peaches, if you ask me," stated Stan, trying to help fill in the breach. Then, having established a long known fact, they walked on in silence, each thinking his own turbulent thoughts.

In Mary Garland's lovely big room at the front of the house, where a wood fire was burning softly, two big wingchairs were placed one on either side of the hearth in an inviting way. She motioned to Florimel to take the pleasanter one where she could see the wide stretch of snowy landscape from the broad low window.

"Sit down, my dear, and we'll talk it over," said Mary Garland, praying in her heart for strength and wisdom to speak the right words.

"You needn't take the trouble to call me 'my dear,'" said

Florimel hatefully, mimicking her tone with an impudent twist in pieshop venacular.

"Oh, I'm sorry!" said Mary Garland. "I didn't realize that might be unpleasant to you."

"Well, I'm not dear to you, of course," explained Florimel, "and there's no use in your pretending that I am. I don't see any point to it. You couldn't possibly love me."

"Why, I don't know," said Mary Garland, studying this curious girl keenly. "I am taking it for granted that you love my son, and that he loves you. And I love my son, therefore for his sake I should love you. For his sake at first of course, and — afterwards — for your own sake, I hope!"

Florimel stared at her. This was a new kind of philosophy that she had never heard before. For the instant her mouth was stopped. At last she said, stirring uneasily,

"Well, I don't think there's any need to bother. It isn't very likely to happen!"

"Why, I don't see why not," said Mary Garland, trying to speak cheerfully. "Why shouldn't you and I go to work and make it happen?"

"Suit yourself," she said with a shrug. "I shan't do anything about it. I'm not interested."

Mary Garland studied her sadly again for a minute or two, and then she said gently:

"I'm sorry, because I think we might have a very happy time together if you felt differently about it."

"Well, I don't feel differently," said the girl with a belligerent lifting of her chin.

"I wonder why you want to take an attitude like that," said Mary Garland sadly. "You know we really could all be much happier together if we liked one another, and were trying to be pleasant to each other. You would have a nicer time yourself, I'm sure, and I know Rex would be much happier. We all would be."

"Well, I'm not in the least interested to have you happy,

not any of you, and as for Rex, he knows what he can do. He can refuse to let you treat him the way you have. He knows his rights and he ought to stand on them and get his property, and then we could go off and live where we liked and you could go on and do as you darn please for all I'd care. You can't expect us to think anything of you when you act that way to us."

"I don't think you will find my son feels that way. He feels that he owes love and loyalty and respect to his family."

"Well, he doesn't! He doesn't owe you a thing! He didn't ask to be born, did he? That's all nonsense! Children don't have to do what their parents say. They don't owe their parents anything at all. It's their own lives they're living, not their parents' lives. Their parents did just as they pleased before them, why shouldn't they? And you can't get around me that way. I'm modern and I don't believe in any of that old time gaff. It's all a lot of bologny! I believe in every man for himself."

"Yes?" said Mary Garland. "Do you happen to know the rest of that quotation? Well, I guess it wouldn't be of any use to talk any more if that is the way you feel. I will excuse you."

"Oh, you don't have to excuse me," said Florimel contemptuously. "I'd go away if I wanted to. There comes Rex. That's what I was waiting for anyway!" And the new daughter-in-law marched out of the room.

Meantime the two girls, Marcia Merrill and Natalie Sargent, walked on silently for almost a block before Natalie said:

"Rex doesn't *look* married, does he?"

Marcia cast a quick glance at her.

"Do people have a special look when they're married?" she asked.

Natalie laughed half apologetically.

"Why, yes, I always fancied they did. Maybe it was imagination. I suppose I shouldn't have said that. I was just thinking aloud. I didn't mean anything."

"I know," said Marcia, "I have queer thoughts like that sometimes too. But I think I would have said 'Rex doesn't look *happy*,' instead of 'married.' He doesn't. He really doesn't! He didn't seem at ease and like himself."

"I guess that was what I meant," said Natalie slowly. "Rex was always so happy, and kind of glad at everything."

"Yes, wasn't he? I'd hate to think that was over for him. He was always the best fun, and seemed so kind of dependable, just like Paul, only perhaps a bit more gay, merrier. I wonder what kind of a girl he's married. That would likely make all the difference in the world."

"Yes, I suppose so," Natalie's eyes were sad and thoughtful, as if she had suddenly been set away from her old friends, as if she were looking backward at a childhood that had been very glad, realizing that it was over forever.

Marcia gave her another quick look and sighed softly. She didn't like to see gay bright Natalie gone suddenly mature.

"Well, we'll get hold of Sylvia by herself some day and find out a lot of things without seeming to ask. She'll tell us. I've only seen her once since they came home, and I thought she looked awfully sad. That was in church this morning. It wasn't like Sylvia to look sad. But then, I suppose it's sad enough business to have Rex married so unexpectedly like that, now while he's hardly more than a kid, no matter who he married."

"Yes," said Natalie. "I think it must be terrible for his mother. I know my mother would feel it if I got married sort of on the sly without letting the family know. I always think of the afterward. No matter what excuse he had for doing it that way, he loses such a lot. No memory of a pleasant wedding with his family present! And he must know they don't like it, no matter how nice she is."

"She couldn't be so nice or she wouldn't have allowed him to do it that way," mused Marcia.

"Don't let's talk that way about her, Marcia," said the other girl. "For there will be an afterward for us all; we've likely got to meet her sometime. It's better for us not to let our minds get prejudiced against her. If we even think that a lot it will show in our expressions, don't you think? And I don't want that to happen through me, anyway. For after all Rex has been our good friend through a lot of happy years, and we can't go back on him just because he's got married impulsively. And maybe it isn't so impulsive after all. Perhaps we'll find that out when we see her."

Marcia gave her a quick touched look.

"That's an ideal way to look at it, Nat. I wish I were as sweet as you are! The old Adam—or Eve!—gets up in me and gets angry at Rex that he could do a thing like that! After knowing you and having you for a companion all these growing-up years, to think he would find *any*body else, no matter how lovely she is! I just can't fogive him for it, Nat!"

"Oh, don't, Marcia!" said Natalie with a grieved look, and a quick catch in her breath. "You know we were just chums! Only children having a good time together! There was never anything between us but friendship!"

"I know!" said Marcia. "Of course there wasn't! I understand and I do suppose that it was the very fact that Rex wasn't grown up yet that made him do a silly thing like this. But honestly, Nat! It seems awful! You know he grew up feeling that all girls were fine and sweet like you and Sylvia, and I'm just afraid that he'll wake up pretty soon and find out that they are not! I'm afraid there is a lot of sorrow in the offing for Rex, and he deserves it too. I thought he had better sense. I really did!"

"Well," said Natalie, "we don't know all about it and let's not speculate. Let's just pray that the afterward won't be so bad."

"Not like Esau's, you mean?" Marcia smiled sadly. " 'Afterward, when he would have inherited the blessing, he was rejected, for he found no place of repentance though he sought it carefully with tears.' "

Natalie gave her friend a look as if her words had been a

knife piercing her heart, and she shrank from the thought in them.

"Oh, not that, Marcia, I hope not that for Rex! Rex loves the Lord, I'm sure. Do you know that verse in Jeremiah twenty-nine, eleven? 'For I know the thoughts that I think toward you, saith the Lord, thoughts of peace, and not of evil, to give you an expected end.' I came on such a beautiful translation of it yesterday, the literal Hebrew. It was so beautiful I learned it. Listen! 'I know the plans that I am planning for you, saith the Lord, plans of peace and not of evil, to give you an afterward, and the things that you long for.' Isn't that wonderful? Let's pray that Rex may have an afterward like that."

"Yes!" said Marcia, as if she were taking a vow. "But you know," she went on, "there's another afterward in the Bible, and I'm thinking that will be God's answer to all this for Rex. 'Now no chastening for the present seemeth to be joyous, but grievous: nevertheless *afterward* it yieldeth the peaceable fruit of righteousness unto them which are exercised thereby.' It looks to me as if Rex had done wrong and it may be necessary for him to have some chastening."

"Yes," said Natalie, "perhaps you're right."

"Well," said Marcia thoughtfully, "let's just put him in God's hands and bear him up continually in prayer."

"Yes," said Natalie softly.

Then they reached the house where the little pupil lived to whom they were carrying a Christmas gift, and their conversation was at an end. But Marcia kept her friend's words continually in her heart, and wondered over the hurt look in Natalie's eyes. Natalie must have cared a good deal, she decided.

14

FLORIMEL had flung into a dress and met Rex at the front door.

"I thought you were going to take me for a walk," she said, her hat in her hand, her coat over her arm.

Rex gave her a quick startled look, trying to read her face. Was more trouble brewing, or was she ready to be reasonable?

"Why sure!" he said, and then gave a quick glance about on the others. "Would any of the rest of you like to go?"

"No, they don't want to go," said Florimel with a rude little laugh. "I want you all to myself for a while."

"Certainly," said Paul courteously. "I couldn't go anyway. I promised mother to do something for her when I got back."

"So did I," said Stan and vanished up the stairs in long strides.

So Rex helped Florimel on with her coat and when it was buttoned she held her small red lips up for a kiss, and nestled against him for an instant the way she used to do in those first days before they came home.

Rex's heart quickened a beat or two. Was she trying to tell him she was sorry for the outrageous way in which she had been acting? Perhaps she and his mother had been having a nice understanding talk, and she was beginning to see how she had misunderstood everyone. So they went out and started down the snowy road.

Florimel was looking very pretty, at least according to her own ideas of beauty. Her lips were very red, and there were blue shadows touched under her eyes that she thought gave her an interesting, sophisticated look. Also she was on her good behavior for the moment, and using all her airs and graces, reminder of their recent brief honeymoon. Almost Rex took new courage as they turned into the street and he begain to point out the places where his friends lived, and try to make her acquainted with the neighborhood, now and then putting in a bit of a happening of his boyhood, letting her get glimpses of himself as he was growing up.

Apparently she was taking it all in eagerly, and she swept him an adoring glance now and then that made him sure she was going to be different now.

He walked her down past the old school house, where he went to school as a little boy, and then past the high school. He showed her the church where he attended Sunday School, though she didn't pay so much attention to that. And then he took her through the snowy park, and told her stories of the holidays there with celebrations. It was all very interesting to Rex himself to be acquainting her with his early life, and Florimel was having her own amusement in seeing the glances of admiration that were being cast at herself and her good-looking husband.

"And now," she said, as they turned, apparently to go back to the house, "where do you skate? You've told me a lot about how you used to skate. Is it a rink? Why can't we go there and skate now? They have skates for rent, don't they?"

He gave her a quick startled look.

"No, it's not a rink," he said, "it's the creek. It's swell down there. We could walk down there and see it, if you're not too tired."

"Tired? Heck, no! Come, let's hurry and get some good skating in before dark! Do they charge much for the skates?"

"Oh, they don't have skates for rent. Everybody owns his own skates of course. But we won't have to buy any. We have plenty of skates at the house. I think we can find a pair to fit you. We'll hunt around and see. But we can't skate today. This is Sunday, you know. Had you forgotten?"

"Sunday? What's that got to do with it? Don't they allow people to skate on Sunday in this town? It must be an awfully hick town."

"Why, no, there isn't any town law against it," said Rex, with a sudden sinking of his heart at her lack of understanding, "but we just don't do it. Most right-minded people around here keep the day sacred."

"What's that to us? Come, let's go get the skates!"

"No," said Rex decidedly, "not today! Our family have never gone in for amusements on Sunday, and I don't either. I don't think it's right."

"Right!" said Florimel in amazement. "What's right? Anything's right that you want to do."

"No," said Rex. "I wasn't brought up that way!"

"Oh, that old stuffy family again! I'm about fed up on them."

"Look here, Florimel. There's one thing I won't stand for and that is for you to discount my family! I don't want to wish them on you, of course, if you really don't like them, but you've got to get acquainted with them to see whether you do or not. After all, you made out to me in the beginning that you had none of your own; I'm only trying to share mine with you!"

"But why should your family care whether you go skating on Sunday? My soul! I never heard such nonsense!"

"Well, it's not just the family, of course, there's God," said Rex reverently. "Sunday is a day set apart to the worship of God. I've always been brought up to make it different from other days and I mean to do it, so we'll just leave that out.

I'll go skating with you tomorrow, but not tonight! Now, come on. It must be supper time."

They walked home in almost entire silence, but as they turned into the drive where the sunset sent a rosy glow over the snowy lawn, and made a gorgeous picture behind the lovely old house, Florimel said with a toss of her head and a deep impatient sigh:

"Well, I don't believe in Sunday, and I *wasn't* brought up that way, see? I certainly don't have to do everything you do."

"No," said Rex sadly, "and of course I don't want to force my standards on you. But neither can I let down and take yours. Neither way is my idea of being happily married." Then he swung open the front door, held it wide for her, and entered into the delightful atmosphere of home, trying to cast off the heaviness that the last few minutes' conversation had cast over his spirits. After all, Florimel had been sweet when they started out. Perhaps little by little she would learn a few things. The misunderstanding was probably all due to the way she was brought up, or rather to the way she was not brought up.

Fae and Stan had the supper on the table when they got there, and were just bringing in a great pot of hot chocolate. There were hot fried oysters that Fae had cooked, and sandwiches; delightful fruit salad, and plenty of chocolate cake. There was a delicious smell of fried oysters and hot chocolate in the air. The walk had made Florimel hungry, and she sat down with quite an appetite, eating without uttering a word.

It was a very quiet atmosphere. Everybody was trying to be on good behavior, and say pleasant things that could not offend the strange new sister-in-law. Mary Garland had a strong sweetness in her face, and eyes full of peace, eyes that had forgotten entirely the unhappy interview of the morning because she had laid it all at her heavenly Father's feet in prayer and left it there.

After the meal was over they all picked up their dishes,

marched out into the big clean kitchen with them, and proceeded to wash and dry them. All but Florimel. Rex had carried hers.

"Have the servants left?" asked Florimel of Stan as she stood in the kitchen doorway and watched them in wonder. Stan was drying the silver in a business like way and putting it away in the sideboard drawers.

"Left?" he said looking at her with a puzzled frown. "Why, you couldn't induce them to leave. They're a part of the family. They think the world and all of mother. No, they've just gone out to church, I guess. They always have Sunday afternoon off."

"Mercy!" said Florimel. "Both of them at once? But why don't you just stack the dishes up and leave them for them to do when they get home?"

"Oh, we like to do them," said Stan, and went whistling off to the dining room with a handful of spoons to put away.

Florimel went back and watched them all. Rex too, with an apron Sylvia had tied around him, looking very masculine, polished away at the glasses as they came from their hot suds, and passed through the hot rinsing water. But she didn't lift her hand to help. She considered that she had washed her share of dishes for the rest of her life, and didn't care to get into any more of that sort of thing.

"Now," said Mary Garland as she wrung out the clean dish towel she had been rinsing and hung it up on the rack, "you've just time for a nice little sing before we all go to church!" She said it with a smile that included Florimel too, but that young woman met her advances like a stone wall, without a lifting of an eyelash.

The rest, however, went gaily into the living room and began to sing hymns. Florimel with curling lip, went also, because there seemed nothing else for her to do just at that moment, and she hadn't as yet acquired a technique that could successfully extract Rex from this musical group which he seemed so much to enjoy.

So she dropped down in a big comfortable chair and watched them disinterestedly, not seeming to take any pleasure at all in the very lovely music they were making. All of them had their instruments, playing and singing too, with the exception of course of the two with their horns, who divided their time between playing and taking a turn at singing with their young sweet voices. Florimel watched them curiously, as if they were a strange breed of animal she had never seen before. She looked at her young husband as if he too were an anomaly to her. She couldn't quite figure out what he saw in all the rest of them, and why, when he was old enough to get away from them all and from their strait-laced life that they had laid down for themselves, he didn't seem to want to go? It was all perplexing to her. She was only interested in it, of course, to know how to pry Rex away from it, and it was thus she studied them. And so the tender lovely melodies and the precious holy words did not touch her.

At last Paul, looking at his watch, said: "Time we went to church, folks," and began to put his violin away. "Go get your bonnets on, ladies!" and he smiled in a general way and looked straight at Florimel.

"Not me!" she said decidedly. "I never go to church. I couldn't be bored that much."

Rex looked at her with a troubled glance, and paused.

"Well, I suppose I—" he began reluctantly.

"Why, Rex," said his mother hesitatingly, "if you want to see your old friends—I heard you say so—you go, and I'll stay with Florimel." There was utter kindliness in the glance she gave her new daughter-in-law, but Florimel gave her only a look of hate.

"Heck! No, you won't! I can stay by myself. It wouldn't be the first time, I guess. I thought I had a husband but it seems he's got too much family. I don't want you to stay, and I won't stay here alone with you, that's certain. If Rex has got to go and see a lot of folks I'll go with him, but heck! I didn't know I was going to let myself in for all this religious stuff! Church! Gosh! What have I come down to!"

Rex had turned perfectly white, and the pupils of his eyes had purply dark places in them like points of deep fire. He bowed his head and looked shamed. He lifted his miserable eyes in apology to the place where his mother had stood, but Mary Garland had gone quietly upstairs, and the others, too, had stolen away. Even Florimel had gone to get ready, presumably, and only Rex stood there alone, staring into the dying fire which Paul had just banked away behind its brass screen for safety. There were things which that moment alone taught Rex, things greater perhaps than any other single moment of his life thus far had taught him. He was seeing the gate to Afterward slowly opening before his shrinking soul.

They all came down presently, ready to go, quietly waiting at the door an instant, Florimel last, insolently, stamping down as if she were very angry at them all.

Rex, standing by the mantel with his elbow on the mantel shelf, his head resting sadly on his hand, watched them all file out, and then desolately roused and came after, taking his hat and coat apathetically from the hall rack as he passed. He followed them out and walked along silently beside that little termagant of a wife, and wondered why he ever got married. Why did anybody get married? What was there in it anyway?

The stars were very bright that Christmas Eve as they walked along together; together, and yet apart. One might almost think of angels up there somewhere gathering to come and make an announcement, winging their way from heights beyond mortal sight. There were snatches of song-carols from a distance, as little groups of young singers went about, from different organizations, various churches and schools.

The air was so clear and cold that the melodies from other streets seemed something tangible like threads of crystal in the moonlight. And then high and clear and mellow there came chimes from a nearby church: "Silent night! Holy night!" and they hushed even their low voices to hear it as they walked.

Then at the next corner Rance Nelius met them, and fell into line, walking with Sylvia as Paul fell back with his mother. Florimel heard Rance say:

"I was hoping I'd meet you. I thought I'd like to go to church with you tonight!" and Florimel wondered. How did they all get that same urge to go to church? Did they really mean it? Could they possibly enjoy it, or was it just superstition?

Then they entered the church and took their seats. Rex and Florimel had to sit across the aisle from the rest, for the church was very full. Presently Rex discovered Marcia Merrill and Natalie Sargent sitting two seats ahead, just where he could see their profiles, and the quiet sense of their reverent presence served to stir him more keenly to see the difference between the two girls who had been brought up as he had been, and the girl he had chosen in his haste to be his lifelong companion. He almost groaned within himself with an unnamed dread of the future.

The service was not long. There was some wonderful music, and a short vivid Christmas message. Florimel listened to some of the music, not at all to the message. For she was studying the people around her and comparing the hats they wore with her own for smartness.

But neither did Rex hear much of the message, for he was beginning to see his own rashness, and the knowledge was very bitter indeed. Perhaps if he had listened he might have caught the meaning of Christmas for himself in all his youth and helplessness, he might have begun to see how he had been depending too much on his family and the way he had been brought up, the traditions of the Christian ages, and not at all on a personal Christ. Though he had been brought up to believe in Jesus Christ as his Saviour, he had never as yet yielded his will and his whole life to Christ. His Christian life, such as it was, had consisted mostly in maintaining great general principles which his dearly beloved and respected family considered right, and which therefore he chose to consider right. But they had been to him heretofore just an atmosphere, a pleasant background and nothing more.

If his family had been openly opposed to his marriage, if they had argued with him and berated him for marrying her, if they had been disagreeable to her and found fault with her, he would have been belligerent at once and defended her even in the things about which he did not agree with her. But they had been lovely to her. They had not reproached him. Even in the brief business talk his mother had had with him, in which she made plain to him the financial arrangements his father had left, she had been gentle and kind, even loving. And Florimel hadn't understood. She had been angry, said all those terrible things. Would he ever be able to make Florimel understand what a wonderful person his mother was, and how his father had been really great and wise! And to think she dared suggest breaking his will! Oh, what had he done to his life and to his family, his dear family? He looked at those two girls ahead of him there in the church, those girls who had been intimate friends before he went away, and shrank from the idea of what they would think of him when they found out what kind of a girl he had married.

Tomorrow—no, tomorrow was Christmas—the next day, he would have to go out and hunt a job. He went over in his mind all the possible places he could go where he might hope to get in. There were one or two friends, intimates of his dear father, who could have been counted on to make a place for his father's son in their prosperous business, that is, if he had finished college and been ready to go into the kind of life their businesses would require. He doubted if they would have a place for such as he was now. Office boy would likely be the best that they could offer. And how could he support a wife on the pay of an office boy? And such a wife as Florimel was evidently going to be. She would want continual money spent upon her, and always on things in which his own tastes could have no part with her.

These plain facts came out in the open there in the church with Florimel sitting sullenly beside him, and those two old friends just ahead where he could see their sweet faces as they listened to the service. Several times during the past twenty-four hours things that Florimel had said in her wrath had made him suspect that he was facing a dubious future; and now, in this holy atmosphere, with sacred words and heavenly melodies in the air, with good Christian people all about him, and still the sound of Florimel's high strident sneers in his memory, he had to face hard facts. He had to consider, at least briefly, the possibilities that might be before him.

There was just one thought that came to him from that service. It was toward the end of the sermon, and at the time it didn't occur to him that it was in any way remarkable or had any particular bearing upon his own case. But afterward in the still watches of the night it came back to him, and went deep into his heart like a sharp prod that was meant to call his attention to danger:

"And to you who are troubled by things in your life that are bringing you disappointment and sorrow, there comes this message of peace, that God has not let anything come to you that is not going to work out some good for you, to the end that His glory may shine forth through you, and that you may pass on this Christmas message of joy and salvation to other lives. Christ was born for you, all those years ago, and some of the hard things had to come to call your attention to your great need of Him in your life. Perhaps you thought you were serving Him already. But come with all the adoring hosts today and worship Him, look into His wonderful face, let Him smile into your heart, and see if He is really born into your life today, for you to love and serve and enjoy as you would a visible Christ born in your home."

After the benediction Florimel pulled his sleeve.

"Come on! Let's get out of here! I'm fed up with all this!"

And Rex too felt that he would like to get out. Somehow he had a sudden shrinking from introducing Florimel to those two girls ahead. He felt self-conscious and mightily uncomfortable, and so he engineered their way willingly out of the crowded Christmas audience and into the quiet of the night. But when they got outside Florimel held back.

"Where were all those young fellows your mother wanted you to meet tonight? She seemed to think you were so set on it."

"Oh, come on," he said impatiently, "if you don't feel up to scratch we'd better get home."

"Oh, no, I don't mind waiting if you've got some interesting fellows you want to see. I always like to meet young men." She laughed foolishly.

"Come on!" he said sharply. "I don't want to see anyone."

"Well, then why did you let your mother make such a fuss about it and fix it so I had to go to your old church?" she said petulantly.

"Come on," said Rex haughtily. "I don't want to wait to see anybody. I'm fed up with the way you're acting, if you want to know the truth." And he took hold of her arm possessively and marched her rapidly down the street. He had no desire to be caught out in front of the church having an altercation with his new wife.

So they went on in a sulky silence to the house, and when the rest of the family got home they were in their room and didn't come down again that night.

Rex had heard them come in, and gave a glance toward Florimel who sat puffing a cigarette in a long wreath of smoke over her head, ignoring him.

"We ought to go down," he said at last with an annoyed glance at her. "This is Christmas Eve."

"What's that got to do with the price of diamonds?" said

Florimel sharply. "I'm fed up, I tell you. I've had enough of your old stuffy religious family. They can't poke their religion down my throat, not on your life they can't. I'm modern, I tell you, and I don't believe that stuff."

Although Rex was not himself deeply spiritual it shocked him to hear a woman's lips speaking that way of matters he had been brought up to consider sacred.

"Don't!" he said sharply. "I don't like it. I won't listen to any more of that rot! If you don't believe yourself for pity's sake keep your mouth shut about what I believe, won't you? I won't stand for any more of it!"

"Oh, you won't, won't you? What'll you do about it?"

But Rex had sense enough to close his lips. He was too angry to trust himself to speak.

After a little Florimel finished her cigarette and flung the stump in a little delicate china tray that graced the bureau, where were several earlier remains of former cigarettes. She got up and fluffed up her hair, added some lipstick and then whirled upon him.

"What's all this Christmas Eve you were wailing about? Why did you think we should go downstairs because it's Christmas Eve?"

Rex drew a deep breath and hesitated. Finally he turned toward her.

"Christmas Eve has always been a very happy time with us," he said. "I know they will expect us down, and probably wait for us. They won't understand if we don't come."

"Oh, for heaven's sake! You always have so many traditions. What do you do when you go down? What kind of a 'happy time,' as you call it? I like to know what I'm getting into."

"Well, first we usually sing Christmas carols a while," he began.

"Nothing doing!" sneered Florimel. "I've listened to all that rot I'm going to. You call that a happy time, I suppose, but I don't. Well, what else?"

"And then after a little we all hang up our stockings," he finished, in a tone that showed that the ceremony meant a lot to him.

But Florimel shouted.

"Hang up your stockings?" She laughed in derision. "What are you? Little babies? Hang up your stockings and expect some nice old Santa Claus to come down the chimney and fill them? Well, I never heard the like. Grown up people doing a silly baby thing like that! What is this family I've married into anyway? A lot of morons? Well, I sure don't want any part in an orgy like that! Preserve me from any more fanatical rites. I've had religion enough to last me for my lifetime."

"Hanging up stockings has nothing to do with religion," said Rex coldly.

"Oh well, what's the difference? Santa Claus or God, it's all one to me. I'm sick of the whole thing! I certainly wish I hadn't married you. I took you for a human being and not a moron!"

Suddenly Rex was aware of an echo of that wish in his own heart, and he was terrified that it should have passed through his mind. He turned and went out of the room, closing the door quietly. But though Florimel listened tensely for a full minute she did not hear him go downstairs. If she had she would have pursued him and found some way to bring him back. She did not hear his stealthy footsteps to the next door which opened into his old boyhood room, nor the quick turning of the key in the latch as he fastened himself in.

Florimel listened for a long time, and finally opened her door to see if she could hear his voice downstairs. But she only heard low words now and then, as if the family might be keeping still to let someone sleep. She even stole a little way down the stairs, and listened some more, but evidently Rex was not there, so she crept back up to her room and sat a long time staring out the window at the lonely strange white world with all those sharp stars up there carrying out this absurd Christmas stuff everybody was so crazy about. Christmas! What had it ever brought to her? It was all a lot of fluey she decided. At last she got tired and went to bed, wondering and fuming in her heart because Rex didn't come back.

But Rex was in his own old room, kneeling beside his boyhood bed, and meeting a God whom he never really had known before. Being searched by God on that Christmas Eve, as he had never been heart-searched before.

15

QUITE early in the morning, before the world had begun to wake up and realize it was Christmas morning, before even the smallest most eager boy had realized that Santa Claus might already have visited his home, and had stolen forth to investigate, there were stealthy footsteps down in the living room, and in the big sun porch where the mammoth Christmas tree had been awaiting its time. Stan and Paul were working silently in the almost dark, with only a tiny light in the far corner of the living room where it was to be set up.

It was an old story, the setting up of that tree, and they had done it so many times that the actual work presented no difficulties. There was a well-made frame with a deep socket that fitted the tree trunk, and it took no time at all to set the tree into the socket. There were accurately measured wires that went around the tree trunk at a certain height and fastened into little hooks well concealed behind pictures, that would steady it and keep it in balance. It was not a great undertaking. But usually there had been three of them to do it. Rex had always been there to help heretofore. Then there were strings of lovely lights ready to wind about among the branches, and attach to the socket on the wall. That would take more time because that had always been Rex's special work, but they went silently on with their work.

Suddenly Rex was among them putting his hand to the work in the old accustomed way.

It was a new Rex, though they didn't know it then. He looked as if he had not slept. They hoped they hadn't wakened him, but they only smiled their welcome in the dim light and were glad he had come. They couldn't see the look of purpose on his strong young face, the look of another kind of assurance from any he had ever had before.

Presently Sylvia came down with Fae just behind, her eyes bright like two morning stars. She helped Sylvia to bring out some boxes from the locker in the sun parlor, and together they worked, Fae putting threads of silver icicles straightly on the branches, handing up handfuls now and then to Rex to put on where she could not reach. Sylvia, with long accustomed skill, built a lovely Bethlehem on the mantel; crumpling green tissue paper for hills with little woolly lambs grazing naturally; stone blocks made very realistic oriental flat-roofed houses, with tiny stone stairways leading up to the housetops in the most unexpected way. When it was finished Paul and Rex hung the great electric star above it all, right over the stone arches where was the stable with the manger and the cattle, and the little figures that represented shepherds and wise men with their camels.

It was wonderful how lovely it all was when it was done, and the brothers and sisters stood for an instant in a group looking it over with the old pleased look in their eyes, and the old Christmas thrill in their hearts. Then they whispered "Merry Christmas!" and stole one by one silently up to their rooms to sleep a little while till the full morning came. But they left behind them all the lights in the tree burning softly under their silver rain, and all the full blaze of blue light from the great star above the mantel as it shone down on the little town of Bethlehem, reminding of long ago. Somehow not even a new and alien sister-in-law could quite dim the joy in their hearts over this morning of Christmas that had always been to them the best day of all the year.

The stars were still shining, and the silver night still held sway over the white earth when there came a silver sound out of the quietness, soft singing, sweet as angel–song, and growing clearer now from the depth of shadows under the windows below.

Was that only two voices at the start, pure and sweet as angel trumpets?

Rex, listening from his sleepless couch, thought it sounded like Marcia and Natalie, as they used to sing in their little-girl days.

> *This is the winter morn*
> *Our Saviour, Christ, was born,*
> *Who left the realms of endless day*
> *To take our sins away.*

Then other voices, a chorus of them. How had they come so quietly there under the windows in the snow?

> *Have ye no carol for the Lord,*
> *To spread His love, His love abroad,*
> *Have ye no carol for the Lord,*
> *To spread His love, His love abroad?*

Then a single voice, ah, that was Natalie's, sweet and tender. It made the tears come to his eyes. A ringing triumphant answer to the chorus:

> *Hosanna! Hosanna! Hosanna in the highest!*

And then Marcia,

> *Hosanna to our King!*

He did not stir. He dared not creep to the window as he used to do when his friends were below singing. He must not let them know he was listening. He must not let Florimel know. He might just listen and know that his God, his new-found God, was going to help him, was sending all this beauty of sound, this lovely silver night with its promise of eternity, for him, and God must have His way in him.

Silently the singers melted away without much sound of their going. The dawn crept up all gold and rose, and the stars were put out. The silver Christmas Eve was over, but the blessedness still lingered in the air. The colored lights from the tree still gleamed, and the great star blazed out in the living room. They must have shone afar and touched the faces of the singers just outside the window. Rex thought of it as he came downstairs and stopped at the door to look at them. He could somehow see their light touching the faces of those two singers, as he had so often seen it in other years, and he was glad they had been there, glad they had seen the star and the tree and the lights, and had had a part in the Christmas morning celebration. Only one thing had been omitted, and that was the gay "Merry Christmas" that had always rung out from the singers on the lawn in years agone, and had been answered from the house. It left a sadness that it had not been complete. Yet, it would not have been the same. Florimel would not have understood.

And then Florimel came down in a bright red dress, with her lips still redder, and looked at him with cold hard gray eyes and a scornful mouth. Florimel had had no part in his real Christmas. He began to doubt if she ever would. But he must not let the others know this. He had married her and he must be loyal to her.

Florimel paused in the living room doorway and surveyed the work of the night.

"Mercy!" she said to Stan. "Couldn't you find any ornaments? That tree looks awfully bare!"

Stan gave a gasp, and then with a bright look at his mother strode up the stairs to his room. His brothers and sisters looked knowingly at one another. All but Rex, in their hearts, knelt suddenly before the Throne and asked for help and quietness.

But then Florimel's eyes traveled to the star.

"Why on earth didn't you put in red lights?" she asked looking at Paul. "Blue makes such a horrid ghastly light. I should think you'd have something bright and gay for a holiday!"

Fae, with her young lips set hard and her eyes stormy, made a sudden dash to the stairs and went up to her room. Paul looked over at Sylvia and grinned, it was so apparent what the children had gone upstairs for. Florimel's quick eyes caught their look and wondered if they were laughing at her. She flashed a look at Sylvia.

"Who built the town?" she asked. "You? Why didn't you put in a few modern houses, and not all those little squat cabins?"

Sylvia tried to smile pleasantly.

"Why, it's Bethlehem, you know. The town where Jesus was born. I guess they didn't have any modern houses there."

"Well, guess again. You never went there, did you? Not so long ago anyway. You don't know what they had there. Why didn't you use a little imagination and bring the thing up to date? If you've got to have Christmas it ought not to be so far behind the times!"

Just then Mary Garland called them to breakfast and they went out to the dining room and stood behind their chairs. Only Florimel drew out her chair and flopped down in it. But when she saw that the rest were standing, she got up again and looked around uncertainly. Was this something she hadn't heard of? She never liked to seem to be lacking in society manners nor sophistication.

They could hear the children's doors opening upstairs, and

they came running lightly downstairs and took their places behind their chairs. Then Sylvia's sweet voice began and they all joined in singing, with heads bent, while Florimel stood wide-eyed and watched them.

> *We thank Thee, Lord, for this our food,*
> *God is love! God is love!*
> *But most of all for Jesus' blood,*
> *God is love! God is love.*
> *These mercies bless and grant that we*
> *May live and feast and reign with Thee.*
> *God is love! God is love!*

Then they all sat down, and everybody said together: "Merry Christmas!"

Everybody except Florimel. She only stared around and kept her lips tightly closed. She had no smiles on her face, nor any holiday air. She was out to be as disagreeable as she could. If the old lady thought she could bring her around by songs and prayers and ceremonies she would find out her mistake. That was Florimel's attitude. She had resolved during the waking hours of her night that today, Christmas Day, should see some progress made toward getting Rex's fortune back into his possession. If it couldn't be done by one method it could by another and she had several plans up her sleeve that she meant to pull off before nightfall. So she ate her nice breakfast unthankfully, and ungaily, and was indignant that the others seemed to look fairly happy in spite of her.

After breakfast they all went into the living room.

Florimel hadn't meant to. She was starting upstairs, and expected Rex to follow her, and she intended to give him plenty to pay him for going off last night and staying away all night.

But Rex, with a determined look on his face, took hold of her firmly and propelled her into the living room, giving her a gentle shove down into a comfortable chair.

"Well, I like that!" she said belligerently. "What do you mean? I didn't want to come here!"

But nobody was paying any attention to her and she subsided because she couldn't quite understand what they were going to do next. Then they broke into song again. Always singing! She couldn't understand it.

> *Praise God from whom all blessings flow,*
> *Praise Him all creatures here below,*
> *Praise Him above ye heavenly host,*
> *Praise Father, Son, and Holy Ghost.*

Before she could get her mind made up to get up and flaunt out, the order changed and each in turn recited a Christmas Bible verse. Florimel didn't know they were Bible verses. She only knew it was something religious, and she looked in wonder from one to the other, as each without being called upon gave a few words. And then to her amazement they all got up and turning knelt by their chairs. All but herself. She wouldn't kneel. Not she! This would be a good time to slip out, now while they were all kneeling and wouldn't see her, and when they got up she just wouldn't be there. It would be a good joke on them.

But suddenly Paul began to pray.

Florimel had never heard a young man pray before. She didn't know any of them did. It was quite interesting. He was talking just like a preacher, as if he were talking to God and He was a real person. Florimel was intrigued by it all. And next Sylvia had a brief prayer; that surprised her, too. A girl praying! What did she think she was, anyway? Some kind of a Sister, or Deaconess or something like they had in charitable associations? But her prayer was short, and Florimel decided that now was her chance to get out before any more religious performances went on. As she edged forward to rise, she heard Rex's voice, quiet calm and steady, not in the least embarrassed or upset, just as if he had done a thing like this before. She turned and looked at him in amazement, realizing that all eyes were closed and they could not see her.

Rex's eyes were shut, too, and his hand was up, half sheltering his face. There, right in the chair beside her, Rex, her new husband, was praying!

"Father in Heaven, we thank Thee for this day on which Thy Son was born into this world. It is so great to know that He came to take our sins upon Himself and pay the penalty for them with His own precious blood. So, today, we confess that we have sinned—I have sinned, Lord, and I ask forgiveness. I thank Thee that I know Thou wilt give it. Bless us all, and help us to walk to please Thee today. Guide us in the way we ought to go. We ask it in the name of Jesus."

Florimel was weak with astonishment. She could scarcely believe that what she had just heard had been real! Yet there he knelt quietly beside her as if he had done nothing strange. She turned wondering eyes as Stan took up the petition in his clear boyish voice, and then little Fae, asking that she might be forgiven for getting angry.

She scarcely took in the short lovely prayer of Mary Garland who put them all in loving care for the day of all days, and then they all arose and there was Florimel yet! She hadn't escaped, and now it was too late to produce the effect she had intended.

"Let's get to work," said Paul smilingly. "It's getting on to time for our dinner guests to arrive. Mother, here's a package for you. You rate first. 'Mother, from her kid daughter.' Open it up, mother, and let's see what the kid has done for you. I'll bet it's a tidy and she made it herself."

Fae's cheeks got rosy red and she looked embarrassed, but she grinned gaily.

"It's not a tidy," she said, "it's some handkerchiefs, and yes, I made them every bit. I hemstitched them!"

"Darling child!" said Mary Garland with her arms about Fae, and her lips against her round pink cheek. Florimel, staring, had a brief vision of what it might have been if she had ever had a mother to love her.

Not that it affected Florimel deeply. She curled her lip and felt superior instead of wistful.

Then Paul laid a little package in Florimel's lap, and she looked down at it as if it were something that might bite her.

"Open it up, sister," said Paul in what was evidently an attempt at brotherliness.

Then Florimel stared at him in wonder. Some months ago she had made an attempt to annex Paul to her list of admirers, but Paul carried his head high, only giving her a lofty impersonal smile, and she soon learned that she had no effect whatever upon him. Therefore she was not in a mood to take him over as a brother-in-law. No sir! If he wouldn't have her for herself he needn't think he could get anywhere with her with that brother stuff. He was too high hat, anyway. She wanted nothing to do with him.

So she only looked down at the package in her lap, and when Rex leaned over and whispered "Open it, Florrie," she tossed her head and said, "No! Not now!"

Paul had always had a reputation for tact, and quickly he produced another package.

"Here's one for you, Sylvia. Come on, let's get this thing going. I don't want to hurry you, but we wouldn't want our guests to arrive while we're at this, would we?"

Then there was a package for Rex, and another one for Florimel, and Paul produced them at the same time, delivering them together, as though to make of no account the fact that Florimel had still her unopened package in her lap.

Rex got red over his, with a glance at his mother. He felt sure this was the new shirts she knew he needed.

"You'll have to — excuse — Florimel," he said, "and me," he added. "We didn't really have much time — or money — to get things after we knew we were coming home. At least Florimel didn't. She didn't know any of you yet, either."

"Of course," said Mary Garland sweetly. "We didn't expect you to. Don't think of it."

"I don't give Christmas presents," said Florimel sharply.

"Oh!" said Fae with a quick catch in her breath. " 'Scuse me a minute," and she hurried out and ran upstairs.

Paul looked at his mother and Sylvia with another grin, and went on distributing presents, and presently everybody had something, and Fae was back serene again, her small face wreathed in smiles over the beautiful pink dress she had found in one of her packages.

And after a while even Florimel began hesitantly to finger some of her gifts curiously. Rex reached over and helped her untie the strings, and for a few minutes she was intrigued by some of the things she had found in her packages. For they were pretty things, not makeshifts. A lovely little hand bag, from Mary Garland, with all the fittings inside. A charming bureau set from Sylvia. Florimel found herself staring at her and wondering why she did it. For she was quite sure that Sylvia didn't like her as a sister-in-law. Did she think she had to do it to keep in right with Rex? She could see that they were all very fond of Rex.

It was growing late in the morning when the great pile of presents was distributed, for some of them had been adorned with pictures and accompanied by original poems that were required to be read aloud, and there was much laughter and fun. Even Florimel smiled once or twice, but for the most part she didn't unbend, and every time Rex got a nice present she looked at it as if she were jealous of it. She didn't want Rex tied down by love to his family. She didn't intend he should be, and she meant to get out and away from here as soon as ever she could. But she meant first to reduce this mother to a place where she would be ready to hand over the last penny that was coming to Rex. So she did not dare to unbend till she had things just where she wanted them.

But as they all got up and began carrying away the presents

that had fallen to their lot, Florimel found she had a goodly pile of things herself, and stood gloating over them. There was a box of Yardley's toilet water, powder and soap. She had never owned any of that. One didn't buy Yardley's on the installment plan. There was a little bottle of expensive perfume, the kind she had always longed for. There was a bangle bracelet with little tinkling things set with bright stones. There were lovely handkerchiefs. Of course as she looked at some of the things the others had, they weren't much, and she tossed her head independently as she thought it over, comparing her things with the fountain pens and watches and really handsome gifts that had been given to some of the "own children." Of course it was all right for them to excuse themselves about not knowing she was coming till it was too late to prepare for her. That was all bologny. If they had approved of the marriage and liked her they would have managed something much more elegant for her. And of course there was still a chance they could give her a wedding present, though it didn't look very likely, the way that tight-fisted mother-in-law was acting about Rex's money. However, she had really fared better than she expected. Of course she hadn't given any of them anything either; she hadn't anything to give them. And if they acted that way about the family money they would never get a cent's worth from her, that was a sure thing.

Nevertheless she took her gifts upstairs and put them away carefully, after she had first tested out some of the Yardley soap and doused one of the new handerchiefs with the wonderful perfume. That she had put it on too freely and was going to be entirely too redolent when she came downstairs didn't bother her in the least. She enjoyed being conspicuous.

She stayed up in her room quite a while prinking, putting her hair into the latest, ugliest mode, and making her lips startling with lipstick. She heard the doorbell and knew the guests must have arrived, but she didn't hurry. She heard Sylvia bringing up that other girl, and she meant to startle her, so she applied herself to putting on a fresh supply of deep dark red nail polish until she looked almost as if her fingers were dripping with red paint.

At last Rex came up after her.

"What are you doing?" he said. "Don't you think you ought to come down? The guests are here. Selma is putting the dinner on the table!"

"I should worry!" said Florimel gaily, beginning to hum the latest jazzy tune and keep time with her feet. She wanted Rex to tell her how pretty she was, but Rex was only staring at her in disgust.

"For mercy's sake go and wash your face!" he said fiercely. "You don't think you look nice with your mouth all smeared up in that bloody way, do you? Those are decent people down there, not movie actresses. Go get your face clean!"

She turned and looked at him in wonder and scorn, the hurt look growing into recklessness.

"Well, if they're too fine to be smart I'd better not go down," she said haughtily. "I dress the way the majority of the world dresses. If they don't like it I can't help it."

"Well, *I* can!" said Rex. "I won't stand for it. I'm not going to have them thinking I married a wild woman. And those painted claws you've got on your hands! Scrub those up and cut your nails. If I ever saw a woman imitate a hottentot you've done it. I can't see how you can bear yourself, looking like that. I wouldn't want to introduce a decent girl to you looking like that! Isn't there some stuff you can put on that will take that red off your nails? My! You make me sick! You look as if you'd been in a battle and got wounded! I'll be back in five minutes to get you. Get washed up quick, and don't let's have any monkey shines!"

He opened the door and went out, slamming it shut before she could rally her astounded senses to cast him a scathing protest. She stood there confounded, trying to invent a worse punishment for him than she had as yet dealt out to him.

But she was terribly hungry, and the door opening even only for a moment had let in the heavenly smell of roasted turkey. She wanted her dinner right away. It was going to be a wonderful dinner. She had been through the kitchen and seen some of the preparations.

She considered for a moment the idea of daring Rex and going down the way she was anyway, but that might upset some of the plans she had been forming for the afternoon and evening. Rex would be furious of course if she insisted on going down this way, and would probably go off with the men somewhere, instead of taking her to some night club to dance as she wanted to do.

She marched over to the mirror and surveyed herself. Then indignantly, baffled for the time being, she went to work at her fingernails ruining all that smart effect that she had labored so hard to produce, just to please a lot of would-be saints who couldn't stand modern ways.

When Rex came back for her he could not find her anywhere, and when he frantically went downstairs there she was talking quite affably to Rance Nelius, as if he were an old friend.

Relieved, he stood across the room and surveyed her, caught a glimpse of her old self as he had seen her first, when she was trying to charm him, smiling with down-drooping lashes and pleasant near-shy glances as she conversed. What kind of a girl was she, anyway? He had married her and he didn't know yet which she was, a shy sweet worried child out in the world on her own, and trying to do her best, or a hard, petulant, spoiled little brat who didn't know how to behave decently and didn't want to know.

He looked at her lips and saw them guiltless of lipstick, showing her pretty white teeth with a winning smile. Rance Nelius seemed to be studying her courteously, trying to understand her. Rex looked at her hands, and amazingly those hideous red fingernails had disappeared, and her fingers were only rosy as nature might have made them. Well, he had conquered her for once. He hadn't really expected to. He had feared he was to have a battle, and dinner was imminent. He didn't want his mother to endure another scene at meal time, with company present, too.

Florimel sat demurely talking, casting now and then a furtive glance at her silent husband. Only a glint of deviltry in the depths of her narrowed gray eyes told of plans.

It was perhaps the stab to her own idea of her beauty that had gone deeper into her selfish soul than anything else. Rex had not thought her lovely when she had dressed up especially to charm him, and now she would pay him back. He was not being nearly as pliable as she had thought he would be. She had supposed in those first days that she would be able to do anything with him, just anything. But now with the family in the background, and all their absurd religious fads and ideas, he seemed to be formidable. But there were ways of breaking that down, and she would try them, soon. He and his precious family should learn that she was not to be daunted. She would have money, and she would wind that smug-faced woman and her two daughters around her finger or she would know the reason why.

They thought they were decent, did they? They thought she was indecent. Well, she would teach them in ways they did not dream of. She would rub their bland smug faces in the dust. She would humiliate them. As she sat there scheming she could think of even more ways to humiliate them than they could possibly find to annoy her.

So her eyes flashed a fire in their battleship-gray depths, and she continued to try her charms on Rance Nelius, just to see if she couldn't make that angel-faced Sylvia look jealous. And to smirk at even that high and mighty brother Paul, just to see if Marcia could be made to look jealous too. Could it be that Marcia was the cause of his snobbishness at college? Maybe they were engaged. The whole family seemed to act as if they belonged together in some special way.

So Florimel, in her thoughts, continued her running line

of comments on the people present, and didn't even know that for the time being the family were as pleased with her as they could ever possibly be, just because she wasn't made up, and was acting like an ordinary pleasant individual. It was more than they had so far had reason to expect.

Then came the call to dinner and they all went out.

16

THE Christmas table was lovely. The guests all exclaimed at its beauty as they paused at the dining room door and surveyed it. Sylvia and Fae had been shut up in the dining room for some time during the morning, with Rance Nelius as soon as he came to help them, and had made it into a place of Christmas festivity.

There was a tiny tree in the center, not tall enough to hide the guests from one another, yet tall enough to partly conceal a goodly group of tiny packages done up in gala ribbons and papers. The tree was adorned with tiny lights, very tiny, and draped thickly with silver rain. It was a thing of beauty in itself. The packages were attached to small silver and red and green ribbons that wandered about and finally reached the different place cards. The place cards were the work of Fae and Stan. They were done in water colors, and inscribed with fitting sentiments, representing hard work and much thought. Some of them bore couplets that were really witty.

So, for a time after they were seated, there was so much to be examined and exclaimed over and delighted in that there was no opportunity for those long embarrassing silences that the Garlands had greatly feared because of the new member of their household.

For the first time in her life Florimel found herself in a group of happy well-mannered people having a very good time, of which she might be a part if she chose. She hadn't intended to choose to be assimilated, but somehow she found herself entering in without her own volition. The little packages under the tree were most engaging and alluring. She found herself wondering what would be in her packages. For just a little while she forgot her role of belligerent daughter-in-law, and really entered into the fun, laughing with the rest over the poetry, and looking quite like a natural young woman. Rex, watching her furtively with relief, decided that after all she might not turn out to be so dreadful. He did not realize yet that he was trying all the time to convince himself that she just didn't understand his family, and that after she did she would love them and behave in a normal manner. He relaxed a little and was able to enjoy his Christmas dinner as much as anybody, with a degree of lightheartedness, rejoicing that he was at home again with those he loved. He was deeply interested in what Rance Nelius was saying about things in the university, and he was able to banish utterly for the time being the wonder that had been creeping into his mind, whether he ever had really loved Florimel at all, and if he didn't what he should do about it. He couldn't do anything about it at the present moment, and if he could what would there be to do anyway? So why think about it? Perhaps all would go well after this beautiful Christmas occasion.

So the dinner went on to its delightful end, with mince pie and plum pudding both to choose from, and everything perfect as everything at home always was perfect on his mother's table.

They adjourned to the living room under the shadow of the great tree, whose lights were just beginning to shine forth and emblazon the dusk that was creeping into the room.

Florimel had her hands full of tiny articles, a Dresden shepherdess, an ivory elephant, three little china dogs, a little black cat with her back arched, an old-fashioned nosegay of roses framed in lace paper, each of which bore a tiny ring which could be fastened to a bangle bracelet. She was actually charmed with them. She sat down in a comfortable chair and began to string a little silver ribbon through their rings, fastening it around her neck. Rex watched her anxiously. If she only would be like that all the time! If she only wouldn't act like a common girl with no manners. Oh, what should he do if she went into one of her frenzies while these two, Marcia and Rance, were here? He couldn't stand the shame of it! Marcia would probably report it all to Natalie Sargent, and he couldn't bear her to know that the wife he had married had turned out all wrong. Natalie, his old friend! Natalie who had been with them a year ago, a part of the merrymaking! And now she was trying to make a happy Christmas for her own family, with a sick father, and an old grandmother, and a mother who was greatly distressed about their changed circumstances.

Suddenly he jerked himself up. He shouldn't be thinking about Natalie. Even if she was one of his very best old friends, a lifelong playmate, he should be thinking about his young wife who really was quite pretty now that she had taken off that hideous make-up, and subdued those beastly finger claws! He shuddered at the thought that she might have come downstairs among them all looking like that. Perhaps she didn't really know that nice people didn't fix themselves up that way. Perhaps he must teach her. After all, she hadn't had any mother to teach her. There was one more thing he wished he had cried out against and that was those long clattery earings. He saw Fae watching her sometimes, with a smothered grin on her lips as if she wanted to laugh at them, and he half resented it, half wanted to laugh with her. Poor little girl! All this wasn't going to be very good for Fae, his little sister. And suddenly he saw that this thing that he had done not only affected himself, but affected his whole family, and those were things he should have thought about before he let himself be persuaded into marriage so hastily. After all, a family had some rights. They had a right to be able to trust every one of themselves to bring no unseemly one among them.

However, he was married, and what was done was done. Was he going to have to regret what he had done all the rest of his life, or was Florimel going to turn out to be all right?

He watched her all the rest of the evening, while she sat there demurely, taking notes of all that went on, taking little part except to play a game or two.

Oh, she was not backward. She was quite ready to take her part. But once or twice when they were playing charades and she was given a part, she grew somewhat hilarious, and her expressions were not all that might have been desired. The high color in his cheeks, the worried look upon his brows might have told her this if she had been alert to discern.

Then they settled down to rest and the suggestion was made that each one sing a song, or recite something, or tell a story, or do some kind of a stunt.

The acts went all around the room. Even Mary Garland told a sweet little story of the first Christmas morning she could remember. And then it came to Florimel, and Marcia Merrill called out pleasantly, "Now, it's your turn, Florimel! What will you do? Sing?"

Nothing loth Florimel arose.

"Okay," she said carelessly. "I'll do a stunt. But mine takes a costume. There comes Selma with a tray of ice cream. I'll go up and get into my togs while you start eating. It won't take me a minute!" and she tripped gaily off up the stairs.

Rex, rousing suddenly to wonder what all this was about, called up the stairs to her:

"I say, Florimel, do you need me to help!"

"Oh no," she called gaily back. "You wouldn't know how!"

and then they could hear the door upstairs shut, and the key turn in the lock.

Florimel did some rapid work upstairs, putting on her make-up freely, daring red lips, ghastly white face, startling dark eyebrows, rosy red cheeks, mascara almost dripping from her eyelashes. There wasn't much time for the finger-nails, but somehow she managed them. She stripped off her shoes and stockings and other garments, slipped her feet into her silver sandals, and put on a brief garment made wholly of white chiffon and swansdown, about the size of a super-latively abbreviated bathing suit. Then with a farewell wave and a blown kiss to her image in the glass she turned and ran lightly, noiselessly down the stairs.

She had not planned all this without thinking of the details.

She had noticed that the victrola had been moved out into the hall near the foot of the stairs to make way for the Christmas tree. It stood in a curve of the stair near the lower step. Now as she paused, still out of sight, she quickly set a record of her own in place, calling out, "Here, I come! Everybody! Hello people!" Then she touched the control and the music whanged out blatantly, eclipsing all pleasant con-versation, utterly taking the room by storm. A strange wild figure dashed into the center of the room right in front of the Christmas tree, and began a series of whirls on the tips of her toes that sent billows of brief down-edged draperies whirling out in a perfect wheel parallel with her waist. Lift-ing a graceful sandaled foot to an incredible height, she whirled on, kicking high at most unexpected moments, as the debauched music of the victrola dictated. She took the breathless audience so unawares that they all sat and stared in wonder, Mary Garland white and speechless at the sight. Could anything be so mad and abandoned as that little crea-ture whirling on with her white limbs kicking higher and higher and her nimble feet, now a-tiptoe, and now in the air. She was like a bit of thistledown suddenly become alive, gifted with bare arms and legs of real flesh and blood.

For several seconds she held the stage, and gave the most daring exhibition she knew. The roomful were speechless with frightened shame of their old friends, and most of all for Rex who really was so decent and fine at heart.

Then suddenly the lights went out as Rex marched into the room. It was utterly dark there except for the soft light of the blue star, which made the whirling dervish look like a thing of mist, unreal, a figment of the imagination. And then the star went out, and the tree, as Stan reached up and disconnected them. Stan was quick to catch an idea.

Rex had reached Florimel's side somehow in the darkness and gathered her naked little form into a firm grasp. Turning he took long strides to the stairs and strode up. They could hear him going, his feet finding their way over the old familiar steps that were just as well known as if he were walking in daylight.

He pushed her from him into the room, with a force that sent her half across the floor and down on her bare pretty knees. One single word he uttered in an angry tone, *"Shame!"* and then he slammed the door behind her, locked it, and hurried downstairs, not even waiting to take out the key.

Paul turned off the victrola with a vicious snap.

"I never used to believe that music could be immoral," he said, "but that sounds as if it came from the bottomless pit. The music of the lost!"

By this time Stan had turned on the lights, and all was as it had been before Florimel made her debut, save that every face bore a look of shock, and distinct pity for him was what Rex read as he looked around.

He stepped into the room.

"I'm sorry!" he said with downcast glance and voice so stern it hardly seemed like Rex. "I hope you will pardon my wife! I guess — perhaps — she didn't know any better!"

And then Mary Garland's voice came sweet and clear, with her eyes on her son.

"Oh, *my dear!*" There was gentlest protest, and utmost sympathy in her voice. The tears were very near the surface, and Rex's eyes went to hers and asked her pardon silently for what he had done. The rest began to try to take up the conversation broken off so unexpectedly. And then suddenly an interruption occurred. A sharp scream from upstairs. Rex turned pale and stepped back into the hall, looking up. Was this another trick?

Florimel had picked herself up from the floor, angry to her heart's core. So, that was the way Rex had taken her reaction to his hatefulness. Well, he would find that he couldn't beat her by locking her in a room. Her knees were smarting and her whole being was filled with wrath, but she hadn't time now to vent it. He would be back in a minute and she would let him see that she was perfectly controlled. He hadn't conquered her by flinging her around like a basketball. He needn't think that just because he could play basketball well, he could order her around and expect her to do just as he said. She would let him see that she was her own mistress, and she would make that mother-in-law understand that she intended to do just as she pleased. She would have a good smoke, and they would all smell cigarette smoke and pretty soon Rex would come and order her to stop, and she would tell him a thing or two. She would tell him that if he didn't let her go down there and finish that dance out she would get a job in a local theater the next day and show the whole town what she was. She would tell him what a good dancer she had been and how all the theaters had been crazy to get her. She wouldn't tell him of course that she had lost her job in the last cheap little vaudeville where she had danced and that she hadn't been able to get another anywhere and that was the reason why she had taken the job at the pieshop.

As her mind wandered over the things she planned to do she got out her cigarette case, selected a cigarette and lighted it, flung herself down in the big luxurious chair by the window, one abandoned bare white leg flung over the arm of the chair, and lolled there enjoying her smoke.

There were other things she could do that would likely bring her mother-in-law to order in a short time. She had heard them talking during the day of the different department stores where the family had charges and she planned to go shopping tomorrow and buy a number of things she wanted, and charge them to her mother-in-law. She would somehow get that money that Mary Garland was keeping away from Rex. If she could make her smart badly enough, in very self-protection she would have to arrange that Rex should have an income.

She was lolling back now with her eyes speculatively on the ceiling, and her right arm over the arm of the upholstered chair. And then, suddenly, she smelled a scorched smell, and looking down she saw her cigarette had scorched a great hole in those cherished old Dolly Varden silk curtains.

She leaned over and watched the silk curl up and turn brown. She moved the little spark of fire up and down, till the curtain was marked up with scorched places.

Suddenly an evil look came into her eyes. Why not go on with that devastation, and finish that curtain? Then they would have to take it down and get some new curtains, and she'd jolly well arrange it so she would do the picking out of the next curtains whether they liked it or not. She'd show them!

She stood up where she could reach higher on the curtain and puffing on her cigarette occasionally to keep it burning brightly she drew a pattern of ugly criss-cross marks all over that beautiful curtain, making great unsightly spots in it over the delicate roses that trailed across its exquisite fabric.

She was standing thus on her tiptoes, to reach a little higher, when she suddenly felt the heat of an actual flame, and before she could even draw back she saw that the inner delicate swiss curtain had caught fire from a smoldering spot and was blazing to the ceiling. It was then she gave that first sharp scream, before she realized what she was doing.

She drew back from the heat of it and cast about her what to do, and suddenly she saw that she had not drawn back from the heat at all, but the heat had followed her, was *on herself!* The flame had caught her chiffon draperies and all at once blazed about her! Clutching at herself in vain attempt to crush out the fire, she began to utter shriek after shriek in terrified horror, and then started and ran about the room wildly, rushing at the door and trying to beat it down, kicking with her frail little silver sandaled foot, then falling down and rolling on the floor in her pain and fright. The door was hopelessly locked against her exit, and her shrieks became horrible.

It was Stan who had seen the rosy light fitfully playing on the snow outside the living room window. He had been standing by the window looking out because he hated to look around the room and see the sorrow on his mother's face.

It was Rance Nelius who had covered the first embarrassing moment after Rex's apology by remarking in a casual tone:

"One of those lights in the star has gone out. Here, let me fix it," and had risen and gone to work at it. And Marcia Merrill had gone over to the tree and straightened out a line or two of the silver rain, just to make it all appear quite natural. But Stan hadn't looked back at them. He was watching that rosy light from the guest room window. What could it be? It seemed to rise and flare widely now almost over to the path to the tennis court, and he turned a frightened face to Paul who sat near by.

"Fire!" he said in a choked voice. "There's a *fire upstairs!*" It was just then that those awful shrieks began. Rex, with fear in his eyes, went tearing upstairs and unlocked that door. What had he done? *What* had *Florimel* done?

He pushed open the door and there lay Florimel in flames at his feet, her gay feather of a costume charred to a crisp and her flesh scorched and raw. She rolled over covering her face with her burned hands, and screaming with all the strength that was left in her fierce young body.

Rex snatched a handsome pink blanket from the foot of the bed and wrapped it around Florimel, caught her up and ran with her to a room at the other side of the house, the old playroom. He put her on the bed there, calling "Mother! Come quick!" and then he rushed back to put out that fire.

But he found Paul and Rance on the spot already. Stan was sending in the alarm to the fire company. Sylvia was there with Marcia and Fae, hastily gathering out precious things that they wanted to save from the fire and carrying them across the hall. The fine old furniture was being moved as far from the window as possible. Sylvia was coming away from the closet with her arms full of Florimel's startling wardrobe when she heard her mother call her. She dropped the garments in a heap in Fae's room and hurried to answer.

It was Sylvia who called up the old family doctor, and then hurried after ointments and old linen.

The young men were beating out the fire as best they could, but it had got a tremendous start before they knew it, and now it bit into the fine old wood of the room, and licked across to the furniture in spite of all they could do.

Rance had dragged out the handsome antique rug, the bed clothing and mattress and pillows, and then began to take down the bed, even before the fire company arrived.

For the next hour there were strenuous times in the old Garland mansion, for the fire had crept up insidiously to the third story before anyone was aware, and was biting into the rafters, the dormer windows, and taking all in its path. When that was discovered they knew there might be a hard fight to save the old mansion.

But Mary Garland was having a fight of her own and did not hear about it until afterward, or she would have thought perhaps they should have taken the patient out of danger.

Florimel was in awful agony, and even when the doctor arrived it was sometime before her pain was relieved.

The doctor sent Fae to telephone for a nurse. Stan was working with the men, doing a man's part. Marcia and Sylvia were getting valuable belongings out of harm's way from fire and water.

Outside the house the beautiful blanket of snow that had been so admired that day by all who passed, was trampled down to the grass. The place under the windows that had reflected so gorgeously the colors of the Christmas tree lights, and where Stan had first seen the rosy glow of the fire, was a black and trodden space, covered now by a great crowd of neighbors and passers-by, the riff-raff that always follows a notable fire.

Paul had flung his coat off and was working with might and main, and so was Rance Nelius. Rex vibrated between the fire and his screaming wife, nearly distracted, unable to think beyond the fact that it was all Florimel's fault and he had brought Florimel there, therefore it was all his fault!

And once when he went into the room where Florimel was being ministered to with tender care and skill, she caught sight of him and screamed again.

"There you are!" she yelled hoarsely. "This is all your fault! You brought me here and it was you who locked me into the room. Why wouldn't I set fire to your old curtains? Priceless curtains, you said they were. Well, I ruined them for you, and I'll ruin more if I get the chance! That's the kind of husband you are, Rex Garland! And you said you wanted to *protect* me!

Her voice rang out wild and clear, out through the windows that were standing wide open. Out above the noises of the engine and the calls of the firemen. People looked at one another in wonder, for not many yet had heard that Rex was married and they did not understand.

But Rex bowed his young head and groaned aloud.

"Oh, Florrie, don't talk that way!" he pleaded, but she only screamed the louder, and Mary Garland came near to her son.

"You'd better go away where she can't see you, Rex. She's beside herself with pain now. She isn't herself, you know. Don't worry, dear. The doctor says her burns are not serious, only very painful."

Rex went away and worked like mad among the men who were fighting the fire. He almost wished that he would get burned or killed or something, so terrible life looked to him just then! And all the time this was going on the Christmas tree stood sweetly shining alone there within the living room, undisturbed by the tumult outside, and the Christmas star beamed out a story of the ages, and a life beyond this life down here. Outside the people who stood staring could see it and remark about its beauty. And one woman who crept up close and crawled under the rope the firemen had stretched to keep the curious out, pressed her nose close to the window to see what the little town on the mantel might be. There in the spot where the carolers just a few hours before had been singing "O Little Town of Bethlehem," they stood and stared, while the end of a perfect day, Christmas Day, was going up in smoke.

But it was over at last. The firemen and the engine and the hook and ladder truck were gone away. Heavy quilts, water soaked, were hung across the empty window spaces. The furniture was out from the beautiful guest room and scattered about in the other rooms. The doctor was gone and the nurse held sway in the old nursery where the spoiled young bride lay under an opiate, her lacerated body swathed in soothing ointments.

Paul had taken Marcia home and now was back. He and Rance Nelius, who had stayed to help, took up their station on the two couches in the living room, with only the soft blue glow of the Christmas star to light them. But Rex was huddled miserably on the top step of the stairs, his face hidden in his hands, his heart facing a swift and terrible retribution that had come so soon and so appalling on the footsteps of his impulsive young act.

Yet he would not hide behind his youth. He had so long boasted of his ability to stand with older boys, to take his stride ahead of time, and always he had been proud of his ability to take what was coming to him, so he must take it now. He would not cry out and protest at fate. He knew it was all his own fault, but this was something he was just finding out in all its clarity.

It was his little sister Fae, sent to her room to go to bed, who finally came and dropped down beside him on the step and put her childish young arm about his neck, her face against his, her soft lips in a tender little vague kiss on his cheek. Rex, grateful for the comfort of her sympathy, roused to slip his arm about her, and stoop to kiss her in return. She was young, but Fae knew that he was pleased with her comfort and she went back to her bed glad of the look he had given her.

Before Mary Garland lay down in her soft dressing gown ready for call if she should be needed to help in the night, she knelt beside her bed and prayed for her boy and his poor silly wife, that all this fiery happening might be overruled to the glory of God and the salvation of all concerned. Then she dropped off to sleep, thinking of the beautiful things in their Christmas Day, and trying to forget the unpleasant happenings. Christmas Day was over, and tomorrow would be another day. And then there was the afterward. What would it be?

17

THE days that followed were very quiet ones for the Garland household, with the exception of the almost constant outcries from the sick room. A few nails were driven to shut off the burned windows from wind and weather; great sheets of celotex nailed across the openings; then the doors were closed and the one-time lovely guest room was alone in its desolation, no longer a cherished part of the fine old home. Everything was kept as still as possible for the sake of the invalid, but the invalid did not seem to appreciate it. She demanded action, much and often. She cried out for diversion and seemed to think they were all to blame for her condition.

It was not that Florimel was in great pain, for all that medical skill could do to relieve her had been done, and there were two nurses, one or the other always in attendance.

After the first few days, as the pain grew less and she began to recover from the shock, she rather enjoyed all this attention from the nurses. None from the family. She would let none of them, not even Rex, lift a hand for her. "No," she would say sharply. "My nurse will attend at that!" As if the nurse were of her own providing, and she had set up a separate household. She demanded fancy dishes, things out of season that were almost impossible to provide, and when they could not be found she went into high hysterics, blaming the family bitterly. Telling the nurse in loud tones that could be heard all over the house how they pretended to be such a holy religious family and yet wouldn't provide just a little something to tempt her appetite. They would let her starve before they would take any trouble to find what she longed for and probably just because it might be a little expensive this time of year they were too tight-fisted to pay for it. One nurse who had long been a friend of the family bore this in patience for a time, till one day when Florimel was really a good deal better, and was carrying on with these high-strikes in fine shape, she turned upon her and told her to hush.

"You've been treated like a young queen!" she said severely, "and you've behaved like a little savage! I've known the Garlands all my life and they are wonderful people and highly thought of by everyone in the community. They've turned heaven and earth to try and get you what you want and it isn't to be had anywhere. As for your appetite you seem to gobble up everything that's sent and I can testify that you've had plenty, and far more than necessary. Flowers on the tray, too, which you as often as not tear to pieces and throw on the floor for me to pick up. You're a spoiled child and have evidently had no bringing up or you would be ashamed of yourself! Now, eat your breakfast and behave yourself or I'll tell the doctor how you are carrying on. You can't expect to get well soon if you act like that!"

For answer Florimel flung her cup of hot coffee from her tray full in the face of the faithful nurse, and screamed out for protection till Mary Garland came to see what was the matter, and then Florimel demanded that the nurse should be dismissed and another supplied who would do as she was told, and not try to insult her.

"But my dear," said Mary Garland gently, "this is the nurse

the doctor got for you. We wouldn't have the authority to dismiss her. This is the nurse who understands cases of burn so well, and knows how to protect you against scars and future troubles arising from your burns."

But Florimel would listen to no one, and demanded to see Rex at once.

Poor Rex was off hunting a job. His haggard face showed what he was going through. Days when he was at home and came in to see Florimel she always spent her time blaming him for the whole affair because he had locked her in her room. His very sleep at night was haunted with her outcries. Once he tried to ask her if there wasn't anybody in the whole world who belonged to her that she would like to see, somebody she loved, who might soothe her and help her to get her self-control. But that only brought on a terrible time of tears and utter exhaustion afterwards.

"You don't love me any more. You want to get rid of me!" she complained in loud tones that could be heard even down in the street.

And once he said in utter despair. "Do you think you would love a person who was acting the way you act?"

It was days before she got over that and would consent to see him again.

But on this day when Rex finally got home again, the despair of another failure to get a job looking from his sorrowful eyes, he came to her at once.

"But that's impossible!" he said when he had heard her demand. "We couldn't think of dismissing Miss Taylor. She's the best to be had. There isn't another nurse around here who can touch her. And she's been with you from the beginning and knows exactly what to do. The doctor would never hear of it. And I'm quite sure my mother is not physically strong enough to nurse you. We could not do without a nurse."

"Heavens, no!" snapped Florimel. "I wouldn't want her pawing around me with her smug sanctimonious ways and her 'my dears.' She makes me sick. How you can stand her

I don't see! She's nothing but a hypocrite!"

Rex turned away from his wife in disgust.

"That'll be about all from you!" he said fiercely, and went away and locked himself into his old boyhood room for hours.

The whole time of the holidays was filled with tumult. The young people, including Paul, Sylvia, Rance and Marcia, with sometimes Natalie Sargent (though never Rex), and always the two children, went skating on the creek, far enough from the house that the echo of their gay laughter could not be heard by the petulant invalid. They attended a couple of concerts, and a meeting or two. They took long hikes when the weather permitted, and once they had a winter picnic in the snow with a fire to broil their sausages, and they did their best each to make it a pleasant time for the others, but the time sometimes hung heavy on their hands, for there seemed to be only one thing they could do for the unhappy invalid and that was to keep the house absolutely quiet. So when they came back home again, they sat down and read, or conversed in low tones, and sighed a good deal.

And of course Rex was entirely aware of all this, though he was never a part of it even when they did their best to make him go for a bit of recreation.

"No," he would say, "I mustn't!"

But in spite of all this tumult and distress Florimel did get better at last. Not too much better. She still demanded her nurse, much as she had wanted her to leave, and she ordered her about most unmercifully.

That word about her being the best nurse to watch out for scars and the like had brought Florimel around to keep her in spite of her dislike, for Florimel cared a great deal whether her young supple body was to be scarred. When her hands were healed enough so she could hold a mirror she spent hours looking at herself in the glass and mourning over the loss of her lovely cloud of red-gold hair, which really had been her only great claim to beauty. Even that the nurse began to suspect had not been wholly natural in color. For it was coming in now where it had been scorched away, a dirty shade of dull yellow and straight as a die. All Florimel's hair except one long heavy lock had been burned away, but she cherished that one lock carefully that she might measure the rest by it.

Amazingly her eyes had not been hurt by the fire.

"I covered them up with my hands," she explained coldly when the nurse wondered about it.

She was allowed to read a little every day if she chose, as soon as she could sit up a little. But she was not fond of reading. The only literature that interested her was movie or fashion magazines. Even those did not hold her long.

The young people of the family stole in to see her now and then, but she did not welcome them. She sneered at their freedom.

"I suppose you folks are gloating over me," she said to Sylvia one day. "I'm shut up here alone with a hateful old nurse and nothing to do, and you are just having the time of your life. You've got your young man, and you've got my husband to yourself. You must be awfully happy. Both your brothers and no wife around to hinder."

Sylvia gave a grave look.

"Rex has not been around with us at all," she said, and sighed. "We scarcely see Rex since you were hurt."

"Oh, *really!* You expect me to believe that, I suppose. I don't know where he is then, he certainly doesn't stay with me, and he hasn't lifted his hand to make me have a pleasant time, me cooped up here with a hateful old nurse."

"I think Rex spends all his time hunting a job. He is really trying very hard to find one. He comes home late every night after we have finished dinner and has to eat his dinner all alone."

"Oh, poor little fellow!" mocked Rex's wife. "Wants a job so much, does he? And your mother is still trying to put that nonsense over on him, when she knows perfectly well that he has money enough to live on in his own right without any job, if she would just give the word. You can't make me believe that!"

"Please don't speak that way of mother," said Sylvia gently trying to control the angry flash that came into her eyes. "If you only knew how mother tries to find ways of pleasing you and helping you to get well you wouldn't think such things of our mother!"

"Oh, she does, does she? Well, I'd like it better if she'd just let up on some of these plans of hers that couldn't please me even if they went through, and would just tell that fool lawyer of hers where to get off and hand over Rex's fortune!"

"Well, you're mistaken about all that, of course," said Sylvia with rising color. "Some day when you are well again perhaps mother will take you down to the lawyer's and let you hear our father's will read, and then you will understand. But until then I guess you and I had better not talk about it."

"Oh, you don't say so!" mocked Florimel. "Okay! Suit yourself. I'll say what I please, of course, and if you don't like it you know what you can do. You don't have to stay around me!"

Florimel always ended her interviews in this way; and then Sylvia would go out.

Later that day Rance Nelius came to take her skating.

It was a lovely clear day, the ice was fine, and the sky without a cloud. Just a brisk cold winter day that brought the color to cheeks and a light to the eyes. The creek was edged with hemlock fringes, tall and graceful, waving in the breeze almost as if they were in tune with the skaters, and were trying to keep time for them.

They were skating hand in hand, with long slow strokes, enjoying every minute of the way. It was getting to be enough for these two just to be together, out in God's day.

"I don't know what to make of Florimel," said Sylvia. "Sometimes I think she is softening and going to be really friendly some day, and then almost in the same breath she flares out and says something perfectly terrible about mother."

"Your wonderful mother! How *can* she?" commented Rance. "I don't see how anybody can help but love her."

He looked down at her and she looked up into his eyes and a warm sweet glance passed between them.

"Oh, I'm glad you've found out how dear mother is!" said Sylvia with a glow in her eyes. "I couldn't really even just *like* anybody that didn't see how wonderful mother is."

"I don't blame you," said he warmly, "and," he added significantly. "I want you to do more than just '*like*' me," and he held her mittened hand in a warm close clasp.

"I do," she said with drooping eyes, and then he slid his other arm within hers and drew her closer to him, her hand in a clasp that thrilled her.

"That's good!" he said earnestly, with a light in his face. It seemed to make her heart quiver with a new joy such as she had never felt before. Then after a moment he said:

"Do you know, you're the only girl that ever made me think I might fall in love some day!"

Her cheeks were rosy red now and her eyes alight.

"That's nice," she said in a comical imitation of his tone a moment before, and then they both laughed merrily, a sweet embarrassed laughter that meant a great deal more than just merriment.

Rance cast a quick glance up and down the creek, saw that they were alone, and putting his arm about her with a sudden tender motion he guided them over to a quiet nook where hemlocks arched the way, and there took her in his arms and laid his lips on hers in a tender kiss that she would never forget. There was something sweet and holy about it, like a solemn ceremony, as if a vow had been sealed.

"There! Now!" he said as he took her hands in his and prepared to go on their way down the creek. "Now, we *belong!*"

"Yes," said Sylvia with a kind of glory in her eyes, "yes, we belong."

He looked at her tenderly.

"Forever?"

"Yes, forever!" said the girl solemnly as if she were registering a vow.

"That means," said Rance searching her eyes deeply, "that some day we shall be married, and always be together. I know you are young yet, and not through your studies, and so am I. I've got to take my place in the world and get ready to take care of you, but, it's nice to know we belong!"

"Oh, yes!" said Sylvia fervently. And then he bent his head and kissed her again. Hand in hand they pursued their way with joy in their hearts, and happiness in their faces.

"We'll talk this over with your mother," said Rance thoughtfully, as they went on, "as soon as an opportunity offers. We don't want to spring any more worries on her."

"Oh, no!" said Sylvia quickly. "But"— she added shyly, "I don't think it will be a worry. She likes you. She said so! She said you were the right kind!"

"Ah!" said Rance. "That's good to hear! May I always be able to hold her good opinion. I know it's going to be wonderful to have a real mother again, that I can claim at least in part."

Then suddenly there were voices ahead! Sylvia recognized them. Paul and Marcia. Paul was going back to college tomorrow, and they were having a farewell skate together.

Rance smiled understandingly.

"I guess those two have some kind of an understanding too," he said. "Have they ever been formally engaged?"

"No," said Sylvia, "they've never said anything about it. But they grew up together. As long ago as I can remember Paul always wanted Marcia invited if we had any company, and he always paired off with her everywhere. They were chums, even when they were quite young. But they never acted silly even then. They were just like nice brothers and sisters."

Rance's eyes lighted.

"I see! Well, you and I didn't have that advantage, but perhaps we'll have just as much love and joy in each other."

Sylvia's eyes answered his with a blaze of present joy.

"Your mother likes Marcia, doesn't she?"

"She loves her," said Sylvia. "She's very happy over those two. Though I don't know whether they've ever really talked it out with mother or not. But we've always taken Marcia for granted. Oh, if only Rex had married someone like that!"

"Don't blame Rex too much," said Rance. "He's really only a kid yet. And I'm afraid this Florimel knew and used the ways of the world far better than he did. But I imagine this experience is going to make him grow up sharply when he awakens to see just what he has done."

"I think he has," said Sylvia. "I think the night of the fire finished that for him. I came on him yesterday morning sitting alone under the unlighted Christmas tree, looking like death. He seems as if he will never be happy again."

"He will," said Rance solemnly, "when he learns to let the Lord have His way with him. God has an afterward for him too, sometime."

"Oh, it's so wonderful that you know Him too!" said Sylvia softly nestling her hand in his for an instant.

And then the other two swept around the nearby curve of the creek and they could answer only by glances. But they went on together now, and somehow it seemed that Paul and Marcia understood about them and were glad.

Then with a shout and an outcry of joy came the other two of the family, Stan and Fae, cutting into the ice with flourishes and curves and dashing at them madly.

"Great!" said Stan. "We thought we might find you here!" and Rance looked down at them joyfully.

"It's going to be great to have all these sisters and brothers," he said in a low tone to Sylvia, and she looked back at him proudly and then smiled at Stan and Fae. Oh, there were going to be no regrets with them when she was married, she thought. But poor, poor Rex! Could they ever be happy in any kind of way over Florimel?

And then when they got home that night, and Rance came in for the evening meal, behold Rex came in just as the bell rang, with a look almost of peace on his worn face, and announced that he had got a job at last. It was only in a foundry, a sort of machine shop. His work was to be most humble, with a very small wage at first, but he was to learn the business and there was a chance to rise. Not very high of course, but perhaps as high as the husband of a girl like Florimel deserved.

He had a very humble attitude, they saw, and it pulled their heart strings to see how thankful the gay bright Rex was over a humble little position like that. An apprentice in a machine shop! When he had been at the head of his college class, and a star in athletics! There was no danger now that handsome, brilliant Rex would ever have too fine an opinion of himself.

It was plain that the lesson had gone deep, all these days in his mother's home, a home that he had well-nigh shattered by his own deed, and no chance of work to help out in any way. Of course his mother wasn't in need of being paid for his and his wife's board. But it had been bitter to his pride to see his mother enduring the impositions that Florimel put upon her, and he unable even to pay the doctor, or for the repairs on the house that her own act had damaged.

Now even the fact that Paul was going back to college without him on the morrow had power to bring a cloud over his face. He seemed to have lived centuries since he left the college town with Florimel. He had grown up and into the knowledge of awful disappointment and sorrow. He had come to find out the ecstatic joys of an hour can turn to dust and ashes on the tongue.

Paul saw that it was not going to be such agony as he had feared for Rex to see him go back to college. For in a way

Rex had grown beyond him, beyond them all. He seemed to have come humbly to God and acknowledged that he was wrong, submitted himself to be made right.

And there seemed to be no longer any question whether Florimel could lead him astray again, for Florimel had overstepped her powers, for good and all, and made it very apparent what she really was.

So Paul spent the evening with Marcia, and then went away early the next morning escorted by Rance who had stayed with him all night, and by Stan who had grown older with all that had passed during that vacation.

But Rex put on overalls and went at an early hour down to his machine shop to begin a time of self-abnegation.

18

REX came home one evening about two weeks after he got his job, walking with a quicker step, and a strong look of purpose in his face. He washed and dressed and went in to see Florimel for a moment, but found her still in a most contemptuous mood. The doctor had told her she might get up, and she had been moving around her room for several days, part of the time. The nurse had told her that she no longer needed her, but she refused to get along without her. The doctor had told her that she might go down to a meal now and then if she felt like it, but she had steadily refused to do this. So when Rex heard the call to dinner he went down by himself.

There was a cosy feeling about the dining room, and the girls and Stan were smiling as he came in. For the first time, almost, since the night of the fire, Rex smiled back, and stooping over his mother, kissed her on the forehead. His heart thrilled faintly as he saw the glad light in her eyes that he had remembered to kiss her, and he felt ashamed that he had omitted it before, so wrapped up in himself and his troubles that he had forgotten a custom of years when they had been separated.

After the blessing which Stan asked, Rex began to talk. There was a strong decision in his voice.

"Moms," he said, "I've just found out that Syl's university has an evening course that is practically free, that is, there would be books, and a trifle for tuition, but I could probably get the books second hand, or borrow them, or something, or maybe Rance or Syl would have some I could use. What would you think if I took an evening course and kept up with my studies so that some day when I'm able to, I could go back and finish. I don't mean finish at our old college of course. That's done forever. But just go evenings and finish somewhere so I could have a diploma and get on a little better. What do you think of it, moms? The reason I ask is, there's a fellow in the machine shop with me who is doing it, and he's never had any college at all, just high school, and he claims he's getting on real well in spite of handicaps. Would you think that was wise? Do you think dad would have thought that was best? At least it would give me something to do evenings that was really worth while, and keep me out of mischief."

He paused and looked at his mother anxiously. Then a voice behind him spoke:

"Yes? And where do I come in? Who's going to amuse me while you go back to your childhood and study your a b c's some more?"

Rex started and paled, and turned quickly. There stood Florimel arrayed in the bright red dress she had worn on Christmas Day before she had changed her apparel. Her hair had begun to grow a little and she had curled it with an iron till it stood in yellow rings around her head, but it wasn't the pretty hair she used to have and she didn't look in the least like her former self. Rex arose quickly and stood looking at her.

"Why, Florimel!" he said "I didn't know you were coming down! Why didn't you tell me? Why didn't you call me to help you down?"

"No, you didn't know I was coming. You didn't ask me, as I remember. But I'm here. I can realize that when I want to do something I have to help myself to it hereafter, do I? That's all right with me, of course, only I shall take the same privilege and do what I want to, and you might as well understand that now as later."

"I'm sorry," said Rex gravely, lifting his chin with that patient humble deference he had been acquiring of late.

"Oh, yes? You're very sorry, I suppose, that I came down and caught you cooking up some scheme with your money-crazy mother for you to go on and get a little more school without my knowing it. But that's all right. Go right on scheming, and let her keep your money. There'll be some way to get it out of her later, and I don't mean maybe. Now that I'm up I'm going to work in real earnest. If I can't do it any other way I'll get a divorce and get alimony, but I'll get it, you'll see!"

"Won't you sit down and have some dinner?" said Rex, moving up a chair for her.

She accepted the chair and let Selma get her a plate and knife and fork, a glass of ice water and a napkin, like a queen whose right it was to have all these things.

They sat down and the dinner proceeded with conversation on safe ordinary lines, but Rex said no more about evening classes at the university, and Florimel sat with grim face and ate her dinner. It did not look much as if the hope were coming true that Mary Garland had expressed once or twice quietly in the privacy of her own room to Sylvia and Paul, that Florimel might be changed by the experience through which she had passed.

"Oh God," she prayed in her heart continually, "help my dear Rex to bear this and acquit himself rightly."

Florimel said no more. She ate a good dinner and afterward let Rex help her upstairs, for there was no mistaking that she was tired. But Rex went about with the old despairing look on his face that he had worn before he got that job.

Late that night when all the household was asleep Rex stole to his mother's room.

"Moms, about that thing I was talking of at the table, don't think any more about it. I can see it wouldn't be best."

"Rex, dear boy," she said putting a loving arm around him, "I am thoroughly in sympathy with your idea, and there'll be a way for you to do it. Don't worry about Florimel. Perhaps you can make her see that it is for the good of you both in the end. But remember that she's been through an awful experience, and don't be too hard on her. Perhaps even yet she may change."

"No, moms, she won't change. She just wants to be ornery, that's all. But I'm glad you thought it was all right. I want to know you approve of what I do. I don't suppose you'll ever forgive me for having got married this way. I'm sure I'll never forgive myself. It's pretty tough to have to take the consequences, but I guess I had all this coming to me. I should have known better, brought up by such a wonderful woman as you are and with my splendid sister and her friends. I knew girls like Marcia and Natalie all my life, and yet I got fooled by a girl like this! When I think about that I can't think of any punishment too bad for me. I deserved it. I want you to know that I think so, moms."

"Dear boy!" Mary Garland stooped and kissed her boy's forehead. "Perhaps after a time you'll find out that what you have gained will be worth all the pain. To have found out that about yourself is worth a great deal. You know what the Bible says: 'Afterward the chastening yieldeth the peaceable fruit of righteousness.' "

Rex shook his head.

"I don't think there'll ever be any such afterward for me," he said desolately. "I'll never have any fruit of righteousness. There won't be a chance. I've just naturally ruined my life and that's all. There'll be no afterward down here for me. I'll even be ashamed to show my face in Heaven!" And he dropped his face in his hands and groaned aloud.

"Son, there is always an afterward, and the blood of Jesus Christ cleanseth us from *all* sin!"

Rex crept to his bed in his old room where he had been staying ever since the fire, comforted somewhat, glad that at least his mother understood and wanted to help.

Florimel got up the next morning and began her program of doing as she pleased, although anybody might wonder what else she had been doing ever since she had been in the house.

She ate her breakfast and as soon as the family were away to school and college, and Mary Garland had gone to attend an all-day missionary meeting, she went to the telephone and did a lot of ordering. From the newspapers and the telephone book she got her numbers, and the very first thing she ordered was a case of champagne, and a carton of fine grade cigarettes. Then she called up a big department store where she had heard the family say they had a charge account, and ordered, from the newspaper advertisements, a new spring suit and the outlandish little perky hat that went with it, a couple of handbags, a handsome suitcase, six pairs of gloves, some lingerie, and several ash trays. She had them all charged and sent to her mother-in-law. Then she settled down to a movie magazine.

The first order that arrived was the champagne, and it came while they were at lunch. Only Fae and her mother were there with Florimel. Stan and Sylvia had telephoned they would take lunch at their schools. There was the sound of an altercation in the kitchen, Selma contending with some delivery man, and then she came to the door.

"Please, Mrs. Garland, would you step here a minute?" she said, in what was meant to be a whisper.

"What is it, Selma? That soap I bought of that man? I thought he needed helping."

"No, Mrs. Garland," said Selma sepulchrally, "it's a case of *champagne!* And I told him you never bought such things. I told him it must be a mistake, but he insisted I should come and tell you. He said it was no mistake, that he had the order with the number written plain."

"Tell him, Selma, that we did not order that champagne. We never order liquor, and we do not intend to pay for it."

"Oh, heavens!" laughed Florimel. "What a fuss about nothing. *I* ordered that champagne, and I wanted it. Do you begrudge me that? You order all sorts of things for me to eat, I thought I might have something I wanted once! Are you such a tightwad that you can't get me a little champagne?"

"*You* ordered it, Florimel?" said Mary Garland in amazement. "But it is charged to *me!*"

"Why sure! You knew I didn't have any charge accounts of my own. You wouldn't fix it so I had any money to buy things with, so I had them charged to you."

Mary Garland's face suddenly froze into stern disapproval.

"I have no charge accounts with liquor dealers," she said, "and they certainly must know that!"

She arose and went into the kitchen, and they could hear her voice speaking very decidedly.

"This is a mistake. I ordered no liquor and I do not want it. You will have to take it away."

"Well, I like that!" said Florimel contemputously. "I wanted a drink of champagne tonight. I don't see what right you had to send back what I bought. If Rex can't get his money out of you one way, I can another."

"No," said Mary Garland firmly, "you can get no money out of me for liquor. You may as well understand that at once."

"Oh, very well," said Florimel airily. "If you prefer to have me go down town and drink it there, I can do that of course, but I might drink too much and then that might be embarrassing to you."

"As you please," said Mary Garland coldly.

So, the next day Florimel went down to the leading hotel in

the city and after her lunch kept ordering more and more drink on some money she had put by for a time of necessity. Then after staggering around the street noisily for a time she was brought home in a taxi, having no money left to pay her taxi fare. Mrs. Garland was out for a few minutes and poor little Fae had to go to her small purse and get out her own cherished money she was saving to get her mother a birthday gift.

The rest of Florimel's purchases of the day before had arrived while she was away. Mrs. Garland, puzzled at the packages that she had not bought, opened each one, and went to interview her daughter-in-law, but found her too drunk to explain more than to say, "Didn't I tell ya I'd get the money outta ya somehow?"

Mary Garland went back to her room and wrapped up those packages to be returned, gave orders to the various department stores to close her accounts with them for *any* order until further notice. But, ignorant of that, the next day Florimel came down in high feather, considering herself to have scored a victory with her mother-in-law.

"Where are my ash trays that I bought yesterday?" she demanded. "I need one."

Mary Garland looked up from the paper she was reading.

"I have sent Stan down to return all the things that you ordered," she said calmly. "You simply cannot buy things on my charge accounts. I have given orders that such service shall be suspended. Now, I think perhaps we had better have a further understanding. It would seem that you have started to carry out your threats against the family, so I have sent for our family lawyer to explain the business situation to you. Then perhaps you will understand that it is not meanness on my part that makes me unwilling to finance Rex in life at this time. You will see that it was a wise and far-seeing father who made all the arrangements, and as it is fixed I have no choice in the matter. My husband explained to me before he died what he was doing, and that he was doing it for the boys' best good. You have not found Paul making any protest against it. You will not find that Rex feels it unfair. But I am sure when you understand that everything you have while you and Rex are here, is a free gift from me, you may not feel that I am as tight-fisted as you have been proclaiming. Now, here comes Mr. Graham and he will explain to you."

Florimel had been so engaged in considering what sharp answer she could give to Rex's mother that she had not heard the door bell ring, and did not realize that the enemy was upon her until Mr. Graham the dignified lawyer walked into the room and was introduced. She gave him a sullen look and favored him with one of her hard stares, which virtually said: "You can't put anything over on me!" and was amazed when her look had no effect whatever upon this great man of the world.

"Mrs. Garland, I understand that you have been enquiring as to your husband's financial standing, so I have brought the full papers and will read them to you. Of course it is a little irregular for a wife to concern herself with such matters. It should rather be your husband who should be told the whole thing first, but as the circumstances are a little peculiar, your husband being not yet of age and not having reached the time when he would be required by law to have the whole matter put before him, I have acceded to Mrs. Garland's request and brought the papers here to read to you, that you may fully understand just how little he has until the time of his majority arrives. Here, first, is the will—" and Mr. Graham unfolded a large legal document and began to read.

Florimel listened with her ever widening gaze to the long important legal terms, until as it went on she began to understand that it was not just a jealous mother's whim that Mary Garland was acting upon, but that they were all up against a great wall of law that had the authority of the land behind it, something a mere girl could not dare to meddle with.

She listened, trying to catch phrases and fathom their meaning, trying to store them away in her memory for future repetition. When the reading was over, and Mr. Graham began to fold the papers and put them away in his brief case, she tossed her head and remarked:

"Well, I've got a lawyer friend that's smart. He knows all the tricks, and can get almost anybody into a corner with all the ways he knows. If I send for him and bring him down to see you, would you read all that stuff to him so he could maybe find a way out for my husband?" She eyed the great lawyer not with contempt, but with the assurance of one who felt she could beat him at his own game.

Mr. Graham looked at her keenly a moment, half smiled, and then answered, still courteously:

"Why, certainly. If your husband consents to such a proceeding, I could not object. You must always remember that this inheritance is your husband's, not yours, and that he would have the final word about it. It could not be done without his knowledge."

Then the lawyer bowed himself out, and Florimel was free to go upstairs and think it over.

Mary Garland went out soon after that for a few minutes on an errand, and when she returned she came around to the kitchen door because she wanted to speak to the grocery boy whose car was standing there. So it happened that she entered the house by the kitchen door instead of the front one, and went straight upstairs to her room. As she started out into the hall later she heard a voice downstairs, loud, strident, talking and laughing immoderately. She paused a moment, wondering who Florimel was talking with. Was she down at the lower hall telephone, or could some caller have come to see her?

That morning Florimel had received a special delivery letter quite early, before breakfast, and Fae had taken it to her door before she left for school. Perhaps some of her old friends had called to see her and the letter had been announcing the arrival. If so, should she invite them to lunch? Probably that would be expected. She hesitated a moment and then came Florimel's voice once more.

"Oh, the old girl has gone to market or to some missionary meeting or something. No, she's not here now. No one in the house but the cook and she's rattling dishes in the kitchen. That's why I called you now. I thought you oughtta know a few things. Sure I got your letter and I know what you mean. I'm glad you got out so soon. I thought you had another month yet to do. But say, that's fine. Only I thought you oughtta know that that alimony business we thought we could pull, is all off. There wouldn't be enough to pay thirty a week even if he was of age, which he won't be for another two and a half years yet, and then he hasta wait another heck of a time till another amount is due. It really wouldn't be worth the risk to try and wait for that. Anyhow he isn't so rich as we were told, and if you'd live in this house for a few weeks you'd find out there wasn't much chance of putting anything over on these wise guys. They know too much, and they don't go on the same principles as the rest of us do. They're religious, and you haveta walk their way if you wanta get on with them. Besides, Rex isn't the same since he came home. He doesn't trust me any more, and I can't put a thing over on him. I think I'd better clear out. I'm perishing for a drink, and a few shows and dances. Where? Oh! All right, only let me know before two o'clock when the whole gang come home from school and I can't get the telephone without somebody hearing. Say, Jeff, I'm fed up with this life. Let's think up a new plan. What? Really? D'ya mean it? Oh *boy!* When? Yes. Where? Okay, I'll be there. Hark! There's the doorbell. I gotta quit, but I'll be there, darling!"

Then the receiver was hung up with a sharp click, and Mary Garland, realizing that she had been listening to a conversation that might mean a great deal, beat a quiet and hasty retreat into her room and closed the door, locked it and knelt down.

"Oh God, what is it? Is it something I should understand? But I don't, and now what shall I do? Anything?"

Long she knelt there praying for her boy. Praying now and then for the girl who seemed so utterly unworthy of him, so involved in all sorts of deceits and worldliness. Almost it seemed to her it must be a world of crime to which she belonged. And yet, was that fair to judge her by that brief conversation which she ought not to have heard at all?

"Oh Lord," she prayed, "I can't do anything. I don't know what to do. Wilt Thou take charge of this matter and work it out for us all in Thy way. Thy will be done!"

So all day as Mary Garland went about her duties, watching meanwhile the mysterious daughter-in-law to see what would develop next, and whether there was aught for her to do to prevent new disaster, her heart was praying, praying.

But all day Florimel went on with her idle listless life. Apparently there were no more phone calls, and Florimel did not appear to intend to go out that day. She stayed in her room except at lunch time when she ate silently and sullenly as usual.

And then when it was almost time for Rex to return from his work, she went to her room to freshen up for the evening meal.

Mrs. Garland could hear the children coming in. They had all been to a basketball game and were full of it, about what this one and that one did. Now if Rex were only a boy again, one of them, coming home as eager as them all. Or, oh God, if he were even a happily married young man with a simple pleasant life to live, a comfortable evening before him with a wife who loved him and would bring him honor, how very glad she would be. If only he had some dear sweet helpful girl like — but no, she must not even think such a thought. God was going to order this affair, and perhaps some day she could look back, and be glad for Florimel. Was that possible? Oh, she had so wanted them all to be a good influence for this new girl. This girl who had come among them under such unforeseen circumstances. She had so hoped they might lead her to Christ, if she was not already a Christian. And they hadn't even been able to make her respect themselves, or their God, it seemed.

Then came Rex. She could hear him walking slowly up the stairs as if he were tired. His steps dragged toward Florimel's door, not as if they loved to go there. Poor Rex! Poor foolish impulsive boy! He was walking as if he had grown suddenly old.

But in a moment she heard him coming back, and toward her door.

"Mother!" he called. "Where are you?" Excitedly he rushed in. "Where is Florimel? Where has she gone?"

"Why, she was here a few minutes ago. I thought she was in her room. I heard her walking around when I came here to dress. That was just twenty minutes ago. She's been around all day."

"But she isn't there!" he said with a startled look on his face, and she noticed his sudden pallor. Could it be that he still cared for her?

"Oh, mother, what can she have done now?"

"Done?" said his mother. "Nonsense, she probably hasn't done anything. She's very likely downstairs reading the paper in the living room."

"No!" said Rex, "the girls are there with Stan trying over a song by the piano. She isn't there. Mother, she *gone!*"

"Oh, but that's not possible!" said his mother sharply with a sudden memory of that strange telephone conversation to part of which she had been an unwilling listener. "Come! We'll go and find her!"

"But she's not there, mother! I looked! She's gone, and all her *things are gone!* I tell you she's *gone!* Now what will she do next? Oh, mother, if you could only cast me out and forget me! If only our friends need not know all this awfulness!

Why couldn't I have died when dad did, before I did all this to you?"

"Hush, Rex! You don't want to frighten your sisters!"

His answer was a groan.

They went to the room that Florimel had been occupying, and found it even as Rex had said, all her clothes were gone, all her trifling trinkets. Her two suitcases were gone. Everything!

And then they found a note stuck into the mirror frame addressed to Rex in her wide uncultured hand.

Dear Rex:

I've gone! I couldn't stand for the life we've been living. And anyhow Jeff got out and I've gone back to him! He's the one I told you I was afraid of, but I was only afraid for fear I'd get in the jug too because I was with him when he got caught. He hasn't done all his time. I don't know how he got out so soon, but anyhow he was sweet and we get on better than you and I did. You were darling at first, till you got back to your beastly religious family, but I think I'm better off with Jeff. There's always some excitement around him, and I don't have to go on the sly to get a drink or smoke. So good by and live happy ever after, only next time be sure you don't go to a fake minister to get married! The joke's on you! If you were rich as I thought you were I would have demanded alimony, but it isn't worth the trouble, so I'm clearing out, and you can go back to your precious college and graduate. Ta ta!

Yours,
Florimel!

P.S. It's no use to hunt us for we have a hiding place where you'd never think to look, and such as you would never *come out alive!*

Rex dropped down on the edge of the bed and looked up from the letter in his hand. Slowly a great light was dawning in his tired young face.

"Oh, mother!" he said dazedly. "She's *gone!* She's gone with *someone else.* She never really belonged to me. She belonged with someone else first. Oh, God has been good! It took a terrible thing like this to show me I was a sinner, I guess, for now I realize I thought I was a pretty good sort. But God has let me find all that out and ruin my life, just so He could save me. And now He's taken her away!" His voice trembled with relief.

Suddenly he looked up.

"You don't think I ought to go and hunt her up, do you, moms? Read the letter. She speaks as if our marriage might not have been real."

Mary Garland read the letter, and then she stooped with thankful tears in her eyes and kissed her boy almost reverently.

"No, dear son, I think not. I think God has solved this for you, and now He has removed at least some of the consequences. You let Him have His way, and He has given you back your life to live, not the old life, but a new one. I think perhaps your 'Afterward' has begun."

About the Author

Grace Livingston Hill is well known as one of the most prolific writers of romantic fiction. Her personal life was fraught with joys and sorrows not unlike those experienced by many of her fictional heroines.

Born in Wellsville, New York, Grace nearly died during the first hours of life. But her loving parents and friends turned to God in prayer. She survived miraculously, thus her thankful father named her Grace.

Grace was always close to her father, a Presbyterian minister, and her mother, a published writer. It was from them that she learned the art of storytelling. When Grace was twelve, a close aunt surprised her with a hardbound, illustrated copy of one of Grace's stories. This was the beginning of Grace's journey into being a published author.

In 1892 Grace married Fred Hill, a young minister, and they soon had two lovely young daughters. Then came 1901, a difficult year for Grace—the year when, within months of each other, both her father and husband died. Suddenly Grace had to find a new place to live (her home was owned by the church where her husband had been pastor). It was a struggle for Grace to raise her young daughters alone, but through everything she kept writing. In 1902 she produced *The Angel of His Presence, The Story of a Whim,* and *An Unwilling Guest.* In 1903 her two books *According to the Pattern* and *Because of Stephen* were published.

It wasn't long before Grace was a well-known author, but she wanted to go beyond just entertaining her readers. She soon included the message of God's salvation through Jesus Christ in each of her books. For Grace, the most important thing she did was not write books but share the message of salvation, a message she felt God wanted her to share through the abilities he had given her.

In all, Grace Livingston Hill wrote more than one hundred books, all of which have sold thousands of copies and have touched the lives of readers around the world with their message of "enduring love" and the true way to lasting happiness: a relationship with God through his Son, Jesus Christ.

In an interview shortly before her death, Grace's devotion to her Lord still shone clear. She commented that whatever she had accomplished had been God's doing. She was only his servant, one who had tried to follow his teaching in all her thoughts and writing.